T0101969

Moth to a Flame:

Tenth Anniversary Edition

Moth to a Flame:

Tenth Anniversary Edition

Ashley Antoinette

www.urbanbooks.net

Urban Books, LLC
300 Farmingdale Road, N.Y.-Route 109
Farmingdale, NY 11735

Moth to a Flame: Tenth Anniversary Edition
Copyright © 2010 Ashley Antoinette

All rights reserved. No part of this book may be repro-
duced in any form or by any means without prior consent
of the Publisher, except brief quotes used in reviews.

ISBN 13: 978-1-64556-055-5
ISBN 10: 1-64556-055-4

First Trade Paperback Printing March 2010
Printed in the United States of America

20 19 18 17 16 15 14 13

*This is a work of fiction. Any references or similarities
to actual events, real people, living or dead, or to real
locales are intended to give the novel a sense of reality.
Any similarity in other names, characters, places, and
incidents is entirely coincidental.*

Distributed by Kensington Publishing Corp.
Submit Orders to:
Customer Service
400 Hahn Road
Westminster, MD 21157-4627
Phone: 1-800-733-3000
Fax: 1-800-659-2436

Dedication

I dedicate this book to my husband. A love so great did not exist until God made us. I appreciate all that you do and all that you are. I love riding shotgun with you in all that we do . . . We knew what it was before anyone else and we are taking this thing all the way to the top. The book game will never be the same.

Acknowledgments

Of course I would like to thank God for all of His blessings. I have been through so many things in my lifetime, and some things I did not always understand, but every experience has taught me a valuable lesson. There was a reason why I encountered every storm. Both the good and bad times gave me the motivation I needed to become a great author. I thank Him for giving me the talent to convey my story to the world.

I'd like to acknowledge my co-author and partner, JaQuavis. The world isn't ready for our true story yet, but it is definitely one for the books. I could not have done this with anyone else but you.

To my mother and father, Jacqueline and Yul. I love you both with all of my heart. Y'all did quite a job when you made me, lol. . . . No, but seriously, I could not ask for better parents. I am so lucky to have both of you and I thank you for all of the sacrifices you have made for me. To my siblings, Mario, Syd, Yul, and Yulanai, I love you guys . . . I know you are all on your way to doing great things. I believe in you all because each of you has always believed in me. To Grandma Symullia Neely, I love you unconditionally and forever. You are the greatest woman I have ever known. To Grandma Annette Snell, I am nothing but a younger version of you. I love you for always supporting me and teaching me how to be a woman. I still have to hear some of your stories because you have lived quite a life and I know you have some good ones to tell. To my Papa, Leslie Neely, you are gone but never forgotten in my heart. To my Great Aunt Pat, I love you. Now you are the one who really reads my books and shows me your undying support. I am so glad that you enjoy what I do and am so grateful to have you in my corner. To my cousin Raven, you know I love you. You are my inspiration and you teach me so many things. I'm glad that I have you to keep my head on straight, remain humble, and to remind me what the word "family" really means. To my Auntie Monya, you are the most generous person I know. I love you very much. To my stepmom, Tammy, I have always admired you and wanted to be just like you. I love you always. Thank you for being here for me and being such a good person in my life. I send love out to all of my family: Amber, Courtney, Jazzy Phe, India, Uncle Sam, Stevie, Chandra, B.J., Wayne, Kiara, Cammy, Jada, Joy, Amir, Zykia, Zannie, Tori, Auntie Lana, Auntie Bubbles, Auntie Lyrica, Auntie Darnesha, Quan, Markise, Aunt Lisa, Margo, and all of the rest of y'all (there are too many to keep naming) but trust me I didn't forget you guys. To my entire family . . . I love you . . . this is getting way to long so I'm wrapping this section up.

To Carl Weber, you are family and I have all the love in the world for you and the entire Urban Books family. Here we are five years later!! Who would've thought that time would bring us this far? I appreciate you for believing in me and my work. You put the money up from the beginning and saw the potential before I had even proven myself. You have watched my talent grow and have supported me from the time I signed my first publishing deal at seventeen. I look forward to doing bigger and better things in the future.

To Tazzy2Bossye aka Tammy Freeman . . . I had to put your government name in here after all that you've done to help me with *Moth to a Flame*. I really appreciate your support and input on my sophomore novel. You have a remarkable talent. There are not many people who can analyze a book the way you do, and I have to say that this one is for you. Readers like you help me perfect my craft.

To Denard, Edd McNair, Brenda Owen, and the entire Urban Books family . . . thank you all for your constant support.

To Natalie Weber aka Nat, thank you for putting up with the many e-mails. I appreciate you for all you do for us and all of the hard work you put in on our behalf. You're the best.

To my girls: Ashley Mustafaa, Tamia Tolbert, Tiffany Deloney, Char Lynn Midock, Donecia "Rudy" Conner, Shonda Gaylord, Sharonda Bowman, Keisha Ervin, and one of my newest friends, Christine Love . . . I appreciate you ladies always. You guys are my truest and dearest friends and I love you. Thank you for always being there.

To my heart, Saquarius "Shay Shay" Holland. You are so grown now that you make me feel old. I love u! Hey, Tee-Tee . . . I know you thought I forgot you, but I didn't. I love you too. Thank you for being here. I'm so glad we are close and I appreciate you so much.

To my cousin, Shenita Hill, and all of her girls behind the wall who support and read our books . . . Shameka Baker, Sharon Brown, Ms. Coretta Scott King, and all the rest of my fans in the Huron Valley Women's Complex, thank you for your support.

To my editor, Maria, it's always a pleasure to work with you. Thank you once again for doing such a great job.

To the hottest graphic designers in the game, Davida Baldwin, from Odd Ball Dsgns and Tony Trischler, from T3 Promotions. I thank you both for your hard work and hot creations when it comes to our covers. You guys always bring you're A-game when it comes to our cover designs and we really appreciate you for summing up our stories in one hot package to be presented to the world.

Acknowledgments

To my biggest fan, Valnavia Brown . . . thank you, hon. I told you I wouldn't forget you. You're the best.

To Perry White, a sixteen-year-old young man who was lost to the streets way too soon. R.I.P.

Last, but certainly not least, to all of the book clubs, book stores, street vendors, and libraries who support the Ashley & JaQuavis and Ashley Antoinette books. I thank y'all for keeping me hot in the game and spreading the word about my books. Coast2Coast, Paper Dolls, Detroit Public Library, Genesee District Library, Thisisformypeople, OOSA, and all of the rest. . . .

Wow! Now that all of that is out of the way, here we go for another round of solo novels, and I'm up to the plate for the second time. The Ashley & JaQuavis books groomed me for this. They prepared me to step out on my own and present this Ashley Antoinette classic to our loyal readers. So many people have contributed to my career so far, and you all are my blessing. I appreciate every single person who picks up my books and every single fan who reaches out to me through e-mails. I do this for you and I thank you for sticking with me from the very beginning. It is because of you that I am so passionate about my work, and because of you that I have been blessed with so much success. So, as I let my pen bleed to give you another story, sit back, relax, and rock with me as I present to you my sophomore novel . . . *Moth to a Flame.*

Always Love,
Ashley Antoinette

Phase 1

Prologue

Raven sped through the city streets with her best friend, Nikki, in the passenger seat. She kept checking her rearview mirror to make sure no one was following her.

"I have to get out of here before he wakes up and finds out I'm gone," she said desperately as she made her way across town, trying to get to Mizan's last trap house. Robbing him blind had been her only option. She had nowhere to go and she had no choice but to leave. He grew more violent as each day passed and she could not take it anymore. She had been forced to take the money and get out of Dodge. If she hadn't, he would have eventually killed her. So far she had $100,000 in her possession, but she had one more stop to make. She had collected from all of Mizan's stash spots except for this last one. Although this dope spot was out of her way on the other side of town, she knew she could not skip it. This spot usually made more money than the rest of them combined, so there was no way that she was leaving town without hitting that safe. After everything he had put her through, she felt like she deserved every cent she was taking. With every tear he had caused her to shed, she had earned it. This was her reparation.

When she finally pulled up to the small yellow house on the city's north side, she turned to Nikki. "I'll be right back. If I'm not out in ten minutes, you pull off." She looked in the backseat at her newborn baby boy who was sleeping soundly. "If anything goes wrong, you take him to the bridge at Mott Park. Ethic will be waiting. He'll take care of him," Raven said urgently. She lowered her head and pulled a pink envelope out of her purse. "If something happens to me, make sure Ethic gets this."

Nikki shook her head and then hugged her friend. "Give it to him yourself. Nothing is going to happen, Rae. Just hurry up so you can get out of here." Nikki stated.

Raven nodded, hopped out of the car, and ran inside the trap house. Mizan's workers were not surprised to see her. She was the only person besides Mizan who came by regularly. The first and the fifteenth were the days that she collected the profit Mizan had made from the streets, only this time she didn't plan on turning them in. She was going to use the money to take her life back. She was purchasing her freedom on Mizan's dime. Because of him, she had lost everything, and now it was payback time. All the black eyes he had given her, all the bruises she had been forced to cover up, all the lies he had told . . . they were all about to come back on him. She was determined to deliver his karma to him personally. By robbing him blind she was going to give him the ultimate "fuck you." and knock him off the throne he had stolen from her father. She was going to take him for everything he had and disappear into the night.

Her hands trembled as she avoided eye contact with Mizan's workers. She watched the money machine as it counted the bills, making a rhythm in her head. The money symbolized her emancipation; all she had to do was make it out of the last stash house and she would be home free. Her foot tapped anxiously against the carpeted floor as she waited impatiently. She turned to look out the window and saw that the coast was still clear.

Hurry the fuck up, she thought eagerly as she tried to remain cool on the outside. Fear pumped through her veins like blood as the last stack was loaded into the machine.

"$135,000," the worker reported as he began to put the money inside a duffel bag. Once she added that to the money she already had in the car she would be almost a quarter of a million dollars richer. That was enough for her to start her life over in a new city. *I can become a new person,* she thought. *He'll never find me.* Raven helped the dude load the cash into the bag, and then grabbed it out of his hands before rushing out of the house.

She popped the trunk and threw it inside before getting into the car. She pulled out of the driveway so fast that she left burnt rubber on the pavement.

"How much is it?"

"Almost a quarter mill in total," Raven said as tears came to her eyes. She gripped her abdomen tightly, feeling sick to her stomach. She was still recuperating from her hard labor, and the pain of moving was making it hard for her to escape, but she had to keep pushing. The pain would be much greater if she stayed with Mizan, and the memories of all of the fucked-up things he had done to her kept her pushing forward. "I can finally get away, Nik. I can use this money to hide out and get away from all of this madness," she whispered as her soul cried.

Her father's face flashed in her mind as she thought of everything that she had been through. Mizan had tried his hardest to break her and she had almost let him. By forgiving him repeatedly she had sent the message that it was acceptable for him to hurt her, but today was her day. Today her entire life was about to change.

"You know you can't come back this time," Nikki said, worried. She knew Raven like the back of her hand. She had attempted to leave Mizan before, but she always came back. Like a moth to a flame, Raven was drawn to Mizan. It was something that no one could ever understand. "You can't let him say he's sorry and you go running home. You have to leave him for good, Raven. If you don't, he is going to kill you."

"I know . . . I'm not going back to him. I swear on everything I love that it's over. I can't take this anymore. He's taken everything away from me and he has hurt everyone I love," she whispered as she reached over and squeezed Nikki's hand. "I'm so sorry, Nik . . . I'm sorry for everything."

"Girl, none of that matters. Let the past be just that—the past. Leave all the bullshit behind. You are getting out now and that's all that counts," Nikki replied.

"I finally have something to fight for." Raven looked back at her sleeping infant. "I just want to keep my baby safe."

Nikki smiled and rubbed her friend's hair gently. "We're going to get you out of here. We're almost there."

As Raven headed toward Mott Park she remembered the day she first met Mizan. She had been so young and naïve to trust him. Now she was caught in his deadly web of deceit, and the closer she got to leaving him the more afraid she became. It would be so much easier for her to stay with him and go with the flow, but she was tired of being his punching bag. She was exhausted from fighting day in and day out. A part of her wanted to turn around and go back home, but as she drove she reminded herself of all the pain he had caused. This is what kept her pushing forward, and kept her foot on the gas. As she made her final escape she thought about her life, reflecting on the very first time she had met Mizan—the man who ruined her life.

Chapter One

Na, na, na, diva is a female version of a hustla of a hustla, of a, of a hustla

"Bitch, why are we bumping this old-ass shit?" Nikki shouted, trying to be heard over the loud subwoofers that vibrated her seat as she bobbed her head to the beat.

"Because ain't no better way to announce me, babes. 'I'm a, a diva I'm a, I'm a, a diva,'" Raven responded with playful arrogance as she whipped her shiny, brand new Lexus Coupe down Clio Road, one of the hottest strips in the entire city. It was the day of the annual Memorial Day celebration, and everybody who was anybody was out riding the strip as they waited for the festivities to begin. Heads turned as everyone tried to catch sight of the infamous Raven Atkins. The lyrics to the song may have been old, but as the local hustlers stopped in their tracks to catch a glimpse of the light-skinned beauty, Raven knew that the words rang true. Around the city of Flint, Michigan, Beyoncé didn't have shit on her. She was hood royalty, the daughter of Benjamin Atkins—the most notorious kingpin the city had seen thus far—and she wore her title well. Her Coach kicks, tight skinny jeans, and casual, white baby tee were simple, but the curves of her voluptuous five feet seven inches frame transformed simple into chic. Niggas were thirsty as they tried to get at her, spitting whack game, each hoping that he would be the lucky one she chose. She was so fly that even the bitches couldn't hate on her; they wanted to, but all they could do was stop and stare while thinking, *she put her shit together so right.* She wasn't the type of chick who bought knockoffs or rocked hundred-dollar weaves done by ten-dollar beauticians, and she definitely wasn't the chick who wore a nice hook-up but accessorized her shit all wrong. No, Raven Atkins was a top-notch bitch with top-notch shit, and when she stepped out, not a hair on her head was out of place. She had gotten it from her mama, learning to be a lady from the best who had ever done it. At only seventeen, Raven knew her position and she played it like little ghetto girls played Double Dutch. She was the princess of the city and just in case anyone didn't know it, she had it tattooed on her wrist and engraved on the plush leather headrests of her car.

"How did you get your dad to let you out the house?" Nikki asked as she pulled down her visor and applied lip gloss.

"He thinks I'm staying the night at your place. You think Auntie Gena will mind?" she asked, turning to her best friend with a concerned look on her face. The last thing she needed was to get caught in a lie by her father. He was extra strict with her, and if he had any idea that she was in the inner city, there would be hell to pay.

"Girl, please . . . it's nothing. You know my mama ain't tripping," Nikki replied as she stepped out of the car. "You drinking?" she asked as she headed into the liquor store.

"You know it," Raven called back, still in the car. "Ciroc and lemonade!"

As she watched her friend disappear inside the store, she smiled. They had been true blue since grade school and she loved her dearly. Where other girls had tried to cling to her to upgrade their status, Nikki was there from the very beginning before her father had arrived into his own. She would never forget the love and loyalty that Nikki had shown her over the years. Which was why whenever Raven got something, so did Nikki. It was like Benjamin had two teenage daughters because whatever he bought for Raven, she conned him into buying a matching item for her girl. As she nodded her head to the music, a shiny black Escalade pulled up next to her. Behind the tint of her Chloe sunglasses she eyed the big-boy toy. The bass from the speaker system could be felt all the way in her car, and the dark-skinned, freshly Caesred eye candy sitting comfortably behind the wheel caused her to raise her glasses and look his way.

He noticed her staring and gave her a nod. He smirked as she lowered her glasses and turned up her radio. Licking his lips, he reached for his own custom system and drowned out her volume. The sounds of Young Jeezy invaded her car. Not one to be outdone, she frowned in displeasure as she turned off her car and walked inside the store. She stepped with a model's precision and commanded attention as her hips swayed from side to side, but the one dude she hoped would be watching had switched his focus to another girl. *What the fuck? Is he serious?* she asked herself as she quickly assessed her competition. A Reebok broad with ass for days had stolen the dude's attention away from her. Even Raven had to admit the girl did have a humongous ass. There was no way her size-ten jeans could compete with that. She rolled her eyes and turned to go into the store, but Nikki was already on her way out.

"What's up? Did you forget something?" Nikki asked.

Giving the dude another glance, she shook her head. "Nah, I was just coming in to see what was taking so long. I'm ready to go inside the club." Raven walked back to her car and gave the dude one last glance before pulling away. She checked her rearview mirror to see if he had stepped out of the car, and noticed that he was sporting out-of-town plates. *Missouri,* she thought. Her interest in him immediately doubled. There was nothing better than putting claims on a fresh out-of-town nigga like him. Flint was so small that everybody knew everybody. An unknown face was a challenge, and the rule always was that the first chick to become wifey won. Raven knew that the dude didn't know who she was, but when he checked her status he would come to his senses. *I might not give the nigga no kick it just for showing out,* she thought. She popped in her Chrisette Michele and pulled out of the parking lot, leaving skid marks on the pavement while Chrisette crooned from her speakers and serenaded the envious onlookers.

"Damn, look at the line to get in," Nikki commented as they pulled into the parking lot of The Palm Tree, a small club on the city's north side.

"You know I'm not waiting in line," Raven stated as she parked and hopped out. She bypassed the entire line, speaking to people she knew as she made her way to the front. The bouncer stopped her dead in her tracks.

"No, no, baby girl . . . Your father is not about to have my fucking head," he said as he refused to let her in. Jerome was one of her father's old bodyguards and he knew the repercussions that could come his way if he allowed her inside.

"Jerome! Don't play me. Come on, let me and my girl in. You know I'm the life of the party." Raven planted one hand on her hip.

"I can't do it, Rae. What you doing out here anyway, ma? You ain't even old enough to be up in here," he reasoned. "You gon' have me lose my job if I let you up in this mu'fucka."

Raven pulled out a wad of money and peeled off two hundred dollar bills. She placed them in his shirt pocket as she smiled sweetly, and stepped into the club, disregarding his protests. "Thank you, Jerome! I'll make sure I tell my daddy you said what up!" she shouted over him as she waved her fingers and strolled in. He shook his head in doubt.

"Nah, if your pops find out don't say shit about me, Rae. I'm serious! I didn't let you in here!" he yelled as she disappeared into the establishment with Nikki holding her hand.

Everybody showed her love as she navigated through the wall-to-wall crowd. "Damn, it ain't even any tables left," Nikki said as she checked her Cartier. "It's not even eleven o'clock and it's already packed."

"I know! I didn't come here to sit down anyway," Raven stated as she made her way to the dance floor. She lifted her hands and swayed arrogantly to the club track as she snapped her fingers. She and Nikki were the center of attention, everyone around them raising their hands to rock with the beat as the twosome did their thing. Conceit was written all over both of their faces. They were so much alike that they played off of each other's movements as they commanded the crowd.

A couple of songs passed before they decided to end their show and make their way over to the bar. Raven felt someone grab her hand. She turned, and smiled when she saw who was trying to get her attention. As her eyes scanned him quickly she saw that he was attractive. He passed all of her tests. In order for a dude to even step to her he had to qualify. She had a rule system and, unlike so many others, her rules were not made to broken.

Rule 1: The dude had to be fine as hell, and as she stared at this dude's grey eyes she had to admit that there wasn't an ugly gene in his body.

Okay, check, she thought.

Rule 2: The dude couldn't be a cornball-ass nigga. There was nothing worse than a corny man, and she could tell if a guy had swag or not just by the way he walked. The dude in front of her didn't try too hard to be cool. He exuded confidence in a casual stroll, and not once did he grab his penis which was a plus in her book. She hated dudes who walked around holding their crotches. It usually meant that there wasn't much to hold on to. The gesture was crass and unattractive, for sure.

Okay, check, she thought, growing more impressed by the second. She continued to inventory him in her head.

Rule 3: Any dude trying to mess with her had to be paid. She came from a long line of hustlers and get-money cats, so any dude trying to impress her would have to be a thoroughbred just like her daddy.

Is he paid? she asked herself. *Yeah, nigga, you paid. That presidential you rocking ain't affordable to many . . . check.*

Rule 4: The nigga shoe game had to be on point, and as she peeped at his brand new Air Jordans she was satisfied. They were official; straight out of Foot Locker, not the hood corner store.

Dude passed her tests with flying colors without having a clue that she had just peeped, his entire style in just a few seconds.

His boyish features made her smile, but she knew that she was fucking with a grown man just from the way he looked at her. He walked up on her as if he knew her, not leaving any personal space between them.

"What up, ma? You getting a lot of love in here. I just came over to find out who the star is," he whispered in her ear. "What's your name?"

"Raven, but you can call me Rae," she answered sweetly.

"Rae, you want to come have a drink with me?" he asked.

"I got my girl with me," she replied as she shook her head to decline his offer. That was one thing she never did: leave her girl on stuck to kick it with a dude.

"Your girl can come too," he stated as he put his arms around Raven and Nikki. He escorted them to his table where a few of his friends were popping bottles and enjoying the club scene.

"I don't even know your name," she whispered in his ear as she cradled a drink in her hand. Her underage lips touched the glass. She sipped the vodka and cranberry while awaiting his response.

"I'm Mizan," he replied as he took her drink from her. "How old are you?"

"Twenty-one," she answered quickly as she snatched her drink back. She already knew she would lie when he asked her. A dude like Mizan could have his pick of the women in the room, and she knew that if she revealed her real age he would instantly dismiss her. "Why? How old are you?"

"I'm twenty-two," he replied.

Just as she was about to respond she spotted the cutie she had seen earlier at the store. Her eyes followed him across the room. He looked good enough to eat and she instantly decided that one day he was going to be her man. She stared at him from across the room, her eyes burning a hole through him. He must have felt the heat because he looked up and their eyes met. Neither of them made it a point to look away too quickly. As she studied every feature on his face she was mesmerized. Everything about him was so on point. His hood swagger was out of this world. She was on cloud nine as people partied around her. Only when the DJ cut the music did she snap out of her trance.

"The fire department is shutting us down! We're over capacity!" he shouted over the microphone. "Party's over!"

Boos and groans erupted throughout the crowd and Raven stood up, Nikki by her side.

"It looks like our night has been cut short," she said, facing Mizan.

"It doesn't have to be. We can kick it back at my place," he answered as he led her out of the club.

Raven frowned and replied, "I don't know you like that." A part of her wanted to roll out with Mizan and his crew, but she knew that if her father ever found out she had gone back to a nigga's crib he would kill her, and probably Mizan too.

"You can give me your number so that I can call you though," she said , with sugar lacing her tone. "We can link up another time."

Mizan pulled out his BlackBerry so that he could swap information with her, but before she could give him her number, gunshots rang out.

Boom! Boom! Boom!

"Aghh!" Raven screamed as she instinctively ducked low and covered her ears. The crowd began to run in all directions. "Nikki!" She reached out, trying to locate her best friend. The sea of panicked faces in the parking lot didn't make it any easier to locate her.

Mizan grabbed her hand and ran toward his car.

"Get in!" he yelled.

"I have to find my girl!" she replied with worry.

"She ran off with one of my niggas. You can call her when you get in the car," Mizan stated with authority.

Boom! Boom! Boom! Boom!

Hearing another round of shots ring out, Raven didn't hesitate to jump inside Mizan's car. Mizan was parked at the edge of the parking lot so he didn't get caught in the barrage of cars trying to get out. She saw her car stuck in the back. "My car . . . I have to get my car."

"I'll bring you back to it once the crowd clears and the shooting stops. You're good with me. Trust me," Mizan said in an attempt to reassure her.

Raven's cell phone vibrated and she quickly answered it when she saw Nikki's picture pop up on the screen.

"Where are you?" Raven answered.

"I'm with one of the dudes from the club. I just wanted to make sure you were straight," Nikki replied.

"Yeah, I'm good. I'm with Mizan, Where you want to meet up?" Raven asked.

"I'm gonna chill with dude for a minute. Let's meet back at your car in a couple hours," Nikki stated.

"A'ight, that's cool."

Mizan reached over and brushed a stray hair from Raven's face. "You good, ma? You look kind of shook over there. You live in Flint so I know you done heard gunshots before, superstar," he teased.

She cut her eyes at him and pursed her lips. "Shut up. I wasn't scared. That ain't nothing new to me," she replied, trying to play tough. But, in actuality, it *was* new to her. Yes, she had heard about the murders and mayhem that her hometown had to offer. She even knew that her father was behind a lot of the madness, but he had kept her far removed from the chaos. So to be so up close to a shootout had indeed shaken her.

"Yeah, a'ight, tough girl," he stated in a disbelieving tone with a smile. "So you gon' let me spend some time with you, ma? Get to know you?"

"Yeah, we can work something out." She blushed, slightly flattered because Mizan was so much older than she was.

He took her back to his north side home and they sat in his driveway. Raven was inexperienced with older men. She was usually confident and commanded the conversation, but with him she felt awkward, as if nothing she had to say would matter to him. To avoid looking stupid she remained quiet. Mizan studied her curiously, and as he stared at her she became insecure. She was conscious of every imperfection on her body. Like most young girls she was cocky, but not truly confident in herself; relying on her looks too much, allowing her intelligence to take a backseat in order to attract a nigga. *Damn, it feel like I got a booger. Is my hair still in place?* She fidgeted in her seat and flicked her long hair behind her shoulders as she took a deep breath.

Cool and collected, Mizan chuckled. "You a'ight over there, shorty? You nervous?"

"I'm good," she responded.

"Nah, you nervous, ma. Loosen up. I got something that will make you feel right," he said as he reached over her and pulled a bag of cush marijuana out of the glove compartment.

"You smoke?" he asked with a mischievous smile.

She nodded. Although she had tried it before she wasn't really a weed head, but she was not about to tell him that. "Yeah, I'm on that with you," she replied, trying to sound cool.

Mizan split the cigar and emptied the legal contents, then replaced it with his own concoction of marijuana and cocaine. Raven noticed that he sprinkled the white powder on top of the cush, and her heart began to speed up anxiously. She knew that some people laced their weed to get a better high, but it wasn't something she was curious about trying. As she watched Mizan's tongue form the blunt, a lump formed in her throat. He lit it and a funny smell filled the car, as a hypnotizing trail of smoke danced around her head. The smoke was seductive as it consumed the car slowly.

Mizan extended his hand to Raven, the glowing tip staring her in the eye.

"Hit this, ma," he choked out as smoke left his mouth.

Peer pressure is a mutha to a seventeen-year-old girl trying to be down. There was no way she was going to tell him no. All the years of preaching and teaching from her parents had been flushed down the drain as soon as an older boy put something new in her head. Her conscience screamed a long *Nooooooo!* Yet she ignored the tiny voice and reached for the blunt. Knowing she was doing wrong, she pouted her perfect pretty lips and puffed on the blunt, causing an amber glow to spark on the tip as she hit the weed.

Her lips went numb as she allowed the smoke into her lungs. She held the blunt out for him to take back, but he shook his head. "You hit that a few more times," he said. Raven leaned back in her seat and continued to blaze, her head relaxed against the headrest.

After smoking it halfway by herself, her eyelids were heavy and she felt so right. The high had her stuck and she smiled dumbly as she put the blunt to Mizan's lips. He toked and then asked, "You feeling a'ight?"

"I'm good," she replied as she coughed.

They sat in his driveway talking and joking for hours. Now that she was at ease, the conversation flowed smoothly and they got to know one another. Once the initial tension went away, she was so comfortable with him and enjoyed his company. Things just flowed between them. Before she knew it, it was time for her to meet back up with Nikki.

"We better go. It's getting late," she said.

"You're welcome to stay the night," Mizan stated in a low tone. He had no problem having an all-night fuck session with her. In fact, it was what he'd had in mind from the first moment he saw her. He wasn't a man of good intentions and a mature woman may have peeped game, but Raven was blind to everything except for his good looks and hood appeal. She felt her love box thump, and she tensed up as Mizan leaned across the seat to kiss her lips. His tongue slid into her mouth so smooth as if he had done this a thousand times before. His tongue tasted like candy. He was teasing her and making the temperature in the car rise from his expert seduction. He kissed her unlike she had ever been kissed before. He was a grown man, and the way his hands touched her neck to pull her closer let her know that anyone she had dealt with before was an amateur. She would have to be careful with her young heart because he could easily capture it. She was playing in an entirely new league, and she hoped she wasn't biting off more than she could chew. Intimidation filled her, but her wet panties urged her on. She was curious, and the pulse of lust that throbbed on her clit had her going crazy. She instantly knew that he was more experienced than she was. His resume of conquests was three pages long and he was about to make her another notch on his belt.

"You want to come in for a minute?" he asked.

"Nigga, I'm not a jump off," she said seriously as she pulled back slightly.

"I'm just trying to kick it with you, shorty. Kill all that attitude."

She loved the way he commanded her. He took charge of her and kept her in check. There was something mysterious about him that she liked.

"Let me just call my girl to let her know what's up." As she looked down at her phone, she saw that it was off. The battery had died so she switched the battery and powered it back on to see that she had missed seven calls. As soon as it's came to life it vibrated in her hands. Nikki's face popped on the caller ID.

"Hey, girl, I was just about to call you," Raven said.

"Bitch, where have you been? I've been blowing you up! Your dad called my house and my mama told him you weren't there. He's been trying to call you. He's pissed the fuck off, Rae. He's got his people out looking for you and everything. You need to get to your car and go to the crib."

"Thanks, girl." Raven tried to keep her cool in front of Mizan, but inside her heart was beating out of her chest and her gut instantly bubbled over. *Fuck . . . fuck . . . fuck!* she shouted in her head as her hands began to sweat. "I need to get back to my car." Her voice trembled a little when she spoke and the pit of her stomach felt hollow. She tried to come up with a lie, but at that moment the only thing she could think of was facing her father's wrath. *My shit was so sloppy tonight. I never get caught up like this,* she thought, beating herself up. *I should have had Nik forward the calls from her mom's house phone to her cell phone. Fuck!*

"Everything a'ight?" Mizan asked as he backed out of the driveway and headed back to the club.

"Yeah, I just need to get back to my car. Can you drive a little bit faster?" she asked, her entire mood changing.

When they got to the club she jumped out of the car. "I'll call you," she stated quickly as she unlocked her whip.

"Yo', where your girl at?" Mizan asked, looking around the deserted parking lot.

"She got into something. I'm good though," Raven responded.

"Nah, ma . . . I'ma follow you home and make sure you get in the house safely," Mizan said.

"No!" Raven shouted. Mizan frowned when he heard the urgency in her voice. She caught herself and finished, "I'm okay. I don't live too far from here. I'll get at you tomorrow."

Raven got into her car and pulled off, pushing her pedal to the floor as she tried to make it home.

***

Raven hit ninety miles per hour on the freeway trying to make it to Grand Blanc. When she finally arrived at her house, all of the lights were on inside. She knew that both her mother and father were waiting for her. It felt like judgment day as she turned off her car and took a deep breath, preparing herself for the worst. Just as she stepped out of her car, she saw a pair of headlights pull into the driveway behind her. She turned around and her eyes widened in a panic when she saw Mizan's car.

"What are you doing here?" she asked as she rushed over to him. She looked back to her front door, and her heart beat out of her chest when she saw the porch light come on.

"It's four o'clock in the morning, shorty. I wasn't gon' let you drive to the crib by yourself. I was just making sure you made it here safely," he said as he got out of the car.

"You've got to go . . . like now!" she stated, but when she saw her parents step outside she knew that it was too late. She was going to have to face the music. There was no lying her way out of this. Her mother and father came over to her.

"Benny Atkins is your pops?" Mizan asked as he looked at her for answers.

A lump formed in her throat. All she could do was nod.

Her father stepped to her and took her chin in his hands. He moved her face from side to side as if to see if his precious daughter had been ruined. "Do you know what time it is? Where have you been?"

"I was on the strip," she admitted, avoiding her father's icy glare. She wanted to lie to him, but insulting his intelligence would just get her in deeper trouble. He stared at her, and then his cold eyes graced Mizan.

"Who the fuck is this nigga and why is he in my driveway?" Benjamin asked as he stared Mizan in his eyes.

"No disrespect, fam . . . I just followed her to the crib to make sure she made it here a'ight. I'm Mizan," he stated as he held out his hand, trying to be cordial. He knew exactly who Benny Atkins was and how he got down. He had also heard that he had a daughter who was off limits. If he had known who Raven was he would've never stepped to her.

Benjamin looked at Mizan's hand and frowned in disapproval. "Who the fuck is this li'l nigga, Raven?" he asked.

"He's just a friend, Daddy," she replied. "Mommy, he's just a friend." Her eyes pleaded with her mother to intervene before her father lost his cool.

Justine Atkins stepped up and shook Mizan's hand. "It's nice to meet you, Mizan, but Raven is only seventeen years old and she has a curfew. Next time we hope that you make sure she abides by it."

Mizan looked at Raven in surprise when he found out she was only seventeen. *Li'l mama bad as hell,* he thought. *But, damn, she's jail bait.* He nodded and replied, "No doubt. I didn't know she had a curfew. The next time we kick it I'll make sure I have her home on time. Good night." Mizan headed back to his car.

Benjamin nodded at Mizan, dismissing him without words. Raven couldn't help but smile because Mizan had clearly said that he was interested in seeing her again. Justine could see the attraction in her daughter's eyes.

"Mizan," Justine called out as she wrapped her silk robe tighter around her body. "We don't let our daughter go out with just anyone. Why don't you stop by tomorrow so we can get to know you better? We're having a fish fry for our youngest daughter's birthday."

Mizan nodded, and winked at a blushing Raven, while Benjamin turned to look at his wife like she was insane.

Justine grabbed her husband's hand and led him into the house as Raven followed close behind.

"What were you doing in the inner city?" Benjamin calmly asked his daughter once they were inside. He didn't have to raise his voice in order to express his anger. Raven could see his temple throbbing, and his red, worried eyes made a streak of guilt run through her.

"I was just chilling, Daddy . . . I knew you wouldn't have let me go if I had asked you," Raven said in a baby's voice. She was a daddy's girl and hated for him to be upset with her. The look of disappointment he gave her made her want to cry.

"Then you come in here with that grown-ass nigga. You're seventeen, Raven. You're still my baby girl. A nigga like that shouldn't even know where you rest your head. I taught you better than that!" he said. He had to stop himself from speaking because he was too angry with her to control his emotions. She didn't understand the magnitude of her irresponsible actions. He had done a lot of dirt over the years. The makings of a boss required a lot of work, and he knew that he was the perfect target for a young nigga looking to come up. Having two daughters and a wife made it that much easier for him to be touched. They were his weakness, especially his beloved Raven. She was his firstborn and he would catch a body if anything ever happened to her. He rubbed his stubby facial hair as he paced back and forth in the foyer. Raven stood before him with tears building in her eyes. He walked over to her and hugged her tightly, kissing the top of her head.

"I love you, Rae. I need you to understand that I'm just trying to keep you safe. There is no point to us living out here in the suburbs if you insist on going back to the hood every chance you get. I'm trying to save you from a lifestyle you can't handle. I want better for you than what

I am. That li'l nigga you brought here tonight is too familiar. Twenty years ago that was me and you deserve better
than that. You deserve the world, Rae. Go and get some
sleep. We've got a busy day tomorrow. I want you up early to help your mama get ready for the party tomorrow."

Raven nodded and ascended the stairs. When she
reached the top she turned and said, "Daddy, what's my
punishment?"

Benjamin shook his head and sighed. He knew the day
would come when a young nigga would come knocking
at his door for his firstborn, but he hoped it would never
be a nigga like Mizan. He wanted to lock her away and
hide the key. If he could he would keep her away from
the world. He had never reprimanded her a day in her
life, and although he wanted to, he wasn't going to today.
As he looked up at her in disappointment, he said, "You
don't punish the ones you love, Rae. Remember that.
Just don't let it happen again. Go to bed, princess."

Raven gave her father a smile and headed to her room.
When she passed her parents' bedroom, she noticed that
her mother's light was still on.

"Hey, Mommy," she said as she peeked inside the room.

"You like that boy, huh?" Justine asked as she patted
the empty spot beside her. Raven sat down on the bed.
Her infectious smile revealed her true feelings about Mizan. "He's cute," her mother said. "How old did you tell
him you were?"

Raven didn't respond and her mother continued, "Raven, he's not one of these little boys you got chasing behind you at your high school. He looks like he's at least
three years older than you. I know what it's like to be
your age and have all the older guys checking for you. It
feels good to have the attention, but this boy has got a lot
more game than you do, Rae. I'm not going to try to tell
you who you can and cannot see. In a few months you

will be eighteen, so I'll leave the decision up to you, but you need to be careful with him."

"I will, ma. I promise," Raven answered as she got up and headed to her room.

"Oh, yeah, and Raven!" her mother called, stopping her in her tracks.

"Yeah, Mommy?" she responded, turning around to look at her.

"The next time you bring your ass in here high I'ma beat the black off of you. Divas don't smoke. You leave that to the niggas. As long as you conduct yourself like a lady then everyone around you will have to treat you like one. Also, Morgan looks up to you. She's your baby sister and she's watching everything you do. She wants to be just like you so you got to show her how to be a lady the same way I showed you, understand?" her mother stated sternly, wisdom lacing her tone.

Raven nodded her head and replied, "Yeah, Mommy, I understand."

"Now go take a shower and wash the smoke out of your hair before your father smells it on you," Justine instructed. She shook her head as she watched her daughter walk out of the room. *I swear, that girl is too much like me when I was her age. I'ma have to keep a close eye on her. She think she's grown, but I'm queen bee up in here. With her little cute self,* Justine thought with a smile while shaking her head. She couldn't help but think back to the day a hood fella came into her life . . . back to the day when she got caught up in the love of her life, Benjamin Atkins.

1975
Sixteen-year-old Justine Washington was a fly girl. In roller skates, a stone-washed mini skirt, and a halter

top she leaned against the banister of TLC Skating Rink while chitchatting with her girlfriends as all the guys rolled by showing off. She was a beautiful distraction as her pretty, long, freshly oiled legs shined underneath the colored strobe light, and she bopped her head to the sounds of Parliament and Funkadelic.

"Hey, Corey!" she called out as the most popular guy in school went past her, full speed. He turned his head and winked at her as he spun on his wheels, trying to impress her. He began to skate backward as they stared at each other while he did circles around her. Staring a moment too long at the most popular girl in school, he lost his balance and went ass first falling to the floor. Justine and her girls cracked up as they turned and skated away.

"Damn, Jus, girl, the boy gon' break his neck trying to get at you," her best friend, Minnie, exclaimed.

Justine laughed as she commanded the skating rink as if she owned it. Her hips swayed from side to side as she raised her hands in the air snapping her fingers to the beat. Everybody who was anybody was there on the Saturday night when the eighteen-and-up crowd commanded the club. With her grown-up looks and fake ID, she had gotten into the rink without problem. She was easily the belle of the ball. Her infatuation with attention came from the lack of it she received at home. Her mother was a mean drunk who despised her daughter for "taking the best years of her life." She blamed Justine for robbing her of her figure, because after she gave birth, she went from a voluptous size twelve to a sloppy twenty-eight. When her mother's size bounced, so did Justine's father, and now her mother was miserable, allowing man after man into her life to make her feel good. Most days she acted as if Justine did not exist, which left Justine feeling alone in a world so cold. With an ab-

sentee father and a selfish mother, this left a huge void in her heart. So any amount of attention she got was a good thing to her, which was why her skirts were always a little high and her blouses cut a little low; to turn heads.

Being center stage, Justine floated on four wheels like a professional, when she noticed she had an audience. Dripping in gold and leaned up against the wall with one foot propped up sat Benny Atkins, the finest man she had ever seen. He was surrounded by an entourage of men, and as he stared at her cooly, she felt power emanating from him. His brown, smooth skin and bedroom eyes were attractive, and she gave him a flirtatious smile, She really got into her moves as Michael Jackson's new hit blared from the speakers. She could tell by his cockiness that he was a little bit older than she. Not once did his eyes leave hers, letting her know that he was definitely staring at something he liked. He nodded at her when the song ended. She skated away with her girls, hoping that she had piqued his interest and that he would try to approach her. But to her surprise, when she turned back to look, their thing had passed. He was kicking it with the fellas and entertaining the next pretty young thing who had crossed his path. This put her in a funk the rest of the night. She purposefully walked past him, switching her wide hips so hard that she thought she had popped them out of place, but to no avail. He did not even notice, being too wrapped up in big-booty Kima, the neighborhood freak.

Smacking her teeth, she turned to her girl Minnie and said, "This is lame. I'm outta here."

"You don't want to hang out in the parking lot. Come on, Jus. You know that everybody's going to stick around for at least an hour," Minnie pleaded.

"Nah, girl, I'm out, but you stay and groove. I'm right around the way so I can walk home. Call me tomorrow," Justine said as she sat down to remove her skates. She hugged her best friend and headed out the door with the rest of the crowd. Dudes were already posted up outside waiting for the unofficial afterparty to begin. She got catcalls and "hey, babys" as she made her way across the lot. On the dark Flint city streets, she strolled carelessly. The city was completely different during that time. Affluence from the General Motors shops kept the residents well fed and crime was a rare occurrence, so she didn't think twice about walking the six blocks to her crib.

She was halfway home when the fear of what she may encounter when she arrived settled in. Her mother's bed was like a revolving door, and oftentimes the men invited inside had roaming eyes and hands. A creepy feeling crawled up her spine as she turned the corner to her street, and saw the Chevy Caprice sitting in her driveway, letting her know that her mother was entertaining company. She was always left to fend for herself and had learned a long time ago that her mother was not her savior. Her mother's motto was that grown bitches took care of themselves. "Since you got tits and ass you's a grown bitch. You quit switching around here and my men might not want a taste," she had said the first time Justine had told her mother about one of her boyfriend's pedophiliac ways. She took a deep breath and used her key to open the door. Her heart skipped a beat when she saw her mother passed out in a liquor-induced coma while her company felt her up. Justine quickly tried to pass, but her path was blocked when her mother's guy friend arose from the couch. A lone tear graced her cheek when she noticed the lustful look filling the man's eyes. He was a new guy. She had never seen him before, but she had seen that look of desire many times. Her eyes fell to the floor. Not again, she thought miserably, already knowing what was to come.

Benny Atkins was the man in his city. Young, fly, and fresh, he was in his prime. Out for a night on the town, he had let his friends talk him into doing something he never did . . . relax. It was a celebration of sorts. Benjamin "Benny" Atkins had secured his first heroine connection, and he could only imagine the type of money he was about to come into. At twenty years old he had the world in the palms of his hands. I'ma show these niggas how to hustle . . . how to get this money, he thought as he crossed one shell toe Adidas over the other, and leaned on his brand new Cadillac Deville. There was only one man standing in his way and that was Sherman Oaks, his old connect. Sherman was a washed-up hustler, a number man who had made the transition to heroine after seeing how much money there was to make during the Vietnam War. But he was a thorn in Benny's side. The old man didn't want to see the young hood star rise above him, and had threatened Benny's life by putting a street contract on his head. Benny wasn't scared. He had mad love in his city and he only had one mentality: hit Sherman before Sherman hit him. Get or get got. They had been playing a game of hide-and-seek with one another for weeks, but when his right-hand man whispered in his ear, "We know where he at," Benny knew that it was his lucky day.

When they pulled up to the small, dilapidated, one-story house, Benny ensured that his gun was loaded. "Keep the car running," he told one of his goons as he and his right-hand man, Wood, got out of the car. "We're in and out." Benny knew that the murder would not take long.

He did not intend on making Sherman suffer. He wasn't about games, only gunplay. One shot to the head would get the job done, and then he would be gone like a thief in the night.

"Please don't do this," she begged as she tried to pull her shirt out of his grasp. "Ma!" she called out. Her cries were useless. Her mother so far gone from the liquor that she could not awaken until after she slept it off.

"Bitch, shut up and take this dick. Consider it a blessing," he said as he backhanded her so hard it sent her flying to the floor. Justine scooted away from him as she held her face, feeling the gash that his watch had made, as hot, salty tears burned the wound. She shook her head and backed up until her back hit the wall. "Please . . ." she sobbed. She watched him look down at her devilishly as he removed his belt and unbuttoned his pants. He removed his gun and placed it near his pants, and got down on the floor, grabbing her legs forcefully as she tried to kick him off.

"No!" she yelled, terrified. "Mama! Wake up!"

"Yeah, I bet you this young pussy tight," he said lustfully as he began to kiss her neck, ignoring her desperate pleas. The scent of him made her stomach turn as her fists beat his chest in protest. He pried her young legs open, forcing them so far apart that pain shot through her lower back. She brought her knee up as hard as she could to his groin, but he moved just in time. "Look, bitch. Be still!" he yelled as he grabbed her head and slammed it as hard as he could against the floor. Justine saw stars as her head fell to the side. Disoriented, she couldn't fight back as bells went off in her head. She could feel his hard penis at her opening as tears trailed her cheeks and graced the floor. Please, God, let him be

quick, she prayed as she reached out in a desperate attempt to save herself.

Benny Atkins kicked in the door and rushed in with his guns aimed, ready to hit anything moving.

"What the fuck!" Sherman cried out as he turned around to see Benny standing behind him. He had been caught in the worst way, with his pants down.

"Fuck you doing, ol' man?" Wood asked in disgust as he looked at Justine sprawled out across the floor, crying.

Benny instantly recognized the girl as the fresh chick from the skating rink, and he trained his pistol on Sherman. "You like little girls, my nigga?" he asked.

"Nah, Benny . . . you know how it is. I was just having a little fun, playa," Sherman said nervously as he pulled up his underwear.

"Don't look like she having too much fun," Benny said, his eyes turning dark with every word he spoke. "Help her up, Wood," he instructed.

Justined was crying so hard that she couldn't get up from the floor. All the while her mother lay clueless on the couch. She felt Wood scoop her in his arms and help her stand.

"Come on, man. You can have the streets, Benny. Just put the gun down. I taught you everything you know, man. Return the favor and put the gun away." Sherman spoke fast so he could buy himself some time.

Benny nodded his head and replied, "I'll tell you what. If babygirl say you can live . . . then you'll live. If not . . ."

Before Benny could finish his sentence gunshots rang out in the house.

Boom! Boom! Boom! Boom!

Justine had grabbed Sherman's gun and shot him without thinking twice. Her hands shook violently, but the hatred in her eyes let Benny know that she had been hurt many times before, and she had just made Sherman pay for it . . . with his life.

Benny walked up to her cautiously and wrapped his hand around the smoking gun. After he removed it from her hands she collapsed into his chest, sobbing.

"It's all right . . . everything's okay," Benny soothed. He nodded to his man and passed him the murder weapon. Wood opened his eyes wide as if to say, "Shorty ain't playing." He took the gun and knew that he was supposed to peform a magic trick by making it disappear.

Benjamin began to walk away, leaving Justine crying and holding herself as she stared at the dead man on her living room floor. But his gut wouldn't let him leave her there like that. When he turned around, he noticed how beautiful she was. In such a delicate state she needed him. She was like a leaf hanging on to a limb, and the winds of life were threatening to blow her away. She needed him. She needed him to stabilize her life. To be her root, her new beginning, her everything. He could sense it in her eyes. Justine was the lady for him. He walked back over to her and removed his coat, wrapping it around her quivering body. "Is there somewhere I can take you?" he asked.

She looked up at him with desperate eyes and shook her head. She had no one. It had just been her for as long as she could remember. Even with the presence of her mother she always felt lonely. No one cared. All she had was herself and a mind full of painful memories that made life seem unbearable.

He looked around at the tiny house, and at her deadbeat mother. There was no way he could leave her there. "You're coming with me. I'ma make sure you're all right," he asserted. He scooped her into his arms and Wood opened the door for them as they made their exit. It was the last time that Justine ever saw her mother. She kissed her old life good-bye.

Benjamin made good on his promise and made sure that Justine was okay. He fell in love with her instantly, and as he rose to the top of the game, so did she. He made her tell him the names of every man who had ever brought her harm, and mysteriously they all had gruesome misfortunes, meeting their fate earlier than they had anticipated at the hands of an upcoming hood legend. He wanted her to know that as long as he was around she had no one to fear. Her life was butter from that day forward. He made her his world and the queen of the streets.

Justine wiped the tears from her eyes as she snapped out of her daydreams. Her husband, Raven's father, had saved her life. Before him she had not known what love was. Now she had two beautiful daughters and anything she could ever want. She had given her life to a hustler, so she knew what it took to be the dopeman's lady . . . and as she reminisced on everything they had been through together, she was positive that Raven was not ready to live the life. *She thinks she's ready, but she's not. She's just a baby . . . my baby,* Justine thought. She did not want the lifestyle of the hood for her daughter, and everything about Mizan spelled H-U-S-T-L-E-R. *Yeah, I'll have to keep my eye on her. Niggas ain't the same no more. They don't make hustlers like Benny anymore. She deserves so much more.* Justine shook old memories from her thoughts and turned off her bedroom light, retiring for the night.

Chapter Two

The next day, the Atkins' brought the hood to their prestigious, affluent community as all of the hustlers in Benjamin's circle came out to show him love at Morgan's birthday cookout. His youngest daughter was deaf, so he always went above and beyond to make her feel as included and loved as possible. It was something they did annually for her, and somehow, every single year, the children's party transformed into an adult party. Raven and Nikki were both wearing swimsuit tops and shorts that left nothing to the imagination. It was unusually hot outside as the sun blazed brightly. Michigan didn't normally warm up until late June, but as Raven watched her little sister and the rest of the kids splashing around in the pool, she was anxious to sit around in her bikini and enjoy the beautiful day. Everybody in the backyard came from nothing, but they were now working with legit businesses while holding reign over the city streets . . . all thanks to the leadership of Benjamin. Benjamin was the king, and the hustlers, along with their wives and children, were the courtship of his kingdom.

"What did your dad say when you came in last night?" Nikki asked nosily.

"He was mad, but he's over it now. My mama invited Mizan to the party. I don't know if he gon' show up though. I haven't heard from him yet. I don't know if he'll call cuz my mama threw salt in the game when she told him my real age," Raven explained.

"Rae! You and Nikki come in here and grab some of this food! Y'all ain't just about to be standing around looking cute. Come help me," Justine called out to the pair.

They went and grabbed the silver pans of side dishes that Justine had whipped up, and carried them outside. Liquor flowed freely and the smell of weed was potent in the air as old school music played inside the house. They may have lived in lavish luxury, but there was nothing snobbish about the royal family. The scent of soul food permeated the air, while the sound of dominoes being smashed on the tabletops resounded throughout the backyard. Benjamin and Justine kept it all the way real, all the time. They were good peoples and enjoyed the family environment as they celebrated their youngest child. They all felt safe because there were no outsiders in their club. Trust was at 100 percent among the men, so they each felt comfortable, so much so that Benjamin allowed everyone to let loose and enjoy the party without putting men on post to guard his home. It was all love because everyone in attendance had pledged their allegiance to Benjamin and vice versa.

"Raven, come over here . . . I want you to meet somebody," Benjamin called out.

"Damn, who is that?" Nikki commented as she lifted her hand to block the sun so she could get a better view.

Raven turned in the direction of her father and lifted her sunglasses when she saw the same dude she had seen the night before at the corner store. "I don't know, but I'm about to find out," she told her friend as she placed her glasses on top of her head and walked over to her father.

"Ethic, this is my daughter, Raven . . . Rae, this is Ethic. He works for me," Benjamin stated. Before they could say anything to each other Justine called Benjamin into the house. "Rae, go to the store and grab some more ice for the coolers!"

"I'm blocked in!" she yelled.

Benjamin pointed to Ethic. "Ethic will take you. He's new in town. It'll give you a chance to get acquainted."

"So you're from Missouri?" Raven asked, making small talk as she and Ethic walked to the front yard.

He nodded as he led her to his car and opened the passenger door for her. She hopped in and then slid over into the driver's seat. When he made it around to the driver's side she held her hand out. "I'll drive," she stated with a smile.

He opened the door and said, "A little girl like you can't handle my whip, ma . . . scoot over."

"Oh, I can handle it just fine. I've ridden bigger things," she insinuated, not moving an inch. "What, you don't want your little girlfriend from yesterday to see me driving your car. No offense, but somebody like you needs to upgrade. I would think you would have a better bitch on your arm," Raven said bluntly.

Ethic scoffed and shook his head at her slick comment. "You should clean up that mouth of yours," he said as he handed her the keys. He got into the passenger side as Raven started the car. She pulled away from the curb. "Don't wreck my shit, ma, this will drive itself. All you got to do is steer," he instructed as he leaned back in his seat.

"I got you . . . I'm not gon' tear up your car," she stated as she eased into traffic. "So was that your girl you were talking to yesterday?" she asked.

"No, that wasn't my lady," he replied.

"So do you have a chick?"

He laughed as he adjusted his fitted cap, pulling it so low on his head that it almost covered his mysterious eyes.

"You ask a lot of questions," he said. "Why are you so interested in me? I'm a grown man. Don't you have little high schoolers or something checking for you?"

"Yeah, but I'm not worried about them . . . I'm checking for you," she admitted.

"Nah, you checking for ol' boy you were with last night," he shot back. "That ho-ass nigga. You should watch the type of company *you* keep."

She smacked her lips and looked at him out of the corner of her eye. "What, you were jealous?"

"You wild, ma," he said as he shook his head at her persistence. He gazed out the window as they rode through the ruthless city.

"I saw you watching me," she said after they'd reached the store and parked. She turned in her seat to face him.

"That was before," he said.

"Before what?" she asked.

"Before you opened your mouth to speak. You're a young'un, ma. You don't know shit about the world around you. You pushing grown woman whips and rocking grown woman clothes." He tapped her temple gently as he leaned close to her ear. "But up here you're still a baby."

"Boy, boo," she replied curtly with a flip of her hand. "I'm a grown-ass woman. I'ma be eighteen in a few months," she stated as if that made her an adult. "How old are you?"

"Twenty-two."

"You can be my old head," she replied flirtatiously. "Admit it, all the rest of these busted bitches ain't what you into. I'm the only girl that's gon' look good on your arm."

"That's the problem, shorty . . . I'm not looking for a girl. I want a woman, and you not there yet." He exited the car, leaving Raven with heavy thoughts on her mind.

Mizan sat in his car with his automatic pistol lying in his lap as he watched people going in and out of the Atkins home. When he had originally lay eyes on Raven he had no clue that she was the daughter of Flint's largest king-pin. His jack boy status kept him in the grimiest parts of the hood, places where Raven would never frequent. They were two individuals living in the same city, but their perceptions of Flint were drastically different. She sat at the top and looked down on the minions who inhabited the murder capital; whereas he was at the bottom clawing his way up inch by inch. Because of their differences in age and hood status, their paths had never crossed before, but all of that changed when the naïve, young girl walked into a small club on his side of town. Now that he knew who she was associated with, she was even more appealing to him. Just from being in her presence he had discovered what not many people knew: Benny Atkins' home address. It was a stick up kid's dream to be able to get inside of the infamous drug dealer's home, and because of Raven he had been extended a personal invitation. He was not about to take the chance of a lifetime for granted. He had his man, Bull, and his brother, Boo, lurking in a parked car a few blocks away with black masks and black gloves, just waiting for the word from Mizan to run up in the house.

I know that mu'fucka keep a safe at his crib, Mizan thought as he studied the home, watching friends of the family as they laughed and joked with one another. He, on the other hand, wasn't there to socialize. After finding out Raven's age he had thought of dismissing her. He didn't fuck with young chicks; the headaches they caused weren't worth the unexplored crevices between their thighs. But Raven was different. She was hood royalty, a sheltered daughter who wanted to be down, and he was about to put her on his team. He knew that it would be easy to capture her head. She was young and impressionable. She would be easy for him to mold. It was the number one rule of any nigga trying to lock down a loyal chick: *Fuck a bitch's mind and the body will follow,* Mizan thought, remembering what his deceased father had taught him when he was coming into adolescence. Mizan could see that Raven was in love with her father. Just from the small time he had seen them interacting, it was obvious that he was the king of her world. Mizan fully intended to break that bond. He wanted Raven for himself. On top of being the flyest little diva in the city, she was his meal ticket. He wanted her on his team. Her loyalty was about to shift from her father to her "new daddy," which was why he gone out of his way to show up to the little shindig.

He saw the black truck that whipped around the corner, and noticed Raven sitting behind the wheel. *Fuck is this mu'fucka she rolling with?* he thought, puzzled. He took the safety off of his pistol and tucked it in his waistband as he exited the car. He leaned against his car as he watched Raven park the vehicle on the curb. When she got out he noticed that she was frowned up, as if she had just got out of a heated discussion, but then she finally saw him. Her frown easily melted away .

"You came!" she said, surprised, her voice rising an octave. She walked across the street to him and hugged him as if she hadn't seen him in years. Mizan embraced her, wrapping one arm around her small waist as he kissed her neck.

"What, you thought I wouldn't?" he replied as he leaned against his car with his hands tucked in his pockets. He wore baggy Sean Jean jeans and a pale yellow designer polo, with fresh kicks. The waves in his fresh cut left her dizzy. He was clean and looked even better than the day before. Even Raven couldn't believe that she had pulled him.

"I thought when you found out how old I was you would crap out," she stated truthfully.

"When do you turn eighteen?" he asked.

"In August."

"Then I guess we'll have to keep this thing friendly until then, n'ah mean?" He licked his lips and looked down at her. He couldn't believe that the beautiful body before him belonged to a girl so young, but he appreciated it all the same. His eyes roamed her scantily clad body and he shook his head at the lovely sight. He glanced up the street and could see his goons obediently waiting to hear the word.

"We can head to the back. Are you hungry? We've got all kinds of food," Raven said as she led the way.

When Mizan walked past Benjamin, he nodded in acknowledgment. He could feel her father's eyes suspiciously trying to figure him out, but Raven was oblivious to it all. She beamed as she walked around proudly on his arm.

Justine watched her daughter and Mizan interact. She could see that Raven was into him and she could also see that her husband wasn't fond of the idea at all. She walked over to him and placed her hand on his back. "Stop frowning, Benny. She's seventeen. At least they are here at the house where we can keep an eye on them," she reasoned.

Benjamin nodded and kissed her cheek, but his frown never wavered. He watched as Mizan whispered in Raven's ear, and his blood boiled. He motioned for Ethic to come over to him.

"I want you to do me a favor, young blood. Keep an eye on that nigga over there with my daughter. I don't like how he move. Something about him ain't right," Benjamin said.

"We're reading out of the same book, fam. I'll keep an eye out," Ethic assured as he sat back and observed while slowly sipping a Heineken. Raven may not have sensed the shade in Mizan, but real recognized real, and every-thing about him spelled phony to Ethic. Even the way he interacted with Raven seemed rehearsed, as if he had his mind on other things. Little did Ethic know, Mizan had his eyes on robbing Benny Atkins.

Mizan wasn't focused on anything, but taking mental notes of his surroundings. He noticed that the only time someone went inside the house was to use the bathroom. Other than that the inside was off limits. It was the perfect setup. While everybody was partying and distracted out back, Mizan was about to hit the inside. He knew that his crew would have to get in and out. As he looked around at all the hustlers and street legends in attendance, he knew that they were strapped. If anything went wrong there would be no turning back. What he was trying to do was reckless, but the life and times of a jack boy often were. It was all or nothing, and Mizan was ready to make his move. "Yo', you got a restroom I can use?" he asked.

"Yeah, it's right inside. Go through the back door, it's the first door on your left," Raven instructed. As soon as he got inside the house, he walked around, making sure the coast was clear. After discovering that no one was in the house, he quickly unlocked the front door, and then headed back to the party.

As he sat back down next to Raven he pulled out his phone.

The front door is unlocked. In and out like a robbery, my niggas. Grab jewelry, money, product . . . every-thing else is too big to carry out of the house unnoticed. Try to find the safe.

"You having a good time?" Raven asked.

Mizan nodded and replied, "It's not my type of scene, but I know I got to put in time with your folk."

Raven's little sister ran up to her soaking wet, and wrapped her arms around her big sister's waist.

"Raven, is this your boyfriend?" Morgan asked through sign language, smiling.

"She can't hear?" Mizan asked.

"Nah, she's been deaf since she was born," Raven informed him.

"What did she say?" he asked.

"She wants to know if you're my man," Raven said with a smirk, putting him on the spot.

"Get out of here. She didn't ask you that shit," he laughed.

"I swear," Raven stated as she laughed too. He smiled and bent down so that he was eye level with Morgan. She was the spitting image of Raven. "She can read your lips so you can talk to her."

"I'm her friend, Mizan. What's your name?"

"Morgan Jacqueline Atkins," she signed proudly, then patted her cheeks as if she were putting on makeup. It was the sign that Raven had made up for her name when she was just a baby.

"Her name is Morgan," Raven interpreted.

Mizan pulled a twenty dollar bill out of his pocket and handed it to Morgan. "Happy Birthday."

Six-year-old Morgan looked at the money in her hands and frowned. "You don't have anything bigger than Andrew?" she signed, revealing her spoiled nature. She had been raised among the hood's elite and was used to them showering her with big face bills whenever they came around.

Raven relayed the message and Mizan looked at the mini-diva, shaking his head. "I got you, shorty . . ." He removed a fifty and handed it to her. "Is that better?"

She smiled brightly and nodded her head. She then tucked the twenty and the fifty dollar bills inside her swimsuit. "Thank you," she signed. Raven just shook her head and chuckled, knowing that her little sister had hustled almost a hundred bucks out of Mizan.

"Okay, can you go play now, Morgan?" Raven said.

"No, Mommy told me to tell you to help me get dressed. I'm tired of swimming. I want to put on my birthday outfit," she replied, her hands moving quickly to let Raven know that she wanted to change now. No exceptions.

Raven sighed and looked at Mizan. "She's such a brat. I'll be right back," she said, then grabbed Morgan's hand and led her into the house.

As Mizan saw Raven disappear inside the house he quickly took out his cell phone, hoping that his goons hadn't already entered.

"Agghhhhhhh!"

When he heard the ear, piercing scream he closed his eyes in regret, knowing that it was too late. "Fuck!" he muttered, knowing that the shit was about to hit the fan.

Justine dropped the plate of food she had in her hand and instantly began running full speed toward the house.

"Benjamin!" she screamed, knowing that something was wrong with her daughters.

Benjamin and an entire army of hustlers rushed toward the house, including Ethic who entered first, pistol in hand. He was ready to shoot anything moving.

When he entered he saw a crying Morgan and Raven in the hands of three masked men.

"Ethic!" Raven screamed as she tried to lunge for him, but she was restrained in a choke hold.

Morgan cried when her father came into view, reaching out as she opened her mouth in fear.

"Oh my God!" Justine cried when she saw what was happening.

"Get the fuck back before I blow this bitch brains all over the floor!" one of the intruders yelled.

Raven closed her eyes as tears streamed down her face. Her captor had a gun firmly planted against her temple. She braced herself, preparing for the worst as she shook like a leaf in the wind. The sounds of her little sister's cries tormented her.

Benjamin's trigger finger itched as he stood in front of his army of lieutenants. Everyone in the room was strapped, but he knew that if even one shot was fired then his two beautiful daughters would be dead. He stepped up next to Ethic and put his hands up.

"Everybody calm down. All I want are my daughters everything else you can take with you." Benjamin tried to conceal the malice in his voice as he stood not even five feet from the masked intruders. Ethic fell back into the crowd and grabbed Justine by the shoulders, ushering her back outside.

"You don't need to see what's about to go down in there," he whispered. "Stay out here . . . No matter what you hear, do not come in. I'ma handle it."

Justine nodded as she gripped his shirt. "Ethic . . . they're my babies."

"I know," he said as he sat her down in the lawn chair. He ran to the front yard, and noticed Mizan's car pulling away from the house. He made a mental note of it. *The nigga girl in there at gunpoint and he disappearing,* Ethic thought, suspicious. Hearing a loud scream come from the house, he knew he didn't have time to press the issue. Putting his suspicions of Mizan in his mental file, he refocused as he approached the front door. He pulled a .38 out of his ankle holster, and with a pistol in each hand he crept up onto the porch. He could see Benjamin through the screen door, and he put his finger to his lips to signal for him to keep his cool.

"Morgan, Raven, everything is going to be okay. Close your eyes," Benjamin said in both sign language and aloud as he stepped closer to the intruders, his hands still raised in the air. He made eye contact with Ethic, who nodded and aimed his two pistols at the two men who had the girls.

Morgan's wide eyes indicated her terror. She wet herself from the overwhelming fear. Raven just did as she was told.

"Didn't I say back the fuck—"

Pow! Pow! Pow!

Before the intruder could get the words out of his mouth, Ethic introduced a hollow point to his brain, shooting both men simultaneously. Before Benjamin could even speak, the third gunman looked like Swiss cheese as his goons let their cannons bark.

The bodies dropped instantly and blood covered Raven and young Morgan. Raven put her hands over her mouth to stifle her cries as she rocked back and forth.

Justine ran into the house and rushed over to her daughters. "You're okay, baby, you're okay," she whispered gratefully as she picked Morgan up, while Benjamin wrapped his arms around their eldest child. Nikki burst through the crowd and fell to the floor to embrace Raven. She cried with her best friend as they both thought of how close death had been.

"Fuck did they get in here?" Benjamin shouted in outrage as he turned to the men in the room. "How did they know where I live?" He leaned into Ethic and shook his hand, embracing him slightly. He was especially grateful to him. "Take my wife and kids someplace safe. I have to find out who was behind this and get these bodies out of here," Benjamin said. He walked over to Justine and told her that she would be leaving with Ethic. She nodded and carried her daughter out of the house. Ethic turned to Raven, who was still holding on to Nikki for dear life. He watched as Benjamin approached her.

"Baby girl, I need you to be strong for Daddy. You're going to go with Ethic," he said.

"No, I want to stay here with you." She couldn't stop the tears from flowing down her cheeks, and the only place she felt safe was in her father's presence.

"You can't, Rae . . . you can't stay here, not tonight. Trust me, baby girl. Ethic will take care of you. Just go with him." He hugged her tightly, and then walked away.

"Call me and let me know you're okay," Nikki whispered in her ear as she hugged her one last time.

Raven nodded, then Ethic put his hand on the small of her back and led her to his car. She was silent as she watched the city streets pass, and she rubbed her sister's hair gently, trying to ease her soul. Her head was spinning, and no matter how hard she tried, she couldn't restore her tough girl visage. When the car stopped moving she looked up and noticed that they were at a house, but nice modest, home. She opened the car door and stepped out without speaking. Her bloody clothes felt disgusting on her body and made her want to throw up. She felt her mouth water and she inhaled deeply to stop herself from becoming sick.

Ethic welcomed them into his three-bedroom, tri-level home. He set them up in his spare rooms, allowing Justine and Morgan to sleep together.

"Thank you, Ethic. My husband speaks very highly of you, and after what you did today, I can see exactly what he says is true," Justine said. "I'm going to put Morgan to bed, but I want to let you know that I appreciate you allowing us to stay here for the night."

"Not a problem. Let me know if you need anything," Ethic said. He turned to Raven, who stood in the hallway, and pointed to the room across the hall. "You can sleep in here."

He stood in the doorway as he watched Raven in front of the dresser mirror. She looked at the blood covering her shirt, and her hands began to shake.

"There are clothes in the drawer and towels in the closet. The bathroom's down the hall," he said.

She nodded, but said nothing as she watched him leave the room. She grabbed the towels and headed for the bathroom. As she stepped into the shower, her tears mixed with the water, and she lowered her head so that it could run through her hair. She closed her eyes and put her hands on the shower walls. This was the first time she realized that the streets were not a game. There was more to them than the glitz and glamour. She had almost lost her life and that fact shook her to the core, causing her stomach to turn. She had never seen a dead body before, and flashes of the men lying with their brains leaking onto the floor plagued her. She just couldn't get the images out of her head. She jumped out of the shower and wrapped a towel around her as she felt vomit tickling her throat.

She leaned over the toilet and heaved violently, her nerves bringing up everything that she had eaten that day. She hugged the toilet as she sank to the floor. A knock at the door caused her to wipe her eyes. She hated to seem like a child, so she grabbed a tissue to soak up her tears as Ethic's voice echoed through the door.

"Raven, everything a'ight?" he asked.

No, everything's not all right, she thought.

He opened the door and saw her sitting on the floor. She stood up as he came in and closed the door. "You okay?" he asked.

She simply nodded because she knew that if she spoke, her floodgates would fail her. Her wet hair hung in her face and made her shiver as she stood in front of Ethic. "I thought they were going to kill me," she whispered, her eyes distant, as if she was recalling everything in her mind.

He put his hand on her neck and massaged it gently as he stared at her empathetically. "But they didn't."

"But they could have," she responded quickly.

He shook his head. "I would not have let that happen."

She fell into his chest and sobbed uncontrollably. Ethic fought with himself, trying to decide if he should hold her, but as he listened to her weep, he realized this was the real Raven: a weak and vulnerable girl who wasn't ready for the lifestyle she so desperately wanted to lead. He wrapped his arms around her and allowed her to release her fear. She was trembling and he thought that her knees may give out beneath her. Scooping her in his arms, he carried her into the spare room. Her eyes were red and puffy as he lay her in the bed.

"I don't want to sleep," she whispered.

"You're safe here. I'll be right here next to you," he promised as he took a seat in the chair next to the bed. He sat facing toward her and leaned down over her as if he was tucking her in. He ran his hand over her face. "Close your eyes, Raven," he whispered. "I'm not going anywhere."

Raven awoke the next day to an empty room. Looking at the clock, she noticed that it was only six in the morning. She arose from the bed and walked out into the hallway. She could hear noise coming from somewhere in the house and she paused mid-step, listening closely. She crept toward the kitchen and realized that the noise was coming from the basement. She crept down the steps, her bare, manicured feet sinking into the plush carpet. She stopped when she saw a shirtless Ethic lifting weights in the basement, his toned chest glistened with sweat as he gritted his teeth while pressing the weights above his head. Raven was in awe as she watched every muscle of his body bulge. Her mouth was wide open as she enjoyed the show. He was the sexiest man she had ever seen in her life. Her attraction to him was more than a schoolgirl crush. She loved him and she didn't even know his last name. Ethic put the weights on their stand and sat up to find her staring at him. Embarrassment flushed her face, but neither of them said a word. He turned his back on her and continued his routine as if she weren't standing there.

"I . . . um . . . I wanted to know if you had heard from my daddy," she said as she leaned against the wall.

"He called late last night. I'll be taking you back home when your moms wake up," he said through clenched teeth as he curled the free weights, working his biceps.

Raven continued to stand there as her eyes roamed his body. He stopped and turned toward her, breathing hard from exhaustion. "Did you want something else?" he asked in an annoyed tone.

Raven was at a loss for words. Of course she wanted something else. She wanted him. The way he had protected her last night reminded her of her father. He was perfect for her and he didn't even know it. She tried to find the courage to tell him how she felt, but she knew that words couldn't express how she was feeling. She walked up on him slowly, almost timidly, afraid of how he was going to react to what she was about to do. There weren't too many people who intimidated her, but Ethic did. He made her nervous, and as she stood in front of him her heart beat out of her chest. She closed her eyes and went for it, standing on the tips of her toes to kiss him.

Ethic stepped back and pushed her away, gently but with enough authority to let her know that she had over stepped her boundaries. "I did what I did yesterday out of the respect I have for your pops. It had nothing to do with you," he said truthfully. His words stung, insulting her and embarrassing her at the same time.

Feeling stupid, Raven scoffed and rolled her eyes as she put her hands on her hips. "Nothing to do with me?"

she repeated in disbelief. "I'm not buying that. I don't know a nigga in the world who would catch a body over somebody they didn't give a damn about."

"Let me make this real clear for you, little girl. I don't have time for you. I already got a lady in my life and I don't have love for no female but her. She has my heart . . . all of it. You could never compete with her," he said before turning his back on her.

Raven shook her head in dismay as she walked back up the steps, enraged and near tears. She couldn't wait to get out of Ethic's presence. She had never been shot down like that before and it bruised her ego, making her feel like she was lacking something that the next chick had. She did not know that what she was feeling was inadequacy. If she were really as grown up as she claimed to be, no man, not even Ethic, would be able to shatter her confidence. Poise could not be broken so easily in a real woman, and her salty disposition over Ethic proved that she was trying to grow up too fast. If she paced herself, she would eventually flourish into that woman, but she had a long way to go. She was missing all of the qualities that it took to be the type of woman Ethic would be attracted to. He was not the average hustler. He wasn't married to the streets like most young men his age. He knew that selling poison to his own people was wrong, and he promised himself that when he made his first million he would exit the game and go legit. His focus was on his hustle, nothing more and nothing less; which was why it would take more than Raven's pretty face to distract him.

When Raven returned to her house, everything was cleaned up and restored as if none of it had ever really happened. She hugged her father tightly, and he told her to go wait for him in his office. He came in and closed the door, then took a seat behind his mahogany desk. Stress was written all over his face. It seemed as though he had aged overnight. Deep lines of worry creased his forehead and bags rimmed his stern, red eyes. His heart was heavy at the fact that his beautiful family had been in harm's way. He was fully aware that in the blink of an eye he could have lost everything. The silence in the room was deafening to Raven. She hated when her father got like this. The anticipation of not knowing what was on his mind was killing her. He leaned over and pinched the bridge of his nose as he took a deep breath.

"I don't want you to see that boy again. If I even see him around our home it's not going to be good for him," Benjamin said in a low but clear tone.

"What? Daddy, why not? What does Mizan have to do with any of this?" she asked.

"I'm not sure that he has anything to do with it, but he was the only outsider here yesterday. I've never had anyone foolish enough to run inside my home. All of a sudden when this kid shows up, three men in masks appear and put my family in danger. I don't believe in coincidences, Raven. You are not to see him again," Benjamin stated.

"But Daddy!" Raven whined. "He was next to me the entire time."

"This is not up for debate, Raven," Benjamin replied sternly. "The nigga is bad news and I don't want you around him. I can't be held responsible for my actions if I see him again so I advise you to not disobey me. If you do, his blood will be on your hands."

Chapter Three

It had been a long time since Benjamin had put in work of his own. Murder had been his game as a young kid, but as a distinguished head of a ruthless Midwest drug connection, he now had people to carry out his homicidal intent. As he looked into Raven's room and watched her sleeping peacefully, he knew it was time to get his feet wet again. This was a situation that he had to handle personally. Sending one of his workers would not get the message across. He had to make the city bleed. The jack boys who had invaded his home had already been taken care of, but now it was time to make an example by touching everyone who was associated with them, including women and children. The devil had lain dormant in him for too long, and now niggas around him thought shit was sweet. For one night, he was about to reveal his cold heart and make the city bleed. Tears came to his eyes and he willed them away before closing Raven's door. After checking on his wife and youngest daughter, he said a short prayer asking God to watch over his family, and left the house.

Ethic waited patiently for Benjamin as he emerged from the house. He popped the locks, giving Benjamin access to his car.

"You ready?" he asked as he grabbed a .45-caliber chrome pistol by the nose and handed it to Benjamin with a gloved hand. Benjamin nodded his head and accepted the weapon. He cocked the weapon back, putting a bullet in the chamber, and nodded as Ethic pulled away from the curb. Jay-Z's *Reasonable Doubt* filled the interior. They needed a real nigga to spit real shit as they prepared to partake in the most real part of the game. They each knew that murder was final and there was no turning back. There was nothing glamorous about this part of their professions. Niggas had violated and now it was time to pay the piper by annihilating everyone the jack boys had ever loved. It would be a hard lesson to teach, but it had to be done so that the streets could learn that Benjamin Atkins was not to be fucked with.

That night, Ethic and Benjamin took the lives of three individuals: the mother of one of the jack boys; the girlfriend and son of the other. All were extinguished because their loved ones had broken the rules and committed the ultimate sin. If the king was going to be overthrown it had to be done right; if not, the repercussions would prove deadly, and Benjamin Atkins ruthlessly reminded the entire city of that on a cold, rainy night. "What about the kid, Mizan?" Ethic asked. "You want to handle that? Something telling me that he's a snake-ass nigga. It was too coincidental that all of this popped off the day he came to your crib."

Benjamin's eyes were cold but his heart was conflicted. Taking the lives of innocent women and a child had him internally disturbed, but he had known that it had to be done.

"Benny, you want me to take care of it?" Ethic asked, seeing the familiar look of uncertainty in the old man's gaze.

Benjamin shook his head and said, "I'm not a hundred percent sure that he was behind this, and because of that I'll give him a pass. If he did have something to do with it, he will get the picture. There's been enough killing tonight."

Ethic didn't understand Benjamin's reasoning, but did not question him. He made a note to be aware of his surroundings and keep an eye out for Mizan. Ethic knew a snake-ass nigga when he saw one, and Mizan was it.

Mizan's entire world went black as he stood over his mother's grave. She was the only person he cared about, the only person who had yet to give up on him, and now she was gone. It wasn't a pained emotion that swept over him, more like rage from being disrespected. He had no doubt that Benjamin Atkins was behind the vicious hit, because he had gotten word that Bull's chick and son had been murdered as well. This was a message to the streets from Benjamin, and Mizan heard it loud and clear. Fortunately, Mizan and his brother Boo had different fathers, giving them different last names, so Benjamin had not been able to link Boo to him, otherwise he would be taking a dirt nap too. *This nigga want to make it personal,* Mizan thought angrily. He pulled out his cell phone and dialed Raven's number. He was even more determined to get at Benjamin now. He was going to fuck up his entire existence, starting with his pretty little daughter Raven. She was his way in and he was going to fuck her in every sense of the word, until he eventually destroyed her father.

Chapter Four

Raven lay in bed wide awake as she waited for her father to come tell her good night. She knew him too well, and he would always come to peek inside her room before he retired to his bedroom. When she heard his footsteps coming down the hall she closed her eyes, pretending to be asleep. She felt him come in and sit on her bed, the weight of his body causing it to sink down.

"Rae, you asleep?" he asked gently.

Raven didn't respond. Benjamin leaned down and kissed her forehead, then tucked the covers tightly around her. "I love you," he said.

I love you too, she responded in her head as she heard him leave the room. Despite his warnings, Raven had been sneaking out to see Mizan almost every night for the past two months. She did not care if her father disapproved. She was feeling him and was willing to do anything to be around him.

She waited another ten minutes just to make sure that he wouldn't come back, before she hopped out of bed, fully clothed. She looked at the clock. She was already twenty minutes late. Mizan had told her to meet him at midnight. *I hope he didn't pull off,* she thought as she opened her second-story bedroom window. She climbed out quietly and crept across the roof, then jumped down onto the top of the garage. She cringed as her feet hit the shingles making a soft thud, and froze to see if anyone had heard her. When she was sure that she was in the clear she climbed down the cable pole that sat directly next to the garage, and walked away into the night.

When she saw Mizan's headlights in the distance she took off running toward him. She tapped his passenger window. The smile he gave her when he saw her was worth all the risk she was taking by sneaking out of her parents' house.

"You ready?" he asked.

She nodded and he pulled off, heading back to his place.

When she entered, she saw rose petals and candles decorating the living room of the three-bedroom house. To a grown woman this might have been routine or even been looked at as game, but to an inexperienced teenager this simple gesture easily won her over. She looked up at him in surprise. "You did all this for me?"

He nodded as he took her hand and pulled her down on the couch. He slid his hand underneath his couch and pulled out a small box filled with pre-rolled blunts. He lifted one out and waved it in front of her face.

"You want to blaze up?" he asked.

Remembering the way that the weed and coke concoction made her feel a smile creased her lips and she nodded eagerly.

"I'm sorry about everything that has happened. My daddy is dead wrong for telling me I can't see you," she said sincerely as they fell into a puff-puff-pass rotation. "He is just overprotective. I don't want him to run you away."

He grabbed her chin and put his fingers to her lips to silence her. He leaned in and kissed her. "I'm not running, ma. There's not a nigga in the world that can keep me from you . . . believe that," he replied, blowing her head up as he continued to kiss her. She was high and every spot he touched made her love gush in anticipation.

Raven felt her body submit to him as his hands roamed all over her. Her heartbeat sped up and was pounding so rapidly that she was sure that it would beat out of her chest. She wanted to be a good girl, to tell him no and make him wait, but the spot between her legs began to pulse and all rational thought went out of the window. To keep a big boy like Mizan she would have to do big-girl things. To stop him now would be a crime.

With his hands palming her breasts beneath her shirt and his fingers teasing her hard nipples, her hormones were in overdrive. It felt so good but at the same time it scared her. Although she talked big shit and flirted openly, Raven was still a virgin. No one had ever touched her the way that Mizan was now. She had never let a guy get this close, but Mizan had set the stage and now it was time for her to perform. Raven pulled back from him breathing heavily as she looked him in the eyes.

"Wait, I don't know what I'm doing," she said, her voice quivering. "I've never done this before," she admitted.

Mizan smirked, feeling like a king with the realization that he was about to be her first. "I'ma show you," he whispered as he got on his knees and removed her jean shorts, revealing her soaking wet panties. He pulled them off and sat back for a minute, enjoying the sight of her pussy, her silky hairs enticing him with the scent of a pure virgin.

"What are you doing?" she whispered insecurely.

"I'ma make you feel good . . . Just relax," he promised. He opened up her southern lips and watched as her juicy peach excreted her natural juices. "Damn, ma," he said in awe as he put his mouth on her clit without hesitation.

"Aghh," she moaned instantly. Her back arched while Mizan put his tongue to work. He put his hands under her ass cheeks and spread her wide open as he licked from her crack all the way to her pearl. She squirmed beneath him. She had never felt anything like it. Even when she would touch herself it never felt so good. Her head fell back in ecstasy and her nipples were tingling as if they were begging for attention. She removed her shirt, exposing her perky D-cups. She took her nipples between her fingers as she grinded into his face. Her moans of passion filled the air. Mizan was a cunnilingus expert and he made love to her with his mouth, knowing that it wouldn't bring her pain. He wasn't ready to break her in yet; he wanted to blow her mind without ever sticking his dick inside of her. He was going to make her wait for it, but in the meantime the sweetness of her satisfied him. He stroked his nine inches while blessing her with oral sex. The way she fed her pussy to him, pushing it against his face, let him know that he was doing it right. She tasted so good, so fresh . . . There was nothing like the taste of unexplored pussy and he lapped up her young juices as if he were sucking on a summer peach. He pulled her to the edge of the couch, both of her thighs encompassing his head as she wound her body, riding his tongue while her perky breasts bounced in the air. He couldn't wait to twist her back out. He knew that it was going to feel like heaven, but he was also aware that she wasn't ready for it yet. In time he would have her right where he wanted her. He began to pull on her clit while his full lips encompassed it, driving her crazy.

"Hmm," he moaned as he continued to suck her into an orgasm. Her legs began to shake and her eyes rolled in the back of her head.

"Ooh, Mizan . . . something's wrong. It's too tender . . . it feels too good," she whispered as tiny bolts of lightning erupted inside her. "What are you doing to me?"

"I'm making you cum," he moaned seductively as she exploded in his mouth.

All of the energy left her body as she melted into the leather couch. A layer of sweat glistened on her body, causing her to stick to the fabric.

He came up for air, wiping his mouth with his hand. He stood, and she was eye level with his penis. She gasped at its size. It was big and thick, with veins protruding from it. The head was blossomed and her eyes bulged as she took it into her hands.

"Put it inside me," she whispered unsurely. She wanted to prove to him that she wasn't a little girl, and make him feel the same bliss he had just bestowed upon her.

"Nah, ma, you're not ready for that . . . I would tear that young pussy up. Stroke it for Daddy," he instructed as she began to rub him up and down slowly. "Wet the tip," he said as he looked down at her. The sight of his toned body made her horny all over again.

Raven had never sucked a dick a day in her life, but she couldn't stop now. *If I don't do it he won't fuck with me anymore. Just quit being a baby and get it over with,* she told herself. Raven knew about chicks at her high school who sucked dick, but they all were labeled hoes for doing so. What she didn't know was that grown women gave super head to their men without hesitation. It had nothing to do with being a ho; little girls worried about trivial things like that. Grown women knew that pleasing their men every now and then kept their kings happy, allowing them to keep their positions, because what wifey won't do, another chick will. So a grown woman covered all her bases by being a freak in the bed but a lady in the streets. The smell of sweaty balls in their faces was a small sacrifice to keep their spots on lock. Raven would have to push her little-girl mentality to the side if she was going to deal with an older dude. She took him into her mouth and instantly began to gag.

"Relax your throat and watch your teeth," Mizan coached patiently, teaching her how to give head as he looked down at her.

Raven attempted again, but her body language was all wrong. The back of her throat was tense, and her teeth too close for comfort.

"Wait a minute, ma . . . hold up. You just need some confidence," he whispered as he pulled out a small bag of cocaine. He moved quickly, laying two lines out on the coffee table in front of him. "Hit this with me," he instructed.

Raven shook her head. "I don't do blow," she whispered.

"It'll make you relax, ma. You'll be hitting me off like a pro," he whispered as he teased her nipples with his fingertips. He leaned down over the table and inhaled one of the lines, using a small straw. "See? That's all there is to it."

Raven slowly got down on her knees and pulled her hair out of her face. She put her face over the cocaine as she gripped.

"Just like that. Now sniff real hard," he coached as he watched her take her first line. The sight of it making his manhood stand at attention.

Raven did as she was told, and as soon as the drug entered her nose she closed her eyes tightly; a horrible stinging sensation took over.

"Give it a minute, ma, it's your first time," Mizan whispered in her ear as he began to kiss her neck. The sight of her was so appealing to him. Just the fact that she was willing to experiment with blow at his request pleased him. She was moldable. Impressionable.

Raven's stomach began to churn and she inhaled deeply. *Oh my God. What the fuck!* she thought miserably, but the more the drug began to ease into her system, the better she began to feel. Her young peach was juicier than it had ever been, and small moans escaped her as Mizan continued to suck on her neck and palm her breasts.

"Suck it for me, ma," he said seductively. The cocaine blocked out everything and this time she did not overanalyze his request. She opened her mouth and invited him in, sucking it timidly.

"Keep it wet and stroke it, ma . . . Not too rough, and don't use your teeth," he said, completely in the moment as she got her groove and he closed his eyes. He began to grind slowly, and she put her hands on his firm buttocks as she pulled him into her. He repositioned himself as he lay on the couch, and pulled her back down on top of him in a 69. He opened her pussy back up, pleasuring her while she gave him head. He tickled her rectum with his wet finger while simultaneously French kissing her lips. She deep throated him, all of a sudden becoming an expert. The more pleasure he gave her, the better job she did, lowering all of her inhibitions.

"Damn, Rae . . . Suck it, ma," he whispered. Raven's mouth felt numb but she kept going, wanting nothing more than to please him; to prove herself to him. They both exploded and Raven stroked him until she had milked him dry, then sat up with a satisfied look on her face. He grabbed her hand and led her into the shower, where they kissed under the stream of water until it ran cold.

When they stepped out, he wrapped a towel around his waist and then held one out for her. She fell into his embrace and stood on her tiptoes to kiss him. She couldn't stop tasting him. Every time he touched her she felt special, and she lowered her head to her chest as she thought about what had just taken place.

"I've never done this with anybody, Mizan. Please don't put my business out there to all of your friends. I know how dudes can be," she whispered.

He lifted her chin and replied, "You're my li'l mama. I don't want another nigga to know what my bitch got. I'll have to kill a nigga for coming at you, trying to take what's mine." He put his hands between her legs and caressed her lips. "This my pussy?" he asked.

She pursed her lips, raised her arched eyebrows, and replied, "It's yours."

He pointed his finger in her face. "Then don't ever give away what belongs to me, Raven," he answered seriously. She grabbed his hand and kissed it as she looked into his eyes.

"I won't," she replied honestly. She had never felt the way Mizan had made her feel, and she had no idea that she had just given her heart away. She was too young to recognize that Mizan was a bad seed. All she saw was his hood swagger and good looks. She was blinded by the idea of being wifey, and the fact that he came from nothing appealed to her even more. Her parents had worked hard to keep her away from the streets, but Mizan's soul was lost in the streets and as long as she was with him, hers would be too. Young and naïve, Raven did not know that she was merely a pawn in Mizan's chess game, and his goal was to take down the king of the streets: her father, Benjamin Atkins.

Mizan pulled into Raven's subdivision at six o'clock in the morning. After staying up all night with him and getting to know one another, she wasn't ready to say good night, but she knew that her mother awoke at 7:00 A.M. sharp. She had to get in before someone discovered she was gone. He let her out at the corner and reached over to open her car door. He kissed her cheek and she exited the car. She headed for her house at the other end of the block. She noticed that all the lights were still out in her

house and she sighed in relief. Just as she was approaching her driveway she heard someone call her name.

"Raven!"

She jumped out of her skin and turned around, knowing she was busted. She put a hand to her chest and exhaled in relief when she saw Ethic sitting in an apple red
Benz. She stepped over to the car, not too excited to see
him.

"What are you doing out here this time of night?" she
asked with her hands on her hips.

"I could be asking you the same thing," he commented
condescendingly.

"I live here so I don't owe you an explanation," she shot
back with a snotty attitude, leaning down so that she
could talk to him through the window.

"Get in," he said in a low tone as he unlocked the doors.

She opened the door and plopped down in the passenger seat.

"Your father asked me to watch the crib. After what
happened at the fish fry he's a little paranoid," he explained. He stared at her intently, making her feel uncomfortable. She felt as if he could see right through her.

"Why are you staring?" she asked.

He ignored her question and posed one of his own.
"Why you fucking with a nigga that can't drop you off at
your doorstep?" Ethic asked, his calm demeanor not revealing any emotion in his tone.

"Why do you care?" Raven asked in confusion. Her
body was beginning to feel sluggish as she came down off
of her cocaine high, and she did not have time for Ethic
to be butting into her business.

"I don't . . . I just think that you should," he responded
bluntly. "Your man is a jack boy. I had my people check
him out after what went down at the party."

"You're going through an awful lot of trouble for some-one who doesn't care," she commented, and folded her arms across her chest. "I don't care how he gets his paper as long as he gets it. I like him and he doesn't think I'm too young to be his girl. Besides, he had nothing to do with what happened. He was with me the entire time," she defended.

Ethic smirked and shook his head. "Open your eyes, little girl."

Tired of hearing him speak, Raven reached for the door. "Just mind your business. You already told me you're not interested in me. I found someone who is. So me and you, we really don't have anything to talk about. You do you and I'll do me," Raven stated as she got out and closed the door.

Ethic got out of the car to go after her. She was half-way across the street before he caught up with her. He grabbed her by the arm and turned her toward him, pull-ing her closely, so that he didn't have to speak too loudly. "Look, Raven, I don't want to see you out in the streets with that nigga, Mizan. I've heard about how he gets down and I have no love for a stick up nigga. I've got a lot of money invested with your pops, and if he's constantly worried about you then his mind ain't on what it should be on, n'ah mean? I'm not trying to get caught slipping, and if I even think your little boyfriend barking up my tree, I'ma snuff his lights out." He looked Raven up and down. "Nigga got you out here climbing out of windows and getting in cars on corners like a ho, and that's the type of nigga you're feeling? You should follow your own advice and be more selective of who you spend your time with, ma."

He was standing so close to her that she could smell the peppermint on his breath. He made her nervous, and the harsh way he came at her made her eyes water. The fact that it bothered Ethic to see her with Mizan made her heart flutter nervously. She didn't want to pull away from him. It felt too good to be in his space, but she did it anyway. It was clear that he wasn't interested, so she couldn't understand why it was so much of a problem for him to see her with another dude.

"I'm not a little girl. I can handle myself. Mizan isn't who you think he is," she replied.

Ethic chuckled slightly as he rubbed the top of his head. "I guess you learned a lot about him in the short time you've known him," he replied sarcastically, making her feel stupid.

"Why are you so mean?" she asked. "You talk to me like I'm beneath you or something, but you want me to listen to you when it comes to my man?" she scoffed, and waved her hand in dismissal.

"Your man?" he asked incredulously.

"Yeah, my man," she stated firmly as she stormed away.

"Raven?" Ethic called out.

She stopped and turned to face him. "What?" she answered with teary eyes.

"I'm not trying to hurt your feelings. I just want you to be careful. You're too green, ma. You're a target simply because of who you are."

Raven put her hand on her hip and looked at him, baffled. "You sure talk about me like you know me. Did you get all of *that* in the short time you have known me? You must forget, I don't know you any better than I know him. So who says you are so trustworthy?"

She walked away and climbed up to her bedroom. When she turned to look out the window, Ethic had gotten back into his car. She pushed him out of her mind and went to sleep.

Chapter Five

Raven pulled up to Nikki's house and honked her horn. She came running out, and hopped into the car.

"Hey, bitch, what's up?" Nikki greeted, as they pulled away.

"I saw Mizan last night," Raven said. She couldn't wait to fill her best friend in on the amazing night she had.

"What? How?"

"He came and got me . . . We went back to his place," Raven said vaguely.

"And, bitch?" Nikki grilled, waiting for Raven to say more.

"And nothing. You don't need to know all my business," Raven replied with laughter, knowing that the suspense was killing Nikki.

"Oh, you know you coming better than that," Nikki said as she leaned her back against the passenger door so that she was facing her best friend. "Did you fuck him?" she asked.

"Not exactly." Raven stated.

"Oh my God, you did! Tell me everything," she said, eager to know the juicy details.

Raven shook her head and replied, "Good girls never tell."

As she pulled up to Hamady High School, Nikki pointed to the rear of the parking lot.

"Well, you did something right, because there go your boy right there," she stated.

Raven parked her car next to Mizan's and smiled. "What are you doing here?" she asked sweetly.

"I wanted to see you." He rested his arm on the top of his steering wheel. "Come take a ride with me for a minute?"

Raven looked at Nikki and said, "If anybody asks, just say you drove my car to school. I'll meet you back here after the last class."

Nikki smiled knowingly. "A'ight, girl, you know I got you. Hey, Mizan."

Mizan nodded, and waited for Raven to switch cars before speeding off. Mizan knew that the way to win Raven over would be to shower her with his time and affection. Financially there was nothing he could give her. He knew that by being the daughter of Benny Atkins she had everything she could ever want, so he wouldn't try to compete with that. He was going to give her what she obviously craved: attention. Mizan made her feel like his world revolved around her. Every move was calculated carefully in an intricate plot to get her to trust him. He wanted her to be so wrapped up in him that she would do anything he asked.

They spent the entire day together chilling and getting high together at his house. Being there with him made her feel like an adult. There were no prying eyes, no boundaries. When she was with Mizan he respected her and let her do what she wanted. She loved the freedom and valued every minute she spent with him. The day ended too soon for her, but she knew she had no choice but to leave. She had to meet Nikki back at the school once classes were over.

"I don't want to leave you," she whispered as she lay on his chest.

"Then stay."

"I can't. I have to get home before my parents wonder where I am, but I want to see you again. Soon," she whispered. "Can you meet me at the school tomorrow morning?"

"Yeah, I'll be there." He kissed her forehead. Mizan was going to have to put a lot of effort into Raven in order for his plan to work, but he was confident that in the end it would all be worth it.

This routine went on for weeks, and the closer she got to Mizan the more she pushed her father away. She was tired of being controlled, and by disobeying Benjamin, she felt like she was proving her independence. She didn't notice that she was simply shifting the control to Mizan. On top of that, the daily weed and cocaine use was slowly turning her out. She found herself sneaking out with Mizan every chance she got. He kept her high and happy. She was quickly falling in love, and when she was not around him, she felt sick. She had a serious love jones for the young thug. She was ostracizing herself from her family but it only made her more dependent on Mizan. She was crazy over him and she told herself that no one was going to stop them from being together. She had no idea that she was mistaking infatuation for love, but in her mind they were one and the same. Now that she had her mind set on being with Mizan, she was determined not to let anyone tear them apart.

"Come and take a ride with me, Rae," Justine requested as she popped her head into her daughter's room.

"Where are we going?" Raven asked. She got up and followed her mother out of the house.

"We're going to the spa. I want to talk to you about something." She lowered her sunglasses onto her face to conceal her eyes. Raven stared out the window, knowing that if her mother wanted to talk, something had to be wrong.

"How was school today?" Justine asked.

"It was good. I'm ready for it to be over, though. I can't wait for graduation next month."

"Raven, I've been around the block more times than you can count. Don't lie to me, little girl. I received a call from your counselor today. You haven't been to school in the past three weeks. Now, you've been leaving the house every morning. Where have you been going?" Justine asked.

Raven tried to think of a reasonable excuse, but Justine raised her hand to stop her. She could see the wheels turning in her daughter's head. "Don't lie to me, Raven. I know you've been sneaking around with Mizan."

"I wouldn't have to sneak if Daddy would just be reasonable."

"Your father has his reasons for everything he does. He's just trying to protect you, Rae," Justine argued. "I can't believe you would do something like this. You barely even know this boy."

"I know him enough to know that I love him, and y'all can't make me stop seeing him. I'll be grown in two months. I can do what I want," Raven replied adamantly.

"Love? Raven, you don't even know what love is yet," Justine said exasperated. "You're too young to even think of making that type of commitment."

"You were my age when you met Daddy," Raven shot back.

Justine gripped the steering wheel of the car tightly as she shook her head in disappointment. "Raven, things were different back then. When I was seventeen I was on my own and paying bills, not living underneath my parents' roof and lying to get my way. You have a month left of high school. Why don't you focus on graduating?

I know you think you love this boy, but it's not the real thing, Rae. I promise you by the end of the summer you will forget all about him."

"Are you going to tell Daddy?" Raven asked.

"Girl, your father knows everything that goes on underneath his roof. I don't lie to my husband. He already knows and you can deal with him when we get home," Justine said as she finally arrived at the spa. She opened the door and got out, noticing that Raven was frozen in her seat like a deer in headlights.

"You might as well get out and come enjoy this spa, because you aren't going anywhere besides school anytime soon. Ain't no point in pouting now. You wanted to act grown and go see that boy, now you have to be a grown woman and accept the consequences."

"Raven, get in here," Benjamin's voice boomed as soon as she stepped in the door. Raven's mother rubbed her back soothingly as she escorted Raven to the study. Ethic was sitting in a chair across from Benjamin, and he stood when he saw her enter the room. "Ethic, can you excuse us for a minute? I need to speak with my daughter. Go and grab something to eat out the kitchen. Make yourself at home." Ethic nodded and left the room as Raven nervously sat in front of her father. Benjamin took his time before he spoke, and sat back in his chair as he loosened his necktie.

"I thought I made myself clear when I told you this the first time, but obviously I did not. I'm going to say this one more time. I don't want to hear about you being around Mizan again." He was reserved, his voice low and calm, but Raven could see his temples throbbing in rage. No one else would have known how upset he was, but Raven and Benjamin shared a special connection. She knew him well enough to see past his controlled demeanor.

"I love him, Daddy," Raven whispered.

Her voice was so low he barely heard her, but a statement so ludicrous he could not miss. "Then you're going to love the nigga to death, Raven, because if you keep fucking with him, I'm going to kill him," Benjamin threatened, fully serious on carrying through if need be.

"Daddy! You're not being fair. You can't tell me who to love," Raven defended, her voice quivering. Her father was the only person she could not stand up to.

"As long as you're living underneath this roof you will not disobey me, Raven. Fair has nothing to do with this. I'm trying to keep you safe," he said.

"Then maybe I don't need to live under your roof!" Raven shouted defiantly, causing Benjamin to stand to his feet.

"Excuse me!" he yelled, raising his voice at her for the first time in his life.

"I'm not going to stop seeing him! You can threaten me all you want. As a matter of fact, I'm out of here!" she screamed as she stormed out of his office.

Benjamin was so upset that he swept all the papers and documents from his desk in one motion. "Fuck!" he screamed as he put his hands on his waistline and paced the room.

Justine came rushing in. "Benjamin, what did you do?" she asked, near tears. "Go upstairs and stop her! She's our baby."

"Let her go. She wants to be grown so I'ma let her get out there and see what it's like. She'll be back home by tomorrow morning," Benjamin stated.

Ethic sat in the living room as he heard the family argue. Morgan peeked her head inside.

"Ethic? Where is Raven going?" she signed to him as she leaned against the door frame.

Ethic, being knowledgeable in many things, knew sign language and surprised her when he signed back, "She's just going out for the night. Don't worry, pretty girl." He patted the seat next to him, and Morgan smiled as she rushed to sit by his side.

"Is she going to go live with her boyfriend?" Morgan signed with a worried expression.

"Nah, shorty, she not going to stay with him," Ethic replied.

He could still hear Justine and Benjamin arguing as Raven descended the stairs with a suitcase in one hand and her keys in the other. Benjamin came into view.

"Leave the car key here," he said, speaking sternly as he stood with one hand in his pocket and the other over his mouth.

Raven stared at her father, and for the first time she found herself disgusted by him. She removed the car key and put it in his hand, and then removed her house key as well. "You can keep that, too. I won't be needing it," she said as she stormed out the front door.

Tears came to Benjamin's eyes as he fought to control his emotions. He was heartbroken that Raven was leaving, but he stubbornly refused to stop her. He had never been in conflict with his daughter. In all of her seventeen years on earth she had never disrespected him so bluntly. As he pictured her face in his mind, everything in him wanted to go after her, but this was not something he would concede. He had seen many young girls led astray by dealing with the wrong man. Raven's judgment was off when it came to Mizan and he would never approve of their relationship. After ten minutes of pacing back and forth, he looked at Ethic and said, "Go make sure she is okay. That's my baby girl," he stated, becoming emotional as he pinched the bridge of his nose. Ethic nodded and began to leave when Benjamin's voice stopped him. "Ethic, don't let her know that I sent you."

Justine grabbed her coat and went to follow Ethic, but Benjamin grabbed her hand. "No, Benny! No! I'm going after my daughter. You can't just send her up out of here like this. What if something happens to my baby?"

"Nothing's going to happen," Benjamin stated. "But she has to learn that she cannot disrespect us underneath this roof. That boy is bad news."

"And you're just going to run her into his arms by acting like this!" she argued.

"Justine!" he said sternly. "I got it. Go and put Morgan to bed. Have I ever let you down?"

Justine's reserve melted as hot tears burned her eyes, threatening to spill over. "No," she whispered.

"Then trust me," he said. He nodded for Ethic to leave, and then watched his wife scoop Morgan up and carry her upstairs.

She stopped midway and turned around. "If something happens to Raven, I will never forgive you, Benjamin. Never."

I'll never forgive myself, he thought as he watched his beautiful wife turn her back on him and ascend the staircase.

Raven cried hysterically as she carried her heavy suitcase down the suburban street. *I can't believe he would take my keys,* she thought, outraged. She wasn't even two blocks away from her house when Ethic pulled up to her. She stuck her middle finger up at him to let him know that she wasn't trying to hear shit he had to say.

"Get in the car," he said, ignoring her childish antics as he rolled slowly next to her. She looked straight ahead, ignoring him. "Raven, get in the car. Where you going? You just said fuck your pops to be with a nigga who don't give a damn about you."

Raven ignored him and carried on. She didn't care that she had no destination. The further away she got from her father, the better.

"Where you going?" he asked. "You think ol' boy gon' take you in now?" he asked. When she didn't answer, Ethic sighed in frustration. "Just get in, ma. Why you got me out here like Keith Sweat, begging you and shit?" he asked.

Raven couldn't help but laugh slightly as she stopped walking. She put her suitcase on the ground and stood with her hand on her hip as she looked tentatively at Ethic.

"Get in," he said.

Knowing that she had no place to go she sighed and lifted her suitcase as she climbed into the car. "Don't take me home. I'm not going back there," she said stubbornly.

Ethic didn't respond as he pulled away from the curb.

He let her into his house and threw his keys down on the coffee table. "Look, I'm not your keeper. I can't tell you, what to do, but if you thinking about having that nigga come and scoop you don't let him know where I live. You take a cab over there or something. 'Cuz if he come down my block, it's gon' be a problem, a'ight?"

Raven nodded her head. "Do you think I'm wrong?" she asked.

"I think you're young," Ethic said. "And I think Mizan knows you're young. You don't let a nigga like him trap your heart, ma. You trying to find yourself, I get that . . . but a dude like that is only gonna get you lost."

The look of disappointment that Ethic gave Raven caused a tear to fall down her cheek. She quickly wiped it away as she watched him disappear behind closed doors.

Part of her wanted to heed Ethic's advice, but to turn around and run home to her father after the scene she had made would make her look foolish. She had defied her father in order to be with Mizan, and now she had to follow through with it. Her pride matched that of a lion's and under no circumstances was she going home. She had argued her way into a corner and now she was on her own. She tapped her foot nervously against the floor as she sat in the dark with her arms crossed tightly over her chest. *Should I call Mizan?* she thought. *I did all of this so that I could be with him.* She picked up her phone and took a deep breath as she dialed his number. She hoped like hell that he was feeling her the same way, because if he wasn't, she had just thrown away all that she had ever known for nothing.

Chapter Six

When Mizan received Raven's phone call he smiled in satisfaction. Things could not have worked out more perfectly for him. The fact that she had gone against the grain just to be with him proved that he had her emotions in his pocket, and an emotional young girl would be easy to manipulate. He was about to offer her a place to rest her head and heart. In return, she would lead him straight to the top of the game where he belonged. As he navigated his way down Miller Road, he pulled out his cell phone to call Raven.

"Hello?" she answered on the first ring.

"Yo', I'm pulling up now. Where you at?" he asked as he turned into the parking lot of the Genesee Valley Mall.

"I'm standing out front of Macy's."

Mizan whipped around the mall until his headlights shined on Raven, revealing her tear-stained face. He got out of the car and grabbed her suitcase, then opened her car door.

"Stop crying, ma. Get in the car. I got you," he said as he buckled her in her seat.

"Thank you for coming to get me," she whispered.

"Don't worry about it, Rae. I told you, you're mine and I take care of what belongs to me," he said. He closed the door and jogged around to his side of the car, then pulled off into the night.

Raven entered Mizan's house and set her suitcase on the floor. "Make yourself at home," he said. He lit up one of his special blunts and passed it to her. She was upset and welcomed the drugs, knowing that they would make everything better. She was slowly growing addicted to the high. She loved the way it solved all of her problems in the blink of an eye. "You don't need anybody but me, remember that."

His words instantly made her lonely world better, and she smiled slightly as he pulled her to him. "Tell me what you're thinking," he said.

"I've just never fought with my daddy before. It doesn't feel right," she whispered. "I just want him to respect my decision, you know?" She looked up to the ceiling and exhaled to stop herself from becoming emotional. "To respect my decision to be with you. He'll come around."

"And if he doesn't, are you prepared to be here with me, ma? I need a woman that's gon' be down for her man through whatever. You got to choose sides. I want to be the only man you're loyal to. N'ah mean?" he stated, his face only inches away from hers.

She nodded. "I am loyal, Mizan. If I wasn't I wouldn't be here right now," she said.

"You better mean it, ma, cuz if I take you in, you've got to be mine. You got to choose me over any nigga, including your pops," he whispered as he circled her nipple with his finger while kissing her neck softly. "You choose me, Rae?"

"I choose you," she gasped. She held her breath as a tickling sensation traveled down her spine, causing her to become wet.

"Can I have it?" he asked as he unbuttoned her jeans with the skill of a Casanova. Her mouth fell open to respond, but no sound came out as he palmed her treasure and added pressure to her clit. She bit her lip and moved her hips from side to side to help him slide off her pants. He had never penetrated Raven, but tonight she hoped that he would take it all the way. She was tired of holding onto her virginity and she thought that she had found the one person who was worthy of her giving it to. Not once did she stop to think that it was something she could never take back. Once Mizan parted her thighs and entered her it would be gone forever, but as she looked into his eyes she felt that he was the man who she would be with. He did not have to be her husband because she felt that the street title of wifey was enough. As he lay her on the floor, she opened her legs and invited him inside. The expectations of a girl so young were of romance and pleasure. She had fantasized about this very moment ever since she had first felt her own fingers play with her clit, but as Mizan stood over her, removing his clothing, her legs began to shake. She had heard about how badly the first time hurt, and subconsciously she knew that once she became intimate with Mizan she really would be his. At seventeen she was now wifey and about to give herself to a grown man. She blocked all thought out of her mind and braced herself as Mizan slipped in between her legs.

When Mizan's nine inches knocked on her doorway to pleasure, she closed her eyes and sucked her teeth to absorb the pain. He slowly worked himself inside of her as tears slipped out of her eyes and she held her breath. With every thrust she could feel her hymen breaking. She knew that it was too much for her to handle, but she could not say no. She had to give it to him. If she did not, there was no way he would keep her around. Her young logic should have told her she was in over her head, but instead she convinced herself that she knew what she was doing.

"You want me to stop?" he asked.

Raven wanted to say yes, but instead shook her head. She knew that she couldn't refuse him after he had taken her into his home. She wanted him to know that she was fully invested in him, and this was her way of submitting to him. She had talked a big game, but now it was time to perform. She had held onto her cherry for seventeen long years and it was time for her to know what the real deal was like.

"Relax, Rae," he whispered as he pumped one good time, breaking her in and gaining access to her fully. Raven's back arched in pain as Mizan began to sex her slowly. Nothing about it felt good; it was painful and the amount of discomfort confused her. She closed her eyes and lay still as Mizan did all the work. He knew that she was inexperienced and did not know what she was doing. "Damn, ma, this shit is heaven," he moaned as her tight walls almost resisted him. The pain that she was receiving was worth the pleasure she was giving to Mizan. The lust in his voice made her feel powerful as if her pussy was enough to keep him on lock . . . enough to make him hers. She expected to feel like a woman when it was over, but nothing had changed. Besides a wet behind, she was still the same little girl she was before. No magical transformation had occurred. "Go clean yourself up and come lay with your man," he said to her, smacking her behind as she walked away.

Raven washed her body and then joined Mizan in the bedroom. As she lay on his chest, a feeling of independence swept over her. What she didn't know was that her separation from her father did not make her free. In the hands of a man like Mizan she was more trapped than she had ever been at home, and only time would reveal the hell that she had gotten herself into.

Raven was jolted out of her sleep when she heard a banging at the door. "Mizan," she whispered as she nudged him awake. "Get up . . . somebody's at the door."

He stood up and frowned when he noticed that it was 4:00 A.M. He grabbed his chrome .45-caliber pistol from the nightstand, and put his finger to his lips to signal her to be quiet. He had robbed plenty of niggas and wasn't taking any chances of someone coming back catching him slipping. She stood nervously with the covers wrapped around her naked body, and walked timidly behind him as he crept into the living room.

Mizan pulled back his living room blinds to see who was on his front porch. He instantly recognized Ethic, and he knew that Raven's father had sent him. What he didn't know was how Ethic knew where he lived.

He snatched open the door, standing shirtless with his pistol in hand.

"Ethic?" Raven called out when she saw him standing there.

"Get your things and let's go. Your father sent me," he stated, completely ignoring Mizan.

Raven went to step closer to Ethic and Mizan quickly put his arm out to halt her. "Mu'fuckas don't got no respect nowadays. Come knocking on my door in the middle of the night asking for my bitch," Mizan said as he kept his hand gripped tightly around his gun.

Ethic smirked as he sniffed and rubbed the bridge of his nose in irritation. He grilled Mizan with malice in his stare, fearless as he stood before him unarmed. Out of nowhere, two niggas with burners appeared beside Ethic. Safeties off and ready to blaze, his goons were just waiting for him to say the word. Mizan shook his head and rubbed his chin, then backed away from the door. Obviously, he had underestimated Ethic's clout in the streets. He chose to back down, losing the battle so that he could win the greater war. It didn't matter if they had come. He was confident that Raven wasn't going anywhere. He didn't need to force her to stay. Outgunned and outnumbered, Mizan knew better than to buck, so he left the decision up to her.

"I ain't into keeping a chick that don't want to be kept," Mizan stated as he looked at Raven, who stood indecisively behind him.

"Raven, get your shit and let's go," Ethic repeated sternly, the bass in his voice causing her to shake. She could see the look of rage on his face. All eyes were on her as they awaited her response.

"I'm not leaving, Ethic," she said. "Tell my daddy that all he did was push me away. Now I'm right where he didn't want me to be." She said, proud of her defiance.

Ethic looked at her sternly, causing her to lower her head to the floor. If she looked him in the eyes she might change her mind, so she avoided his stare.

Mizan wrapped his arm around Raven and a smug look crossed his face. He pulled her close and kissed her cheek, never taking his eyes off of Ethic.

"Go back in the bedroom," Mizan whispered in her ear. When Raven disappeared from sight, Mizan stood toe to toe with Ethic.

"See, my nigga, I'm Daddy now," Mizan stated.

Ethic wanted to snatch Raven out of the house and deliver her back to her father, but it wasn't his place. He wasn't Captain-Save-a-Ho, and if she refused to leave, he was not going to make her. He nodded and stepped off the porch, as his trained dogs kept their pistols aimed in Mizan's direction. "I'ma see you, my nigga," Ethic threatened.

"I look forward to it," Mizan shouted back, unimpressed by Ethic's intimidation skills. They were two men at odds, both fearless, each ruthless in his own way. A war between them would be the greatest the streets had ever seen, but today was not the day to spark it. "You gentlemen have a good day," Mizan said mockingly as he watched them pull away.

He headed back to his bedroom to find Raven looking out the window. Her eyes were watching the taillights of Ethic's car disappear into the night.

"Another nigga come to my door for you and I'ma body him," Mizan whispered in her ear.

She turned to him and wrapped her arms around his neck. Seeing Mizan stand up to Ethic made her feel secure, as if no matter who came for her, he would always be there to handle it.

"You don't have to worry about me going anywhere," she replied. "No matter how many people he sends here for me. I'm never gonna leave you. I'll always come back to you." When Raven spoke the words, she had no idea how true they would one day be.

Chapter Seven

Raven awoke when she felt Mizan get out of bed. They had been living together for two months and almost every night he would leave to hit the streets. She had become used to the routine. She knew how he made his money. The bloody clothes and small sums of cash told her that the rumors she had been hearing about him being a stick-up kid were true, but she didn't care. She knew that he would never harm her, and as long as he treated her well she didn't question him or complain. She had not spoken to her father since the day she stormed out.

After hearing the news from Ethic that she had refused to leave Mizan, Benjamin stubbornly decided to cut his daughter off until she came to her senses. The sting of betrayal hurt him only because it was coming from the one person who he felt would always take his side. Raven was his baby girl and her behavior cut him deeply.

Raven missed her father dearly, but she was unwilling to give up her new relationship just to appease him. Her eighteenth birthday was in a week and she would officially be grown. She knew that on that day she would no longer owe her father any explanations. He would either respect her decision or be cut out of her life. The choice was up to him. She knew that she had given up a life of luxury in order to ride for Mizan. The small Susan Street house was a far cry from her lavish mini-mansion in Grand Blanc, but the trade was worth it to her. For the past eight weeks all she had seen was his face. They had been holed up the way that only new lovers can be, sexing each other every minute of every day. Once Mizan had broken her in, Raven couldn't get enough of him. The things he did to her body were amazing and only made her fall deeper in love. The only time they were apart was when he had to handle his business, and she always waited patiently for him to return.

"What time will you be home?" she asked.

"I don't know. I won't be long, though, ma," he said shortly.

"I just get so lonely here by myself sometimes," Raven said, knowing that he didn't want her to leave unless he was with her. He told Raven it was because he wanted to keep her safe, but in reality he wanted to keep her contained. He didn't need anyone putting anything in her head to make her stray, so he kept her secluded. He even kept her away from her friends and family. Raven didn't know it, but her parents had called her almost every day trying to reach her. Mizan had contacted her phone carrier and had their numbers blocked so that they could not connect their calls. They wouldn't hear from Raven until he allowed her to call, and he had planted so many seeds in her head about her parents controlling ways, that Raven had cut them off completely out of anger.

"I'll try to make it back quick, a'ight?" he said.

She nodded and pulled his gun out of the nightstand beside her. She handed it to him and rolled her eyes. She knew he was just trying to game her. "Yeah, okay, boy," she replied with a smirk.

Mizan loaded the clip and leaned over to kiss her lips before leaving. When she heard the door lock, she put the pillow over her face and went back to sleep.

Raven awoke the next morning, nauseated. She ran to the bathroom. She couldn't make it to the toilet, so she leaned over the sink and vomited profusely. She brushed her teeth and then wiped her face with a cold towel, trying to stop the hot flashes that swept over her. She took a deep breath as her stomach continued to feel as if she were riding a huge wave. She held on to the sink as she became dizzy. *What is wrong with me?* she thought. She didn't have much time to think before she leaned over again and dry heaved. She got in the shower and cleaned herself as best she could. *I need to go to the doctor,* she thought. *Something doesn't feel right.* She went to her purse to retrieve her cell phone and dialed Nikki's number. It had been awhile since she talked to her, but she knew that her best friend would take her where she needed to go without holding grudges or acting petty.

"Damn, bitch, I was beginning to think you had lost my number," Nikki greeted, as soon as she picked up the phone.

"Never that, hon. I've just been busy with Mizan. You know how it is," Raven said as she breathed heavily into the phone.

"Yeah, I know . . . Niggas wanna take up all your time like you didn't have a life before they came along. It must be nice. I wish I had that problem." She paused when she heard Raven groan slightly. "You okay? You don't sound too good."

Raven put her hand to her head and noticed that her temperature was elevated. "I feel like shit. Can you come by and take me to the doctor? Mizan isn't here and I can't wait for him to come home," she explained.

"Just give me the address and I'll be there in a few," Nikki said without hesitation.

"I'm on the north side on Susan Street," Raven replied, barely able to get the words out before she was throwing up again.

After giving Nikki directions, Raven lay on the bed until she heard her friend knocking at the door. She went to open it, and Nikki's eyes widened in surprise.

"Damn, Raven, what the fuck Mizan been doing to you? You must been getting a lot of dick because your ass is for sho' spreading." Nikki put her hands on her hips.

"Girl, shut up and take me to the doctor." Raven closed her eyes as she felt more nausea hitting her. "Oh my God, it must be something I ate."

"You're throwing up?" Nikki asked curiously. She eyed her best friend and began to shake her head in disbelief. "Bitch, you're pregnant!"

"What?" Raven exclaimed. "Get the fuck out of here. Don't be putting that on me. I am not pregnant."

Nikki took Raven's hand and pulled her into the bedroom to stand her in front of a mirror. "Look at yourself, girl. You're wide as fuck, out here looking like a video model. Your hips ain't ever been that wide, and you had a cute shape but your butt ain't ever been that big, either, bitch. Don't front!" Nikki laughed. "Even your face has rounded out a little bit. On top of that you're throwing up. You don't need a doctor to tell you what I already know. Don't act like it's impossible. You've been hiding out in this house with him for two months . . . You're not on birth control?"

A panicked look crossed Raven's face as she thought of herself with a baby. "Oh, shit," she whispered as her legs gave out on her and she flopped down on the bed. "Pregnant?" This wasn't supposed to happen to her. Living with Mizan was one thing, but to have his baby took their relationship to an entirely new level. She wasn't sure if she was ready for that, and, most importantly, she was afraid of how Mizan would feel if it turned out to be true. Having a baby was irreversible. Her life would be forever changed. Nikki noticed the look of uncertainty on Raven's face.

"There's only one way to find out for sure." Nikki shrugged. "Let's go get a test."

"I can't. I need to wait for Mizan to come back," Raven said.

"We're just running to the store . . . come on," Nikki replied with a frown.

Raven pulled out her cell phone to check in with Mizan. She didn't want him to come back and find her gone. When she got his voicemail she sighed and flipped her phone closed. "He's not answering and I don't feel like going to the store anyway. Can you just go pick it up and bring it back for me?" she asked.

Nikki nodded uncertain. It seemed to her that Raven had been locked down, but she didn't want to seem like she was hating so she simply agreed. "Yeah, I'll be right back."

Raven paced back and forth anxiously. Ten minutes felt like hours. She met Nikki at the door and snatched the test out of her hand. As soon as she peed on the stick, two lines began to appear.

She put her hand over her mouth. "I'm pregnant," she whispered as she turned to look at Nikki.

"Y'all didn't use condoms?" Nikki asked.

"Yes!" Raven yelled hysterically.

"Every time, Rae? All it takes is one slip-up," Nikki stated seriously with sympathetic eyes.

"I mean, no, not every time, but most of the time, and when we didn't he pulled out," Raven exclaimed in bewilderment. "This shit is unreal. This cannot be happening."

"What are you gon' do?" Nikki asked.

"I don't know," Raven replied absently. All she could think of was how Mizan was going to react.

Mizan and Rich sat in the car watching Benjamin Atkins. They had been following him for months in an attempt to learn his routine.

"You see that? I bet you that's his connect," Mizan said, referring to an older black woman getting out of a car. They watched as Benjamin helped the woman out and escorted her into a small bakery.

"Man, that old bitch ain't his connect," Rich said. "We wasting our time with all this stalking bullshit. You trying to do too much. You playing house with his daughter, trying to get her to lead you to the safe . . . You been fucking that bitch for months and we're still in the same position. I'm starting to think you got ol' girl around for another reason. I say we quit playing games and run in his spot."

Mizan shook his head. "We tried that already, remember?" He thought of the three members of his crew who had gotten aired out by Benjamin. "Nah, we got to take our time on this one. Tie all loose ends. I got Raven under control. I've been popping holes in the condoms."

"I know I heard you wrong, fam. You trying to get shorty pregnant?" Rich asked in disbelief.

Mizan nodded as he continued to watch the bakery, never taking his eyes off Benjamin.

"A pregnant bitch is loyal to her man above anyone else. Once she's carrying my seed she'll do anything I ask her to," Mizan explained.

"And if she doesn't?" Rich shot back.

"She will."

"And you really think that the old lady is supplying Benjamin with the birds?" Mizan's plan didn't make sense to Rich, and he wanted to make sure that all of his bases were covered before he went up against the hood legend.

Mizan pointed toward the bakery, Rich turned to see Benjamin and his goons carrying pie boxes out of the shop and loading them into one of the shop's delivery vans.

"I know Benny Atkins ain't eating a hundred pies, my nigga." Mizan smiled and started his car so that he could follow the delivery truck. He knew that he was close to the biggest come-up of his life. Ever since he had met Raven he had been watching her pops. For Benjamin to be such a legend in the streets he moved like a rookie. He had gotten comfortable and was too easy a mark. Benjamin picked up 100 kilos of cocaine from the old woman twice a month. Same day, same time, rain or shine. It never failed. Mizan had meticulously observed Benjamin, wanting to learn as much about him as he possibly could before attempting to rob him. He estimated there to be close to half a million dollars worth of product in that safe, and he wanted it all. He knew that strong, arming his way into the house would be suicide. His only way in was Raven, and it was only a matter of time before he convinced her to rob her own father blind.

Raven's hands were sweaty as she sat next to Nikki with her knees tucked to her chest. They hadn't spoken a word for hours. Raven had asked Nikki to stay with her until Mizan came home. She didn't know how she was going to break the news, and she needed her girl for support. When Raven heard keys in the front door, her stomach tightened and she stood up.

"Hey, baby," she said, as a thousand butterflies fluttered in her stomach.

Mizan came in and stood silently as he looked from Raven to Nikki. "I thought I told you not to invite anybody over here," he stated with no emotion.

"I know, but I needed some company. I . . . I was feeling sick today," she replied. "That's why I called Nikki over. I have something I need to tell you."

Mizan stared at her blankly as he waited for her to continue, but in his head he already knew what was about to come out of her mouth.

"I'm pregnant," she whispered. Her voice shook and was so low that he almost didn't hear her.

On the inside he smiled, but on the outside he remained calm. He put his hands on top of his head and closed his eyes as if it was the worst news he could have gotten.

"You're what?" he asked.

"I'm pregnant," she replied, her eyes on the floor as her heart tore in half from the devastated look on his face. She looked back at Nikki, who came and stood beside her, grabbing her hand because she knew that it was not the reaction Raven had been hoping for. "Say something," Raven pleaded. "Are you mad?" she asked as tears began to accumulate in her eyes.

"No, I'm not mad, baby. Calm down." Mizan approached her and kissed her forehead. "There's just a lot of stuff you don't know. I can't bring a baby into my world right now. I've got to go . . . I need to clear my head."

"Where are you going?" she asked. "You just got home." Her questions bounced off his back as he walked out the door.

Mizan smiled deviously as he pulled away in his car. Raven was vulnerable to his manipulation. Her emotions were all over the place. He knew that she thought he was going to leave her, and he was sure that at that moment she would do anything in her power to keep him. He was about to set his plans into motion. He was tired of being on the bottom, robbing petty niggas for petty cash. He was ready to inherit the throne, and he was going to enjoy contributing to Benjamin Atkins' fall from grace.

"Don't touch Raven," Mizan instructed as he pulled the ski mask over his face. "I don't give a fuck about that other bitch, but Raven belongs to me."

"I think you're feeling her and don't want to admit it," Rich replied.

"I don't give a fuck about a bitch. This is about a dollar. I've got to do this. It'll make her desperate to get this money, and where do you think she's going to go get it?" Mizan asked. He didn't wait for Rich to reply. "Right back home to Daddy."

Mizan and Rich got out of the car and approached Mizan's house with pistols in hand. Mizan knocked on the door. He knew that Raven had a bad habit of opening the door to see who was outside, instead of looking through the peephole, and as soon as he saw it crack he kicked it open. The impact of the door caused Raven to fall to the floor.

"Nikki!" she screamed as she scrambled backward, away from the two masked men.

Nikki came rushing into the room, but instantly turned on her heels when she realized what was happening. Rich went running after her, grabbing her by the hair. "Bitch, where you think you going?" he asked.

"No!" Nikki screamed as she kicked and swung, trying to free herself of his hold. Rich covered her mouth with his hand and she bit down as hard as she could.

"Aghh fuck! You bitch!" he hollered as he backhanded her across the face.

"Nikki!" Raven screamed as she was snatched up from the floor. Snot and tears covered her face as she pushed her assailant off of her. She had no idea that the man behind the mask was Mizan, and the fear she felt paralyzed her.

"Raven!" Nikki yelled, hysterical. They called for each other as if they could save one another, as if they weren't in the same predicament.

The men manhandled the girls, dragging them down the hallway toward the bedroom.

"No! No please!" Raven screamed as she held on to the walls. Mizan held her with such force that her nails broke and her fingertips bled. "No!"

"Shut that bitch up!" Rich screamed.

They forced the girls onto the bed, sticking their guns in the center of their foreheads. Rich went into action. He was the only one who could speak because they would have recognized Mizan's voice.

"Put your hands out," Rich instructed. The girls huddled together, hugging each other for dear life. Mizan snatched Raven's hands so hard that she felt like her wrists were breaking.

"What do you want?" Raven yelled.

"We want our money. That nigga Mizan been dodging me for weeks. Now we're here to collect," Rich said harshly, planting the mental seed so that Mizan could grow it later. "Where the money?"

"I don't know!" she responded.

"Too bad for you," Rich replied in a sinister tone.

She sniffled loudly as Mizan zip-tied her wrists together in front of her. When Nikki saw Raven's wrists getting bound, she knew what they had in store for them. *They're going to kill us,* she thought. She knew that she didn't have anything to lose. She ran for the door full speed. She got all the way to the front door, but as soon as she opened it Rich came barreling into her from behind, causing the weight of her body to slam the door.

"Where you going, bitch?" he asked through clenched teeth as he threw her down on the floor. He mounted her, licking his lips as he noticed her ripe body for the first time. "Now I'ma have to teach you a lesson," he said as he unbuckled his pants, preparing to have a little fun.

As Nikki looked up into the eyes of the man in front of her she began to sob, her chest heaving up and down as her head fell to the side. She felt him get on top of her and slide her shaky legs open. She closed her eyes and re-fused to look. She didn't want to be a witness to the rape that was about to occur.

Mizan looked down at Raven as she sat with her head down and her hands in front of her body. As he pointed his gun to her head, she was so afraid that she shook vi-olently. He pushed her back on the bed and got on top of her, staring her directly in her eyes.

"Please don't do this," she cried as she listened to the screams of Nikki coming from the next room. He ig-nored her pleas and opened her legs. She used all of her strength to keep them closed, but he was too strong and pulled them apart with such force, she thought they may have broken.

His ultimate goal was to scare her into submission. He had to make her think that her back was against a wall so that when he asked her to do the unthinkable, she would agree.

When she saw him unzip his pants she knew there was no stopping him. She took a deep breath and forced her-self to stop crying as he positioned himself on top of her. She was waiting for the pain to come. She was prepared to scream with Nikki as they were tortured together. She closed her eyes and swallowed the lump in her throat while her heart beat rapidly. She stifled her cries, and she felt a cold hand on her thigh she tensed in terror.

"When Mizan find out you did this to me, he's going to kill you. You bitch-ass nigga," she whispered hatefully as she trembled and stared her attacker in the eyes.

Mizan paused and looked down at Raven. He was sur-prised at her loyalty. Despite the threat of danger, Raven had stood behind her man. He scoffed and got to his feet as he zipped his pants back up. He had always demanded her loyalty, but with the words that had just come out of her mouth she had gained his in return. He saw Raven in a new light, and in that moment he decided to keep her around after he got rid of her father.

Boom! Out of nowhere a loud blast erupted through the house. "Nik!" Raven screamed out for her, and when Nikki didn't respond she knew what it meant.

Mizan rushed out of the room. When he saw the bloodbath in front of him, he snatched Rich up by the neck and pushed him toward the door.

Raven ran into the room, not caring that they had guns pointed in her direction. She had to check on Nikki. She knew in her heart that she had been shot, but when she saw her lying in the middle of the floor naked, a pool of blood surrounding her head, she fell to her knees beside her.

"No . . . no, Nik . . . wake up!" she whispered as she cradled her bloody face in her hands. Raven tried to press her hands against the bullet hole in her temple, but nothing she did would stop the profuse flow of blood as it seeped onto the floor.

Raven crawled to the house phone and picked it up, her shaky hand barely able to dial 911. "Please, I need help," she muttered hopelessly.

Rich lunged toward her to snatch the phone from her hand, but Mizan grabbed his forearm forcefully and stared him in the eye. The look he gave Rich spoke a thousand words. He had meant what he said: Rich was not to touch Raven. Oddly, Mizan knew he felt something deeper for Raven then he was willing to admit, and he gave her one last look before pushing Rich out the front door.

"Fuck did you do?" he screamed at Rich as soon as they were in the getaway car.

"Shit got out of hand," Rich said nonchalantly as he peeled off the ski mask.

"You stupid mu'fucka. Now my crib is a fucking crime scene. I said scare the bitch, not kill her," Mizan said, enraged. He hit the steering wheel in frustration and put as much distance between himself and his house as possible. "Fuck!" he shouted. He hadn't meant for anyone to get seriously hurt. *Fuck it, what's done is done,* he thought. His cell phone began to vibrate and he pulled it off his hip to see that it was Raven, trying to reach him. He picked it up.

"Yo'?" he answered coolly.

"I . . . I need you to come home. She's shot . . . . They came in here . . . They tied me up." She sobbed uncontrollably. She was so terrified that she couldn't piece her words together intelligibly.

Mizan played his role perfectly, like a skilled actor. "What? Rae, I can't understand you. Calm down and tell me what went down." He tried to appear rational.

Raven didn't have the strength to repeat herself, and all he heard were her wails accompanied by sirens. "I'm on my way," he shouted, then hung up the phone.

He pulled up to Rich's house and they both went inside, where Mizan quickly changed clothes. Before Mizan left, he said, "Keep your mouth shut about what happened tonight. I'll let you know when we're hitting the safe. Until then, lay low."

Rich nodded and Mizan pulled off into the night, heading back to his house to come to the rescue of the woman he had just terrorized.

Chapter Eight

Flashing red, white, and blue lights were scattered all over Mizan's street when he pulled onto his block. He made sure that he tucked his pistol underneath his seat before he got out to search for Raven. He saw her standing on the front yard, speaking with a police officer, and he hesitantly made his way over to her. When she saw him she broke down, running to him as if he could take all of her pain away. She melted into his embrace as he wrapped his arms around her.

"It's okay, ma . . . I'm right here," he whispered in her ear. "What happened?" he asked.

Before she could respond a police officer interrupted them. He attempted to finish questioning Raven, but in her current state she wasn't much help. She refused to say too much. All she could think of was Nikki and how close she had come to ending up just like her. There were policemen and paramedics everywhere, and all Raven wanted to do was get away from all the madness.

"Let's get you out of here," Mizan said, touching her with such care that he even fooled himself into thinking his concern was genuine. She began to walk away with him, but stopped suddenly when she heard a paramedic call out for help behind her.

"We have a pulse in here! We need to get her to a hospital before we lose her!"

Raven turned around and ran back toward the house. "She's alive?" Raven called out in shock. She had seen all of the blood that had come out of Nikki. "They shot her in the head," she whispered in pure disbelief. A police officer stopped her from getting too close to the gurney that Nikki lay on. "Is she all right? I just want to know if she's okay!" she shouted. "She needs me!"

Mizan grabbed Raven by her waist and carried her away kicking and screaming. "I have to be with her!" she yelled. She spoke with such persistence that Mizan had to oblige. He grabbed her by the shoulders to calm her down.

"We will meet her at the hospital," he assured her.

The waiting room was eerily silent as Raven sat between Mizan and Nikki's mother. They had been there for five hours anticipating the results of the emergency surgery that Nikki was undergoing.

"I don't understand this . . . I don't understand how this happened to my baby," Nikki's mother said.

"I'm so sorry, Auntie Gena," Raven whispered as she put her face in her hands.

"I can't just sit here and wait. I need to find out what's going on in there!"

Nikki's mother stormed off, an emotional wreck, while Raven leaned against Mizan. It was 4:00 A.M. and Raven's body begged her to rest, but she could not sleep until she found out if her best friend would make it.

"Who were they, Mizan?" she asked quietly.

Mizan rubbed his freshly cut Caesar and appeared to be searching for an answer.

"Tell me the truth. I think I deserve to know," she continued.

"I owe somebody a lot of money . . . the type of money that people will kill over," he said. "That's why I don't like for you to leave the house without me. That's why I don't like a lot of people to know where I rest my head. That's why I can't allow you to have this baby."

"What?" she whispered as she looked at him sadly.

"I owe these niggas a hundred stacks, Raven," he informed her. "They'll touch you and everybody I love for that type of dough. I can't put you and my baby in harm's way like that, ma. We got to end this now. I can't fuck with you like that no more."

"What! What do you mean you can't fuck with me, Mizan? I gave up everything for you. Where am I supposed to go?" she asked. "I love you. I don't want to be without you."

"It's not safe with me, Rae. That could have been you up in that operating room," he said passionately. It was odd, because even though Mizan had orchestrated the entire night's events, he meant what he was telling her. He did have feelings for her, but they were so unfamiliar to him. He had never felt love before. It had never been given to him, therefore he didn't know how to give it to someone else. His love came in the form of control and chaos. "I don't have a hundred thousand, Raven. That's the only way these niggas gon' stop gunning for me."

"You can't leave me alone," she whispered as a huge teardrop fell from her eyes, splattering on the floor at her feet. "You told me you would take care of me. I can't go home now. You can't do this to me, Mizan. If you do, everything they said about you will be true."

"I have to, ma," he said, laying it on thick as his eyelids filled with phony tears. Mizan delivered an Oscar worthy performance as he gripped her hand. He stood to leave, but before he could take two steps in the other direction, she spoke.

"What if I can get you the money?" she said.

"I can't ask you to do that, ma. I don't want you involved."

"Mizan, my best friend is in there dying. I was tied up and almost raped with your baby inside of me," she whispered frantically. "I'm already involved. I can get you the money . . . Let me help."

"If you thinking about going to your old man, it is not going to work, Raven. Your father hates me. The nigga will see me slumped in the gutter before he comes out of his pocket for me," Mizan said truthfully.

"That's why I'm not going to ask him," she replied. "I know the combination to his safe. He gave it to me and my mother so that if anything ever happened to him we would have access to his paper. If this is what it takes for us to be together, then I'll do it."

"That's your father," Mizan said, playing devil's advocate. He wanted to be sure that she planned every aspect of the setup. He did not want her to ever put two and two together. In her eyes, she would be the one who thought of the entire thing.

"You're my man," she replied sincerely. "I'll do anything for you."

Raven stared at Mizan as she picked up the phone and dialed her father's number. It had been such a long time since she had last seen him. Her leg jumped around nervously, causing her high heel to tap against the tiled floor. She counted the number of times the phone rang. She couldn't believe what she was about to do. To set up the man who had raised her was eating her up inside, but the greater threat of losing Mizan was what stopped her from hanging up the phone. She thought of the baby growing inside of her—the one that she desperately wanted—and knew that if she did not do this, Mizan would leave. It wasn't something that she was willing to let happen.

"Hello?" Benjamin finally answered.

"Hey, Daddy," she whispered. Hearing his voice was therapy to her weary soul. There was never a problem that he could not fix. Her father had been the keeper of her heart until Mizan had come along and stolen it away.

"Baby girl . . . I'm glad you called," he said. "Your mama has been trying to call you. She's been worried sick over you."

Raven smiled. She knew that he really wanted to say he had been worried. "I miss you too, Daddy," she replied, her voice shaky. Mizan stared at her intensely, adding pressure to the already tense situation. She closed her eyes to block him out and opened her mouth to speak. She knew that the next words out of her mouth would establish her allegiance to Mizan. "I really need to see you. I don't want to fight with you anymore. I just want my daddy back." She bit her fingernails while fighting the moisture that built up in her eyes.

"I want my baby girl back too," Benjamin replied. "I only want what's best for you, Raven. I love you."

"I love you too, Daddy. Can we meet for breakfast so that we can talk?" she asked.

"Yeah, I would like that," he replied. "I'll pick you up at two o'clock."

"Okay, Daddy, see you soon," she said before closing her cell phone. She looked up at Mizan. "I don't feel right about this," she told him. "He will hate me after this."

"We will make it look like a robbery, ma, don't worry. You just keep him away from the house for at least an hour. Where is your moms and sister?" he asked.

"It's Sunday. They go to church every Sunday morning," Raven replied.

"Everything will be okay, a'ight? Trust your man," Mizan stated as he stood and rubbed her hair. He gripped her shoulders gently and pulled her to her feet. "Go get dressed. You want to be ready when your pops get here.

Remember, give me an hour to get in and out. What's the combination to the safe?"

"Eight-fourteen-twenty-four," she muttered hesitantly. As the numbers rolled off of her tongue, a wave of extreme guilt swept over her. She lifted her head to the sky. *God, please don't let anything go wrong. Just make everything okay.* Raven had to put her faith somewhere because the pit in her stomach was telling her that this could blow up in her face.

A smile came to Raven's face when she heard the sound of Al Green coming down the street. Only her father would cruise to the old school music with such pride. She shook her head in embarrassment as he pulled his pearl Cadillac STS into the driveway. She rushed into her bedroom, went into her candy dish, and took out a small amount of cocaine. She felt badly for indulging in the white candy while she was pregnant, but she needed it. She was hooked on it, loving the euphoric feeling it gave her, and she figured a little bit wouldn't hurt. It was how she started every day, but she knew that she would especially need it today in order to deal with the lecture her father was sure to give her. She hit the line like a pro and then rushed outside. She was genuinely happy to see her dad and she smiled brightly as she hopped in the car.

"Hey, Daddy," she greeted him as she leaned over to kiss his cheek.

"You flew up out there before I could even get in the driveway good," he commented as he looked at the small house. "I'm not welcomed in your house? He got you living here and I can't come inside?"

Raven sighed. *Here he go,* she thought. "Daddy, you can come in." She opened her car door and headed back inside with her father on her heels. She knew that he only wanted to come inside to be nosy. He turned his nose up almost as soon as he stepped foot inside.

"This is where he has my baby girl laying her head at night?" he asked, his tone insinuating disapproval.

"Daddy, don't start. I'm not with Mizan because of what he has," she said. "As a matter of fact, I'm not even trying to get into all of that. Let's just go have a nice breakfast."

"You know you deserve more than this. I don't look down on a nigga because he doesn't make a lot of money. I just don't respect how he makes his money and you are above this lifestyle. I didn't raise you to play housewife, Raven, cuz that's all this is . . . You're playing house."

"It's not like that, Daddy," she replied. "I know you don't like him, but I really need you to give him a chance."

Benjamin shook his head. "That's not going to happen, Raven. He has no morals. No code. I can't throw stones because I'm not society's most honorable citizen either. I know that some people might think what I do is wrong. I'm a hustler. I sell drugs, but the difference between me and Mizan is that I take care of those who take care of me. I'm loyal. I know a snake when I see one, and whenever you are ready to come back home, my door will always be open."

As he took in his daughter's appearance he noticed that she had changed. She was no longer the delicate flower he had nurtured. Being with Mizan had hardened her around the edges. Her eyes were red and her lips had taken on a slightly darker tint; a clear indication that she had been smoking weed. He had no clue that his baby girl had graduated to snorting soft, but if he had known it would only intensify his desire to snatch her out of Mizan's clutches and force her to come home. "Let's get out of here," he whispered.

He led the way back to his car and opened the door for Raven before getting in himself. He reached into his glove box and pulled out the key to Raven's Lexus.

"I'm not giving this to you because I agree with how you're living. I'm giving it to you because I want you to have your own. Whenever you want to leave, you have a way out," he said.

Raven gave her father a half smile as she put her hand on her stomach. *Should I tell him I'm pregnant?* She desperately wanted her father's blessing, but she was not ready to deal with him knowing about her baby. *Mizan was right. He would have never helped us.* Hearing her father speak so critically of Mizan only made her feel more confident in her choice to help Mizan. She put on a fake smile as she rode shotgun with her father through the city streets.

Entering the Atkins home was a piece of cake. With the security code Raven had provided, and the combination to the safe, Mizan and Rich entered without arising suspicion. They quickly made their way up the carpeted stairs and entered the master bedroom. They followed Raven's instructions precisely, walking up to the bookshelf that made up one entire wall. Mizan scanned the second shelf until he located *The Art of War.* He removed the book and behind it sat a red button. He pressed it and the entire wall slid to the side, revealing a hidden panic room. Mizan instantly noticed the wall safe inside. With ease, he opened the safe, and when he saw the neatly stacked kilos of cocaine, he rubbed his hands together greedily.

"Whoo!" he shouted in excitement. There was more cocaine in the safe than he had ever anticipated. After months of planning it was finally his time to come into his own. He opened the four duffel bags he had brought, and he and Rich emptied the safe.

"One hundred and twenty bricks," he stated in disbelief. He was about to make the streets snow and couldn't wait to put in work. He pulled out one kilo and placed it back in the safe, leaving the door wide open.

"What are you doing, fam? Take all that shit. What you putting one back for?" Rich asked.

"That one brick is going to take care of my main competition," Mizan replied as he darted down the steps with the duffel bags in hand. He hit the panic button on the alarm before leaving, which sent a direct message to the police department. "When the police get here they're gonna find that brick. It's enough to send Benny Atkins away for the rest of his life, and the streets will be wide open for the taking."

When Raven saw the police cars in front of her father's house, she immediately thought the worst. The neighbors had come out to watch the scene. They stood around the Atkins' property, trying to get a glimpse of what was going on.

"Oh my God . . . Did Mommy and Morgan go to church this morning?" she asked, fearing the worst. Her father ignored the question, but she could see his brow furrow in concern. They stepped out of the car and Benjamin rushed up the walkway only to be stopped by a plain-clothes detective.

"Whoa, who are you? You can't go in there," the detective said.

"I'm the owner of this house. What is going on? Are my wife and daughter inside?" he asked. Raven stood in the background, terrified, as she shook her head, praying that nothing had gone wrong and that her family was safe.

The detective moved his hand to his pistol. "Sir, I'm going to need you to step back and put your hands up slowly." He raised his gun and aimed it at Benjamin's chest.

"Fuck is wrong with you? Answer my question! What is going on inside my house? Where is my wife? Justine!" he screamed as he pushed past the detective, fearing that something had happened to his wife and child.

"Daddy, wait!" Raven shouted.

Benjamin was stopped by two uniformed police officers. "Get your fucking hands off of me!" he yelled. "I own this house. I need to get inside." He reached into his jacket pocket.

"He has a gun!" one of the officers shouted. Before Benjamin could protest, the officers opened fire.

"Daddy!" Raven screamed as she witnessed her father's body go limp. He seemed to fall in slow motion in front of her face, and when his body hit the pavement, a sickening thud echoed from his head hitting the ground. A wallet fell out of his hand, revealing that he had only been reaching for identification to prove that he was the owner of the house. "Daddy!" Raven ran for her father, but was held back from getting too close. "He didn't have a gun! What did you do?" she screamed in agony as her legs gave out under her and she collapsed in the detective's arms. She hit him furiously. "What did you do?" she cried.

Raven stared at the blood on her hands as she sat on the floor in the hospital. She was waiting by the morgue for her mother and sister to arrive. She hadn't the heart to call her mother herself, so she'd allowed the hospital to do it. She heard her mother's wails through the phone. *This is all my fault,* she thought. Her pale skin was flushed red from constant crying. She could not wrap her mind around the fact that her father was gone. She regretted their foolish fighting. Now she would never have a chance to say she was sorry, or to make things right. In the blink of an eye he had been taken from her. She was now a fatherless child, and the ache she felt in her soul was one she would live with for the rest of her life. She looked at her vibrating cell phone and ignored it. Mizan had been calling her all day, but she did not have the energy to speak to him. She was sure he had heard what had happened, but she was not trying to hear anything from anyone. Nobody could take away the emptiness she felt inside. No one would ever understand what she had lost.

"Raven?"

She heard her mother's voice and looked up. Justine came down the hall, holding Morgan's hand. Ethic stood by her side as he escorted them inside.

"Mommy?" Raven called as she stood up. She ran to her mother and hugged her tightly. "I'm so sorry, Mommy . . . I'm sorry," she whispered. She buried her face in Justine's shoulders as they embraced each other and Morgan. "They shot him right in front of my face. They killed him," Raven sobbed.

Justine felt as if her heart had been ripped from her chest as she held her daughters. She had been with Benjamin since she was a young girl. He was the love of her life, and to have him taken away so suddenly felt like torture.

"Mrs. Atkins?" a woman in a white lab coat interrupted.

Justine looked up and nodded as she wiped her nose with a tissue. "Yes, I'm Mrs. Atkins," she confirmed.

She spoke with so much sorrow that she brought tears to the woman's eyes. "I am so very sorry for your loss. Your daughter is still a minor so she could not legally identify the body. I hate to put you through this, but. . . ."

"I'll identify him," she replied. "I'd like to see what they did to him."

The woman led Justine away, and Morgan clung to Raven.

"What happened to Daddy, Rae?" Morgan signed as she cried from uncertainty. She did not know exactly what was going on but she could feel the sadness in the air.

Raven was speechless. She was so caught up in her own grief that she was choking on it, unable to respond to her little sister's question. Ethic had been standing back to allow them their intimate moments, but he could see that Raven was traumatized. He bent down to face Morgan. "Your daddy is with the angels. He is watching over you right now, so wipe your face. You don't want him to see you crying," Ethic signed back.

Morgan wiped her tears and Raven turned her back to them because she could not stop herself from breaking down. It was so unfair. She felt like seventeen years was not enough time with her father. Ethic came up behind her and put his hand on her back. She turned into him and cried on his shoulder.

"I was fighting with him . . . For months I haven't talked to him," she said.

"Don't think about that. None of that matters now. He knew you loved him," Ethic assured her.

"I don't know how I let this happen," Raven said as she shook her head. Something inside of her was telling her that Mizan's setup was the reason why the police had gotten involved. "How did this happen?"

"I don't know, ma . . . but I'm gon' find out," he stated.

Justine emerged from the coroner's office. Distress was written all over her face as she reached for Morgan. "I can't believe he's gone," she said. "I just need to go home . . . Raven, will you stay with us tonight? I need both of my girls with me."

Raven desperately wanted to be near her family, but she knew that Mizan wouldn't want her staying the night away from home. "I can't, ma. I can't go back there right now. I can't get the image of Daddy laying on the grass out of my head," she replied.

Justine touched Raven's cheek gently and gave her a half smile. "I understand, baby. Tomorrow then?" she asked.

Raven nodded in agreement. "Tomorrow, I promise."

"I would really love for you to come home. We are all we have left. We have to stick together," Justine said solemnly. She turned to Ethic. "Thank you for rushing here to be with us, Ethic. You were like the son Benjamin never had, and he trusted you."

"Do you need anything?" Ethic asked.

Justine looked to the floor as her bottom lip quivered. "What I need you can't give me, Ethic. No one can." She walked away, holding Morgan's hand.

Ethic turned to Raven. "How did you get here?"

"I rode in the ambulance with my daddy."

"Let me take you home," he said. He removed his Sean John hoodie and wrapped it around her shoulders, then led her outside to his car. Raven's nerves were shot, and she breathed deeply, trying to calm down. She desperately needed a line of coke to take the edge off. She needed it to take her away. She sniffled loudly as her nose ran, and she became antsy. Ethic noticed her erratic behavior, but he dismissed it. He wanted to give her the benefit of the doubt, and assumed that she was grieving over what had happened. They did not speak as he took her back to Mizan's. Her world had been turned upside down and she was sure that it was her fault. Something had gone wrong. *Mizan told me that this would be easy. . . . that nobody would get hurt,* she thought.

Ethic could see that Raven was deeply affected by Benjamin's death. Everyone knew that she was the apple of her father's eye, and he was sure that this would affect her more than anyone else. "I'm sorry, Raven," Ethic said. The way he spoke her name reminded her of her father, and she put her face in her hands and sobbed quietly. Ethic rubbed her back gently with one hand as he steered the car with the other. "Let it out, ma. You don't got to play tough. Let it out."

As soon as Ethic pulled in front of her house, Mizan stepped out onto the porch to make his presence known. Ethic turned Raven's face toward him, his touch like electricity running up and down her spine. "You sure you don't want to stay with your moms tonight?" he asked. "You don't have to play this game anymore. You can go back home."

"Raven!" Mizan called, causing her to jump in her seat.

"I've got to go, Ethic," she said nervously, her wide eyes filled with emotion. She opened the door and Ethic grabbed her hand gently.

"Just because your father is gon' doesn't mean you don't still have an army of niggas behind you. All you got to do is say the word. I don't like your nigga. The only reason he's still breathing is because of you," Ethic whispered.

"Rae!" Mizan's voice was like the bark of a pit bull.

Raven pulled back her hand. "I'm sorry, I got to go," she said again. She walked up to the house, never looking back as she went inside. Mizan put both of his hands up as if to tell Ethic that he was ready to pop off anytime.

Ethic bit his inner cheek as he tried to control his temper. He had never been the type to start a fight, but if Mizan wanted to push him to the edge, he would have no problem finishing one. He got his money low key. He avoided the flash and the spotlight so that he could keep a low profile and avoid unwanted attention from the police. Mizan, however, was pulling his card and provoking him to start a beef. Ethic knew that Mizan was intimidated by him. The look in Raven's eyes when she looked at Ethic infuriated Mizan, which is why he was itching to take him off the map. *I don't want your bitch,* Ethic thought as he backed out of the driveway. Ethic did not have to prove his gangster. He had only been in Flint for a few months and his name already rang bells in the street. As a man of few words, he didn't speak unless he had something important to say. At first, the hustlers in Flint had taken his passive personality as a weakness, but after he proved that he was about his gunplay, he commanded the respect of his peers. Ethic hoped that he didn't have to make an example out of Mizan, because once Ethic pressed "go" on his murder game, there would be no stopping him.

Mizan stepped back into the house and approached Raven. Before she could say a word he wrapped one hand around her throat. He pushed her head against the wall so hard that the drywall dented behind her. "Fuck is wrong with you? I've been calling your phone all fucking day. You were too busy out fucking with that nigga to answer my calls, bitch," he said harshly as he chastised her with a finger in her face. Raven grabbed at his hand for release. She couldn't breathe and her eyes bulged from the lack of oxygen. "This the second time that mu'fucka done came to my house on your behalf. You fucking him?" Mizan yelled through clenched teeth as he pounded her head against the wall repeatedly.

She fell to her knees when he released, her and grabbed the back of her head as an instant headache formed in her skull. She sobbed as she braced herself on the floor while nursing her injured neck. She stared at him in contempt.

"I'm not fucking him! He works for my father! He's dead, Mizan! I've been at the hospital all day. Ethic just brought me home!" she yelled. "You told me nothing would go wrong!"

Mizan's rage melted away as he processed what she had just said. "Nothing was supposed to go wrong," he said defensively. "What happened?"

"When we showed up there were police everywhere! Daddy thought something bad had happened to my mom. He was just trying to get inside to see. They shot him, Mizan! He's gone." She curled up on the floor, lying on her side, her back facing Mizan. The immeasurable pain that plagued her heart was almost too much to handle. It was torture.

Mizan smiled wickedly. He hadn't intended for Benjamin to die, but now that it had happened, the reality of his situation was bittersweet. Bitter for Raven, but oh-so-sweet for him. Now he could take over the streets without fear of Benjamin's retribution. He looked at Raven on the floor and lay down beside her. He wrapped his arms around her.

"Everything's good now, ma . . . The world is mine, and as long as you are loyal I will share it with you."

Raven closed her eyes as she felt Mizan's lips grace the back of her neck. To her it felt like the kiss of death. She loved him, but now it seemed like everything she had done to please him had turned her soul black.

Chapter Nine

During the week that Raven was picking out caskets and flowers, Mizan was scoping out corners and trap houses. He played the sympathetic boyfriend well, but his only concern was taking over her father's empire. He knew that he would have competition from the low-level workers who had hustled beneath Benjamin. They would want to see an insider move up and take reign of the streets, but Mizan wasn't having it. He had already killed the head of the operation; now it was time for the body to fall.

He had a week until the funeral. It was street code that the next king could not be crowned until the one before him was put to rest. A meeting had been planned, seven of Benjamin's highest lieutenants, to be held directly after the services, but unfortunately for them Mizan had other things in store. He had seven days to hit seven men, all of whom were in line to succeed their boss.

The ruthlessness that it took to make it to the top was something that most men did not possess, but Mizan was the grimiest of character and would stop at nothing to get what he wanted. No one would be spared. If anyone stood in his way they would be taken care of, including Raven. The fact that he had claimed Benny Atkins' daughter as his prize made him feel superior, as if he had delivered the ultimate slap to the face of Flint's kingpin. Everyone in town knew that Raven was Benjamin's most treasured loved one, but she had chosen Mizan over him.

He had plucked Benjamin's most delicate flower and now she belonged to him. She was the perfect trophy as long as she stayed in check.

Mizan was not green to the game, however. He had convinced Raven to betray her own father so he knew that her loyalty to anyone else would never be rock solid. If he even smelled the foul scent of disloyalty he would tie all loose ends. He had become soft on her, but even she was expendable. It was all in the game. She had wanted to live the street life, and now that she was in it, there was no walking away.

Yul "Big Baby" Snell left his home at 2:00 A.M. He had no clue that it was his day to die. His name fit him perfectly. His baby-boy features made him a hot commodity to the ladies around town, despite the platinum wedding band on his chubby finger. He had been working for Benny Atkins since he was fourteen years old and he had put in work over the years. A born hustler, he could sell sand to a beach. The way he moved weight he should have been a millionaire by now, but he was a known trick and couldn't help but spend his money on maintaining his women. As Mizan followed him through the city streets, there was no doubt in his mind that he was going to meet one of his A.M. jump offs.

He followed him out of the city limits until he pulled up to a black-and-white cottage-style home. Mizan cut his headlights and parked a block away, then watched Big Baby exit the car. Mizan's eyes scanned the house carefully, trying to figure out how many people were inside. The house was dark except for one room, and when he saw a voluptuous woman answer the door wearing skimpy lingerie, he knew she was alone.

"Damn," Mizan whispered as he admired the woman's physique. "I'ma give you time to hit that one last time. You deserve that." He shook his head as he screwed the silencer on to his ratchet. He hoped Big Baby had the best orgasm of his life, because it would surely be his last.

Mizan slipped on leather gloves, got out of his car, and crept toward Big Baby's shiny Denali truck. Unfortunately for Big Baby, he had been too preoccupied to lock his car doors. He had practically invited Mizan to hide in the backseat. *Pussy make this nigga go dumb,* Mizan thought, knowing that he would never give another man a chance to catch him slipping. To kill Mizan would be like hunting a lion: most times the lion ended up being the last one standing. He checked his watch and prepared for a long wait as he stretched out on the floor. The windows were tinted, so he didn't have to worry about Big Baby seeing him before he got in the car.

Fuck, dude taking all day to handle his business, Mizan thought after two hours of waiting. Finally, Big Baby emerged from the house. As soon as he entered the vehicle, Mizan popped off.

Psst. . . .

The gunshot was barely a whisper as it sent a hollow point flying through Big Baby's skull. He never saw it coming. His head slumped forward and rested on his horn. The blaring noise erupted and Mizan saw lights coming on in the surrounding houses. He quickly hopped out and jogged to his car, then pulled away, disappearing into the night.

One down, six to go.

After the first hit, Mizan's conscience took a backseat. He did not care what he had to do; he was determined to get to the top. No life was worth more than his potential reign over the city, and as he thought about the hit he was about to do, he smiled. Leslie Philips was next on his list. There was only one problem: he never traveled alone. Les always kept a bodyguard around him. *This nigga on some real John Gotti–type shit,* Mizan thought with a smirk. It was smart for Les to keep extra protection around him, but Mizan thought outside of the box. If he could not get close to his vic, then he was going to use the people who could. Les hired the best bodyguard in town, a hood nigga by the name of Mario, who wasn't afraid to get it popping. Mario was a known shooter and had lay a few souls to rest with his gunplay. He was a gangster, but Mizan had graduated to goon status a long time ago, and even though he had no personal beef with Mario, he was a target by association.

When Mario pulled away from his home to go put in work for Leslie, Mizan sprang into action and got out of the car. He screwed on a silencer as he made his way up the manicured lawn to the front door of Mario's house. He knocked lightly, and when a dark-skinned beauty opened the door with her new-born in her arms, Mizan pushed her back into the house and pointed the gun in her face. She tried to run, but Mizan grabbed her forcefully by her hair.

"Ah, ah, ah," he chastised as he pushed her toward the couch.

"Please . . ." she began to beg.

"Bitch, shut up," he said. "If you do exactly what I say, you and your brat will live to see another day."

She cried as she cradled her child to her chest.

Mizan pointed his gun toward the phone. "Call him," he instructed.

"Call who?" she exclaimed through her tears, playing dumb.

Mizan smacked her across the face swiftly. The weight of the gun in his hand caused her lip to burst on contact, and she whimpered as she put her hands up to shield her child.

"Call him," Mizan repeated calmly.

His face was covered by a red bandana. All she could see were his eyes, and she noticed the crazed look in his stare. Her hand shook as she conceded and picked up the phone to dial. Mizan snatched the phone from the girl's hand.

"What up, Kim?" Mario answered.

"Didn't anybody tell you never to leave your wife and kid at home alone?" Mizan said mockingly into the phone. He kept his pistol on the chocolate-kiss beauty before him. She cried as she held her baby tighter.

"Who the fuck is this?" Mario replied. "If you put one fucking hand on my wife—"

"Look, I don't got time for the rah-rah shit, my nigga. I've got a proposition for you. We both got a problem right now. My problem is riding shotgun in your car as we speak and can be handled with one bullet. Your problem is this gun I'm pointing at wifey. Somebody gon' die tonight, my nigga. One of us gon' have to get it popping, but it's up to you to decide if it's me or you, n'ah mean?"

There was a long silence on the other end of the phone. Mizan continued, "You've got a choice to make. You handle my problem and I can make yours disappear."

Mario hesitated for a long time, feeling like a snake for contemplating the proposal; but when it came down to it he had to make sure that his family was all right. He couldn't afford to pull any slick shit and fake the funk with Mizan. He had to kill or his family would be killed. He reached inside his jacket pocket and gripped his pistol discreetly underneath the fabric. He looked his man in the eye and said, "I'm sorry, fam." He regretfully pulled the trigger.

When Mizan heard the gunshot go off in his ear, he smiled deviously. "Smart choice," he said as he hung up. Mizan looked down at the traumatized woman. She was so afraid that she had peed on herself.

"Get on the ground," he ordered.

"Please don't do this," she pleaded.

"Bitch, you got two seconds to get your ass on the ground before I pop your melon," Mizan threatened. The girl reluctantly did as she was told and lay her baby on a pillow beside her. She closed her eyes and waited for the shot that would end her life.

"Count to sixty," he ordered.

As she began to count, Mizan made his exit. By the time she was at twenty he was pulling away from the scene and thinking about a way to hit the next man on his list.

Mizan ran through Benjamin's lietenants like a john ran through whores on a Saturday night. With ease and efficiency, he touched each and every one of them except Ethic. He knew that killing him would prove to be much more difficult, and he took his time, giving himself time to watch his prey so that he was fully prepared. Ethic was respected in the city, and Mizan knew that after he got rid of him, he would inherit the throne. He wanted to make an example of Ethic, and the perfect stage on which to murder him would be at Benjamin Atkins' funeral. Mizan could not wait for his time to arrive.

The funeral came too quickly for Raven. A dreadful feeling filled the pit of her stomach because she knew that this would be the last time she would ever see her father's face. The emptiness she felt inside mixed with the morning sickness she was experiencing had her on an emotional roller coaster. As she dressed in the bedroom mirror, tears slid down her cheeks like raindrops on a windowpane. There was no reason to wear makeup; her crying would only wash it away. She closed her eyes and gripped her stomach while she thought of the child inside of her. The black Donna Karan dress she wore concealed her baby bump well. She wasn't ready to share her news with the world just yet. She did not want people judging her. She knew that her situation looked bad. She was a high school dropout who was pregnant and living with a man her parents hated. *Everybody think I'm too young to know what I'm doing, but I know what I feel, and I love Mizan. They don't understand. They don't see what I see. When I turn eighteen everything will be good. They will have to respect my decisions then,* she thought. She only had a month to go before she was legal, and decided it would be better if she waited until then to inform her mother of her condition. She tried to think of how she would tell Justine, and she instinctively pictured her father there to hear the news too. She quickly wiped a tear away, realizing that she would never again share a milestone with her father. He would never walk her down the aisle at her wedding. He would never hold her child or even be there to hold her hand while she gave birth.

I didn't even tell him he was going to be a grandfather. Why didn't I just tell him when I had the chance? she asked herself. It was important for her father to at least know that she was about to be a mother. She had imagined them being one big happy family. Everything they had fought about seemed so petty now. She looked down at the photo of herself when she was a little girl that sat on the dresser. She removed it from the frame and placed it in her purse, deciding to put it in his casket before he was lowered into the ground. She felt like there was a piece of her missing. A huge chunk of her life had been removed, and now she was on her own. She took a deep breath and walked into the living room to find Mizan sitting on the couch, blazing a spliff.

"Why aren't you dressed?" she asked. She frowned at the sweatpants and T-shirt he was wearing.

"Dressed for what?" he responded casually, as if her father's death was insignificant in his world.

"You know for what, Mizan," she replied. "I need you there. I'm burying him today and I don't think I can do it by myself."

"You're not going to be by yourself. Your moms will be there. I didn't rock with your pops like that. I wasn't a fake nigga when he was breathing and I ain't a fake nigga now that's he's sleeping, n'ah mean?" he asked. "Plus, I got to handle some business."

"That's real fucked up, Mizan," Raven shot back defiantly. "Can you just show your face at least out of respect?"

Mizan looked at Raven sternly as he stood up, a hint of anger glittering in his eyes. He calmly smashed the blunt out in an ashtray on the coffee table before he approached her. He stood in front of her, his tall frame looming over her. "Out of respect?" Mizan repeated as if he hadn't heard her right.

Raven placed one hand on her hip and cocked her head to the side. "Yes, out of resp—"

Before Raven could get the sentence out, Mizan slapped the taste out of her mouth. Raven's head spun halfway around her neck. He had slapped her so hard that her right ear was ringing and her face went numb.

Raven had so much pent-up emotion that she snapped and attacked back. "What is wrong with you?" she screamed as she swung her arms wildly.

Unfazed by her punches, Mizan hemmed her in quickly, holding her firmly against the wall. He held her face so tightly that his fingertips made bruises appear on her pale skin.

"Let me go!" she cried as tears of contempt burned her eyes.

"Bitch, let me tell you something. Fuck your pops. I'm not impressed by him or what he did in the streets. Don't get me twisted with none of them ho-ass niggas he had working for him. You better watch your fucking mouth when you talk to me. You tell me to respect another man in my house again and I will break your jaw. I don't give a damn if he was your father or not. I'ma give you a pass right now because I know you're not thinking straight, but after today you better remember one thing. I'm Daddy now," he said through clenched teeth. The rage brewing in his eyes terrified Raven. It was the second time he had put his hands on her. After it had happened the first time, she had made an excuse for him. She blamed herself, thinking that he loved her so much that she was the only person who could take him there. Now it had happened again, and although it broke her down, somewhere inside she accepted his actions. She justified them, thinking that he only acted that way because he cared about her. She closed her eyes as he held her in place. She was so young, so vulnerable. She was a little girl trying to do big-girl things, and her decision to live with Mizan was slowly proving to be more than she could handle. Following his lead had led to her father's death, but for some odd reason she did not want to leave. She could never see herself willingly letting Mizan go. Her young heart was under siege and being held captive by Mizan. No matter what he did to her or how much he took her through, she would always be there for him, which was why she slowly submitted to him. She stopped fighting back, and as Mizan looked down at her crying face, his grip loosened.

He had never meant to fall for Raven. She was only supposed to be a pawn in his plot to get on top, but the young, fair-skinned beauty before him was the hottest chick in the game. All she needed was a bit of grooming. He let her go and she slid down the wall until her bottom hit the floor.

He sauntered out of the room casually, as if a conflict between them had never occurred. "Fix yourself up. You don't want to be late," he said before he disappeared down the hall.

Raven grabbed her car keys off the table and ran all the way to her car. When she was locked safely inside she pulled down the visor and examined her damaged face. *Fuck him! I'm done with him. That's the last time he's going to put his hands on me.* She wanted to mean the words, but she knew that all he had to do was say he was sorry and she would go right back. She wiped the wetness away and pulled out of the driveway, heading for her parents' home.

She tried her best to cover the red marks on her face and neck, but no amount of foundation would hide them. Her skin was too light and the bruises too deep to conceal. She got out of the car and reluctantly walked into the house.

"Rae!" Morgan signed. She instantly brightened up at the sight of her older sister. She ran over to hug Raven.

"Hey, Stank," she greeted glumly as she wrapped her arms around her. Morgan's royal blue dress made her look like a princess. Raven smiled and wished she could go back to that age when everything in the world seemed so simple.

"What happened to your face?" Morgan signed curiously.

"Nothing, Morgan. I fell, that's all. I'm going to talk to Mommy. I'll be right back," she signed back insecurely. She made her way up the stairs and entered her parents' bedroom. The scent of her father still lingered in the air, and she froze at the doorway.

"It doesn't even feel like he is gone," Justine stated. Her back was turned to Raven as she stood with a champagne flute in her hand, but she was a mother and she felt her daughter's presence behind her. "I am going to miss that man."

"Me too, Mommy," Raven whispered. She inched into the room and took a seat on the bed. Raven lowered her head and remained quiet until her mother turned around.

When Justine saw the bruises on her daughter's face, her mouth fell open. Her hand went numb, sending her glass to the floor where it shattered, spilling champagne on the hardwood floor.

"Oh, baby," Justine whispered as she put her hands on her daughter's face. Water immediately built up in Raven's eyes.

"He hit me, Mommy. He told me he loved me and then he took it away," Raven sobbed.

"Oh, my precious baby girl," Justine said, her voice filled with hurt. She wished that she could take away the pain that her daughter was feeling, but when a man breaks your heart there is nothing anyone can say to help it mend. "How many times?"

"Twice," Raven replied honestly. "He's good to me though, Mommy. I love him, but sometimes the look in his eyes scares me, Mommy."

Justine sat next to Raven and wrapped her arm around her, while Raven's head rested on her mother's shoulder.

"We didn't want this for you, Rae. You were supposed to marry a doctor or lawyer. A senator or engineer. We tried our hardest to keep you from falling in love with a thug because this entire street life is a game, and every player has a position. You chose to be wifey, Rae, and a wifey is not the same thing as a wife. That's what you young girls have mixed up. You think being a man's main woman gives you prestige. You think it gives you clout, but it makes you look like a fool, Raven. Being wifey means that there is a mistress behind you and a ho behind her. You all are ranked. You should not have to be number one, because when a man really loves you, he will make you his wife. The wives are the only ones who matter, but even they go through the heartache. The bruises, the blowout fights, being called bitches and hoes . . . it's all a part of the game."

"It's not like this all the time though, Ma. Most of the time we're good. I just can't believe that Mizan would do this to me," Raven exclaimed as she sniffled loudly, releasing the weight from her shoulders. She was handing her burdens down to her mother, the one person she knew she could trust.

"That's the type of man you chose, Rae. No matter how well they treat you in the beginning, they can't help but discipline you every once in a while. And when they do it, they do it hard. A man who lives his life in the street can't help it. It's all they know. They either saw it happen to their mamas growing up, or they have so much anger built up inside of them that they take it out on you. It's the price you pay for the lifestyle you lead. You can find a man who won't touch you, Rae. He'll treat you as if you were made of gold, but he'll be a square-ass nigga. Your father spoiled you, Raven, and he started something that only a street-savvy man can finish. That's what draws you to Mizan, and that's what attracts you to Ethic."

"To Ethic?" Raven exclaimed.

"Yes, Ethic," Justine stated matter-of-factly. "Don't think I don't notice how you look at him."

"Ethic's not feeling me," Raven replied honestly. "Trust me. I've tried."

"Raven, you have all the things that a man like Ethic desires. You just don't know how to use what you got to get what you want, that's all. You will learn that as you mature into a woman. Ethic is not your average hustler. He will take care of the lady he chooses, but he doesn't want someone he has to carry every step of the way. He needs a partner who can help him get money. Not just spend it."

"I just want a man like Daddy. Daddy was perfect," Raven replied with an exasperated sigh.

Justine couldn't help but laugh at that one. "Girl, your daddy was far from perfect. There is no such thing as the perfect man, Rae. That's why I never taught you about Prince Charming as a little girl. Men cheat. They lie. They manipulate. They control. All men have flaws. You just have to find the one who works for you. Marriage is founded on love and tolerance because you have to put up with a lot of bullshit."

"At least Daddy didn't hit you. I never even heard Daddy raise his voice at you," Raven replied proudly.

"Just because you never saw or heard us fight does not mean that it did not happen. Daddy hit me, Rae. He did not abuse me, but he and I had our fair share of fights. Mostly when we were young, but it did happen. He knew what being with a man like Mizan would mean for you. Why do you think he was so against it? Men are possessive, especially hustlers. They see us as their trophies, as objects, which is why they can be so gentle one moment and so hostile the next. If you want to be with Mizan, this is what you are going to have to deal with. Don't think that he is going to change, because he won't. A woman can't change a man, but a man can change a woman in the worst way. Do you love him?" Justine asked.

"I do," Raven replied.

"Then you punish him hard this time. Don't go rushing right back to him. You let him know that you have someplace else to go, so that next time he will think twice before he raises a hand to you," Justine instructed. She touched her daughter's stomach and smiled. "You have a baby to think about. You and Mizan are going to be okay. You two have created something so precious together. It's not just about the two of you anymore. You have to think of what's to come."

Raven looked up in shock. "How did you know I was pregnant?"

"Someone once told me that when you lose someone you love, you gain someone you love. I believe that. Plus, wide hips don't run in our family and you're looking a little bit too thick, baby," Justine teased, making her daughter smile. "Now, come on. Let's get your face together so we can go say good-bye to your father."

Chapter Ten

Every hustler in Flint came out to say good-bye to the infamous Benny Atkins. Mt. Pisgah Baptist was filled with the elite of the underworld as they piled into the church to pay their respects.

As Raven sat next to her sister and mother they all held hands, anxiously looking out of the tinted limousine windows. The rainy day matched their somber mood; it seemed fitting for the occasion. They each dreaded the task ahead of them; unprepared to say farewell to the man they loved. Their lives felt so incomplete without the head of their household. While on the outside they presented a strong, united front, on the inside they were broken and torn. The limo came to a stop in front of the church doors where Ethic stood waiting, dapper in a black Ralph Lauren suit. He was well groomed, from his fresh Caesar haircut to his clear, manicured nails. He had cleaned up nicely, and the sight of him made Raven insecure. She went into her purse and pulled out her M•A•C compact to examine the bruises on her face and neck. Her mother had helped her cover them as best she could, but there was only so much that makeup could do. Raven's skin was so light that she could almost pass for white, and on a complexion so fair nothing could be hidden. Ethic opened the door for them and they all exited the car. Raven got out last and turned her head so that he would not see her face as she made her way into the church.

The condolences of her father's associates came one after another and Raven quickly grew overwhelmed in the
sea of faces. She smiled graciously, but she did not hear a
word they said. She was on autopilot. She had to turn her
emotions completely off to prevent herself from breaking down. Her mother led the way through the crowded
church with grace, holding on to Morgan and accepting
the attention like the queen she was. Raven, on the other hand, felt trapped. She felt claustrophobic in the tiny
space, and she began to hyperventilate. She grabbed her
chest as she took a deep breath and stopped walking.
This is too much. I'm not ready for this, she thought. If
she had been high she could have floated through the
entire funeral, but she had chosen not to hit lines that
morning on purpose. She owed her father more than that.
She would never show up at his funeral under the influence of narcotics. She wanted to feel every emotion and
remember every detail of their final farewell. This day
was the last day she would ever see him again and
she was ill prepared. She had no idea how hard it was to
let someone go until she stepped foot inside Mt. Pisgah.
Just as she was about to retreat, she felt a reassuring
hand on the small of her back.

"Everything's gon' be a'ight, ma. I promise," Ethic whispered in her ear as he gently pushed her toward her seat.
He played bodyguard to her and prevented anyone else
from speaking to her. He then escorted her to her father's
casket. Raven's body trembled with every step she took.

"I can't do this," she whispered. She turned to leave, but
Ethic pulled her into his body. His solid frame felt safe . . .
secure . . . right. She closed her eyes tightly. "I can't . . . I
can't do this. I don't want to do this," she whispered over
and over as she began to cry; huge tears cascaded onto
Ethic's suit.

"You can. You can do this. If you don't, you're going to regret it for the rest of your life. I got you. Let's go see your father," Ethic whispered privately as all of the attendees' eyes focused on the two of them. He was so supportive and attentive. He was doing what she had needed Mizan to be there to do.

Ethic put her arm in his and held her hand as he walked her down the aisle. She finally reached her father's casket. A sob escaped her when she saw his face. She hardly recognized the man lying in front of her. Her father had always appeared so strong, so in control, so powerful. The man before her resembled the exact opposite. His ashen, wrinkled face was hardly recognizable.

"What did they do to you?" she asked aloud as she searched for any trace of familiarity in her father's face. She went into her Gucci clutch and removed the photo of herself. By leaving it with him she felt that he would always have a piece of her. She leaned over her father and kissed his face, while placing the photo inside of his suit jacket pocket. "I love you Daddy. I will always love you."

When Raven made it to the front pew she exhaled in relief. She was grateful for all the sympathy people were showing her family, but hearing the sadness in their voices only intensified her own grief. "Thank you," she said to Ethic. Without him, she would have never made it down the aisle.

Ethic didn't reply. He simply nodded and went to take his seat. The service was one big blur to Raven because she never took her eyes off her father's body. This was the last time she would ever see him in the flesh, and she wanted to absorb all of him while she still had a chance.

Justine sat reserved through the service, allowing her tears to flow freely, but never making a sound. Appearances had always been important to Benjamin, and she acted accordingly, as he had taught her many years ago.

She wanted her husband's legacy to live on and refused to put on a show. She carried herself like a true lady. Although she wanted to scream from the pain she was feeling, she remained reserved as she gripped her daughters' hands.

Morgan appeared to be the most heartbroken of them all. At six years old, she did not understand why her father had been taken away from her. Her usual grown persona reverted to the innocent child that she was. She was crushed, and she buried her head in Raven's shoulder as she cried through the entire eulogy. She felt cheated because Raven had gotten to know their father. She had gotten to impress him and make him proud. Morgan felt like she had received the short end of the stick because before her time to shine had come, Benjamin had been murdered.

Benjamin had left his three beautiful girls behind, and his death affected them all, changing the courses of their lives forever.

Mizan sat outside the church waiting patiently for Ethic to emerge. He was the last person on his list to hit and he had undoubtedly been the hardest to touch. Ethic had arrived at the church in one of the family's limos, not knowing that Mizan had attached an explosive device beneath the vehicle. He was just waiting for the right moment to detonate the bomb. The funeral would be the perfect place to make an example out of Ethic. After today, everyone in the city would know not to fuck with Mizan. He was going hard and he wanted any nigga who was thinking of coming at him to think twice before testing his hand. Three hours passed and finally mourners began to flow out of the church. As they came through the doors, Mizan sat up in his seat, scanning each head, trying to get a glimpse of Ethic. He held a small metal box tightly in his palm, and wiggled his index finger over the red button. He literally held Ethic's life in his hands.

He watched as Raven and her family came out of the church. His eyes followed her every move. The natural sway of her hips caused him to smirk, because he knew that she belonged to him. *I own that,* he thought arrogantly. He was proud to have her on his arm. There was nothing like a boss having a bad bitch by his side. He felt badly for putting his hands on her, but if she wanted to be his girl, she had to learn to respect him before all others, including her father. If she did not learn the easy way, he was going to teach her the hard way. Her father had placed her on a pedestal so high that she carried her superior attitude with pride. Mizan planned on knocking her so far down that her confidence level would be at an all-time low. Raven was hardheaded, but by the time he was done with her she would be the perfect wifey: beautiful, obedient, and dependent.

"Where is this nigga?" he mumbled to himself as he refocused his attention on the doors of the church. He slouched down in his seat to avoid being noticed by anyone. "He went in so he got to come out." Mizan's eyes narrowed when he finally noticed Ethic exit the building. He smirked in satisfaction knowing that he was about to gain the upper hand.

Ethic walked out of the building with an entourage of bodyguards following him. His presence was powerful and commanded respect, as he stepped with the confidence of Denzel toward his limo. Ethic knew that he was a moving target. Six of Benjamin's most trusted lieutenants had been murdered in the past week, and he was sure that he was next on the list. He did not know who was behind the takeover, but he fully intended on finding out. To the average eye, it seemed Ethic had come to town and been enlisted by Benjamin. The streets knew him as Benny Atkins' up-and-coming protégé, but they were sadly mistaken. Ethic was the birdman and the old woman who Benjamin had copped his work from was Ethic's great aunt Dot. His intention was to move like a ghost through the streets of Flint. A real boss didn't reveal his status and Ethic had no problem humbling himself in order to remain inconspicuous in such a ruthless environment.

Hailing from humble roots in Kansas City, he had a drug ring that stretched all over the Midwest. He had an operation in almost every state, and Benny Atkins had been one of his biggest buyers. Benjamin had intended on increasing the number of bricks he ordered on consignment, and before Ethic agreed to the deal he wanted to personally ensure that his bricks were in safe hands. He came to Flint and joined Benjamin's operation to remain low key. No one, except Benjamin and Aunt Dot, knew that he was the connect. Now he had more than a hundred bricks missing and his largest customer was dead. Ethic was not a fool. Yes, the police had killed Benjamin, but he was well aware that someone else had played a role in how everything had gone down. He did not know who, but he planned to find out.

He unfastened the buttons on his suit as he walked underneath the umbrella one of his goons held for him. He nodded at the limo driver and went to get into the car, but halted when he noticed Raven getting inside of the car with her family.

He stepped out and grabbed the umbrella from his goon. "I'm good, fam. Follow me in your whip," he instructed as he walked off toward Raven.

She looked up, and when she saw him approaching, she tried to hurry into the car.

"Raven!" he called.

She turned around nervously and looked at the ground while she shuffled her feet from side to side. She felt like she had to be accountable to Ethic, almost in the same way that she was accountable to her father, and the last thing she wanted him to do was notice her face. She did not want Ethic to know that Mizan had hit her.

"Come take a ride with me," he said. He was always so authoritative with her. He never gave her room to say no. "I need to rap with you about. . . ."

Knowing that she could not avoid the inevitable, she lifted her head and looked Ethic in the face. There was no hiding behind the dim church lights now. She was out in the daylight and every imperfection on her once exquisite face could be seen. He stopped speaking midsentence as he stared at her damaged face. He grabbed her chin and turned her head from side to side so that he could see all that had been done, yet he showed no emotion. No anger. No sympathy. No nothing. He was stoic and expressionless.

Ethic exhaled as he stared at Raven. He had seen so many young girls go down the path that she had chosen in the name of love, but he knew what love looked like, and what he was staring at was not it.

"He did this to you?" he asked, his voice even. On behalf of her father, Ethic had no problem stepping in and handling the situation with Mizan, but he was not going to waste his time. He knew the routine of chicks who got sucked into abusive relationships. They always went back, and Ethic did not have time to be in the middle of a lover's quarrel, because once he intervened there would be no turning back. Ethic did not play games. He would murder Mizan, and from the look in Raven's eyes, he knew that she did not want that.

Raven nodded her head, admitting that Mizan had
hurt her, as she willed away the tears in her eyes.

"Are you going to leave him?" he asked.

Just as he had suspected, she shook her head and replied, "He didn't mean to. Things just got out of hand. We
just need a little time apart . . . some space, you know?"

He averted his gaze from her in disappointment. Seeing as though Raven was bred from strong stock, he had
expected her to be smarter than the average chick, but
she was just the same. She would not realize that Mizan
was no good until it was too late, and if she did not want
to help herself by leaving him alone, there was nothing
that Ethic could do. He would not step in to her rescue
because she was right where she wanted to be; no one
was making her stay except herself. He put the umbrella
over her head and said, "Walk with me."

Mizan's nostrils flared when he saw Raven conversing
with Ethic. Everything in him wanted to get out of the car
and snatch her out of her Gucci pumps, but he remained
inside his vehicle, seething.

"Fuck the nigga touching her face for?" he asked aloud
as he felt a streak of jealousy pulse through him. He knew
that Raven was vulnerable right now because of the fight
they had gotten into before she had left home, and the
fact that Ethic was so close to his girl bothered Mizan. He
noticed the intimate way she looked at Ethic. Everything
about her interaction with him seemed intimate. *Bitch is
too fucking friendly with this nigga,* he thought bitterly.
Mizan sensed the respect and humility that Raven had
for Ethic, which only made him angrier. He knew that
she did not hold him in such high regard.

When they began to walk around the block, Mizan's
finger began to itch. He wanted to detonate the bomb so

badly that he was biting his inner cheek in anticipation. Ethic had disrespected him one too many times. *Dude is way too close to my bitch,* Mizan thought as a silent rage pulsed through him. He watched on, his heart beating a mile a minute. He was waiting for the perfect opportunity to push the button that would make Ethic extinct.

"I'm going back to Missouri," Ethic said.

"What?" Raven exclaimed. She stopped walking and turned toward him in shock.

"I thought you should know." He went into his jacket pocket and pulled out a white envelope. "There is twenty thousand and a number where you can reach me," he explained. "I know things may get tough for you now that your pops is gone, but if you ever need me, don't hesitate to call."

"Why are you leaving?" She tucked the envelope inside her purse.

"Because it's time for me to go." I have business back home that I need to tend to."

"What about your business here?"

"Your father was my only business in Flint. I don't have anything keeping me here and there is too much going down right now. It wasn't a coincidence that the cops were waiting at your father's house when he got home. Benny had hundred and twenty bricks of cocaine sitting in his safe. The cops only found one. That tells me that this entire thing was a setup, and whoever has those bricks are plotting a takeover. Every nigga who was affiliated with your father is a target. They're being knocked off one by one. I'm not the type to get caught up in the crossfire."

"And what about the people you are leaving behind? Are we supposed to just get caught up in the crossfire?

My father was grooming you. He chose you to take his spot," Raven objected heatedly. She had already lost enough, and although Ethic was fairly new in her life, she refused to watch him walk out of it. His temperament and swagger were mirror images of her father's. "You can't leave."

Ethic chuckled as he massaged the bridge of his nose. The more he got to know Raven, the less he thought of her. Everything in her world was so black and white. Good or bad. There was no in-between with her. She thought she was so knowledgeable about the hood, but in actuality she didn't know anything. She was green to the game, and chicks like her would lead to a hustler's downfall; she was their worst nightmare. A wifey with beauty but no brains. "This ain't a movie, Raven. This shit here is real life and you don't know anything about the streets. I haven't been groomed by a nigga in a long time. Little boys are groomed and I'm a grown man. I didn't work for your father. I worked *with* him and there is a difference. I don't owe your pops anything more than what I've already given."

"What about me?" Raven asked.

"You have a nigga that should be taking care of you. That's his job and if he ain't doing that, then you have my number," Ethic reassured her.

Raven nodded and began to choke up. "It just seems like my entire world is changing," she said glumly. She thought about the baby growing inside of her, and of Nikki lying up in a hospital, then of her father's death. Everything had gotten so complicated in her life. She had experienced more pain in the past few months then she ever had in her time on this earth.

"You made it change, ma," Ethic replied. "When you're ready to change it back, you know how to find me," he said as he turned to leave.

She watched him walk away. Everything from his posture to his stride spelled power and honor. He was so
much like her father that it was scary. As she felt the ache
from the bruises on her face she knew that she deserved
more. She wanted a man like Ethic . . . like her father. A
man who would never hurt her. "Ethic!" she called out
just before he reached his limo.

He turned toward her to see what she wanted.

"What do I have to do?" she asked.

"What?"

"To be with you . . . What do I have to do?" she asked
with tears in her eyes. "Just tell me what I have to do and
I'll do it."

Ethic sighed because he was fully aware of Raven's
attraction to him. Her heart was young and so was her
mind, which was why Mizan was able to manipulate
her so easily. Ethic knew she wanted something she
wasn't ready to handle. He stretched out his hand and
she grabbed it, allowing him to pull her near. He put his
hands on the sides of her face and stared her in the eyes.

The intensity between their gazes made Raven's heart
melt. "I'll do anything for you, Ethic. Just tell me who I
have to be to get you to like me." Her voice was almost
pleading, childlike as her tears graced his hands. She
was pouring her premature heart out to him. Every other
time she had attempted to come at him she was on that
fly-girl, slick-mouth, princess of the streets–type stuff,
but this time was completely different. She was open. She
was letting him see how sincere her attraction for him really was. It didn't take a teenage girl much to know when
she was in love, and ever since the first time she saw Ethic she had been smitten. Ethic was the man she wanted,
but Mizan was the man she could actually have. Mizan
was simply her heart's substitute.

Ethic shook his head at the dilemma that faced him. "That right there is why I can't fuck with you, Raven. You don't even know who you are yet. You're seventeen, ma. Don't be so eager to do grown-up things," he replied. "You're moving too fast." He stepped to the side and motioned for her to get inside of the awaiting car. "I'll take you home."

Mizan hit the steering wheel in pure rage as he watched Raven get into the limo with Ethic. He was steaming. He could feel his body temperature rise as he watched the black Lincoln pull away. "Stupid bitch," he mumbled. He knew that he could not finish the job with Raven in harm's way. He contemplated pressing the button anyway. He reasoned with himself that Raven could be replaced, but he knew that she could not. She had managed to secure a small piece of his loyalty and it was enough to stop him from sending the car up in smoke. He pulled out his phone and dialed her number immediately. Envy filled his heart. Raven belonged to him and Ethic was too close for comfort. He followed the luxury car as it pulled away from the church. He was not willing to let Ethic slip through the cracks. Ethic was a problem and Mizan had every intention of getting rid of him . . . one way or another.

Raven sent Mizan to voice mail as she rode in the back of the limo with Ethic. She leaned against him comfortably as he held her tightly, but she knew that there was nothing romantic about his embrace. Ethic did what he did for her out of duty; as a tribute to her father. But still she cherished every second and stored every single detail of him in her memory, even down to the scent of his Issey

Miyake cologne. He stroked her hair and they rode in silence until they pulled up to her house. She closed her eyes and sat still, wishing that she did not have to get out of the car, but when she felt Ethic move to exit she knew that the moment had passed. Reality was a cold, hard smack in the face.

She followed him out of the car and stood in front of him. Her vision was cloudy and she shook her head and waved her hands in front of her face. "Aghh, I can't stop," she yelled softly in embarrassment, referring to her tears.

"I didn't ask you to," Ethic replied. He pulled her close and wrapped his arms around her waist. "You take care of yourself, Raven."

Raven gave him a weak smile and nodded. "You too," she replied. She watched him walk back to the limo, and as he pulled away she stood in the middle of her street. She wished that her life was a fairy tale and that the man she loved would turn around to sweep her off her feet, but she wasn't that type of princess. The daughter of a street king never got her prince.

Just as the limo reached the corner, Raven turned to see her mother and sister coming out of the house. Justine held her arms out for her oldest daughter. She recognized the signs of heartbreak on her face, but before Raven could take a step in her mother's direction, a loud explosion rang in her ears. The deafening sound seemed to shake the entire block.

She turned to the direction it had come from and her heart fell out of her chest. "No!" she screamed as she ran toward the burning limousine at the end of the street. She ran full speed toward the blaze as she watched the fire consume the car. She could hear her mother and sister screaming her name in the background, but she ignored them as her feet moved forward, carrying her as fast as they could toward the wreckage.

The front of the car was in pieces all over the road and the back was burning quickly. She knew that at any moment the fire would reach the gas tank. She reached for the door, causing the skin on her hand to burn excruciatingly.

"Aghhhh!" she screamed in pain. She removed her jacket and used it to block her hand from the simmering metal door handle. She could still feel the heat and it took everything in her not to let it go. Finally she snatched the door open and saw Ethic lying on the limo floor, unconscious. "Ethic!" she yelled. She could barely see through all the smoke. She felt hands pulling at her, trying to get her away from the car.

"No! Please help him!" she yelled as she turned to see a firefighter dragging her to safety. "I have to get to him!"

Paramedics and fire trucks surrounded the scene and immediately went to work putting out the blaze. They pulled Ethic's body from the car as Raven was rushed into an ambulance and whisked off to the hospital.

Chapter Eleven

Raven closed her worried eyes as she lay back in the hospital bed. Ethic had been rushed into surgery as soon as he entered the hospital and she had not heard anything since. Second degree burns covered her hand, causing her great pain, but it was nothing compared to what she knew Ethic was going through.

"Have you heard anything yet, Mommy?" Raven asked.

Justine held a sleeping Morgan in her arms as she regretfully shook her head at Raven's question. "Ethic will be okay, Raven. Your father went twenty years in the game without ever getting involved in a war. Violence has never been this close to us. Now that he's gone, it is knocking at the front door," Justine stated in disbelief.

A knock at the door interrupted their conversation, and a young black woman came in. Her white lab coat, tired eyes, and hanging stethoscope let Raven know that she was a doctor. The girl could not have been a day older than twenty-five. Most black girls her age were wifed up or seeking a baller to get out of the hood, but the young lady before her was degreed up and making a way for herself. Raven knew that the doctor before her was the ideal daughter to someone. She was the perfect example of who Benjamin and Justine had hoped Raven would someday become. Raven lowered her eyes self-consciously, feeling as if she had let her parents down. In her city there were no doctors or lawyers to look up to. The role models of Flint's youth were dope boys and the women who loved them. According to that scale she was successful. She had been snagged by Mizan, and although he had not been a part of her father's prestigious street organization, he was still knee-deep in the game, which gave her bragging rights all her own. It was a dire mentality, but it was life.

Raven rolled her eyes at the doctor, letting the young woman know where she stood before any words were ever exchanged.

"Hello, Raven, I'm Dr. Daniels and I'm an OBGYN. Your blood work indicates that you are pregnant. Were you aware of this?" she asked.

"Yeah, I know," Raven replied shortly.

"Well, I would like to do an ultrasound and get you started on prenatal vitamins. It's important that we nourish the baby early," the doctor answered.

Raven agreed, and as she allowed the doctor to place her feet in the stirrups her legs began to shake. She gripped the metal siding on the bed and held on to it for dear life. Her body tensed as the doctor inserted two gloved fingers into her vagina. "What are you doing?" Raven asked.

"I'm examining your cervix to make sure it is healthy. Just relax," she coached.

Raven took a deep breath and closed her eyes to calm herself. She felt a cold gel on her stomach.

"Open your eyes and look at your baby," Dr. Daniels instructed.

A steady rhythm resembling the sound of running water filled the room, and Raven turned her head to look at the monitor. She had no idea what she was looking at. The screen was filled with a black background and white shadows all over it, but the one thing she was sure of was the pulsing dot in the middle. The steady throb that could be heard throughout the room was her baby's heartbeat. She smiled in disbelief at the miracle that was happening inside of her, and for the first time since her father passed, she felt happiness. "Is it a boy or girl?" she asked with stars in her eyes. Justine lay Morgan down in the chair, then stood to be by Raven's side.

The doctor removed the gel from her stomach, print-ed an ultrasound photo for Raven to take, and stood up. "It's too early to tell, but we will know soon. Now, Raven, your blood work also detected traces of cocaine in your system."

"Cocaine? Raven!" Justine uttered as she looked at her daughter with a broken heart.

"It's not like that, ma. I don't use it all the time. I just tried it once," Raven lied, but Justine knew her daughter all too well.

"Your drug use is detrimental to your health and the baby's health," Dr. Daniels stated. "If you care about this child, it is imperative that you discontinue all use of any type of narcotic."

Raven smacked her lips. "Didn't I just say I don't use drugs? It was a mistake. One time . . . that's it!" she said, feeling as if she was being judged by the successful young black woman.

The doctor nodded unsurely and changed the subject. "I'm going to write you a prescription for the vitamins and give you a moment alone. Congratulations," she said with a friendly smile. She then turned to Justine. "There are two gentlemen here for you. They would like to speak with you."

Raven sat up and began to dress. She looked curiously in her mother's direction as she exited the room. Hop-ping up from the hospital bed, she inched over to the door and peeked outside the glass pane.

It did not take much to see that the gentlemen talking to her mother were cops. She cracked the door so that she could hear what was going on.

"Justine Atkins, we would like to ask you a few questions about the business dealings of your husband, Benjamin Atkins," the taller man said.

"I just buried my husband today and my daughter was involved in an accident. I'm not up for answering anybody's questions," Justine replied.

"Mrs. Atkins, I'm going to be straight with you," the man said as he leaned into Justine. "Your husband was being investigated by the Federal Bureau of Investigation. I have a warrant for your arrest."

"My arrest!" Justine exclaimed.

"For aiding and abetting a criminal enterprise, drug trafficking, and tax evasion. Now, we know that you were just spending your husband's money, but we have to get somebody. It's not going to be him for obvious reasons and it doesn't have to be you. All you have to do is cooperate and tell us who was supplying your husband," the agent said.

Justine did not reply, and both federal agents could see the defiance on her face. Just like every inner-city youth, she had been bred with a "fuck the police" attitude. They were determined to get her to crack. The men had their backs to Raven, but her mother faced her. When their eyes met, Raven saw an emotion in her mother that she had never seen before: fear. No words needed to be spoken between them for Raven to get the message her mother was trying to send. They were in trouble. When her father died, their entire lives had been thrown out of balance.

When the cops inspected the house, they had found a secret room that Benjamin had built beneath his basement floor. It was not in the original floor plan of the home, so Benjamin never expected anyone other than himself and his family to ever be able to locate the room. After tearing the house up from top to bottom, they finally located it and hit the jackpot. Inside it, they found re-cords of every drug transaction Benjamin had ever made, including the minor role that his wife had played in his operation by counting up his profits for him over the years. Benjamin was detailed down to the very last gram of cocaine in his possession. They also recovered income tax returns that had been doctored by a C.P.A. stating that Benjamin was making a modest income of $50,000 annually. It was obvious that the lifestyle the kingpin was living could not be maintained on that amount, so they hit him with underreported income to the Internal Revenue Service. The room was so incriminating that if the notorious Benny Atkins had ever gone to trial he would have surely lost. He was meticulous in keeping track of how much money he was making and had thought he had kept the information hidden well, but when the feds are on a hunt they are relentless until they find what they are looking for. The only thing he left out was the name of his connect, and the feds wanted that name, even if it meant bulldozing Justine to get it.

Justine nodded her head and said, "I will tell you gen-tlemen everything you want to know. Please give me a minute to check on my daughters. Then we can go have coffee in the cafeteria so that I can answer your ques-tions."

The men stepped to the side so that Justine could reen-ter the hospital room.

"Mommy, what's going on?" Raven whispered fran-tically. Justine backed her daughter into the room and held on to her forearms desperately.

"Listen to me, Raven. I need you right now, sweet-ie. When you see me and those men get on the eleva-tor you take your little sister and get out of here. Take the stairs and get as far away from this hospital as you can. They're going to arrest me and when that happens they will try to throw you and Morgan into the system. I grew up fending for myself, Raven. I grew up in the gutter around people who didn't care about me. All I had was myself and I don't want that for my daughters. I want you two to always be there for one another. To always have one another 'cuz at the end of the day family is all that matters. You two can't be separated. That cannot happen, Raven. You hear me? You take Morgan and get out of here. Take care of her, baby. You both are my angels. Your father and I never meant for things to end like this, but it's up to you now, Raven. You have to make sure that the two of you stay together," she said seriously as a ball of emotion stuck in her throat.

"Mommy, no . . . You can't go to jail," Raven replied. "Just tell them what they want to know!"

"I can't, Rae. The game does not work like that. There's more to being a hustler's wife than spending the money. The queen falls right next to the king. It's my time to fall, but I need you to take care of your sister. You will be eighteen soon and then they won't be able to touch you. Until then, hide, do everything you can to stop them from placing you both in the system. I'm going to let them think that I'm cooperating, but as soon as they find out I'm not, they will come looking for you." Justine stated.

Raven tried to absorb everything her mother was saying, but it was all too much. Her head spun as she was besieged with her mother's instructions. Justine rushed over to her youngest daughter and shook her out of her sleep. "Morgan, wake up, baby. Mommy's got to go away for a while, but Raven's going to take care of you. I need you to listen to your sister at all times, okay? Respect her and love her. The two of you are all you have," she signed. With every word she expressed, her heart tore in half. The shine of fresh sentiment glistened in her eyes as she thought of all of the things that had led up to this moment. All of the foreign cars, big faces, designer clothes, and exotic trips were not worth the heartache she felt. Being the dope man's wife was not worth the consequence of being separated from her most prized possessions: Raven and Morgan.

Morgan wiped her sleepy eyes and yawned, oblivious to what was about to go down. "Okay, Mommy, I will," she signed. Justine hugged her daughters tightly, and Raven's chest swelled with unrelenting burden. It felt like they were saying good-bye, as if they would never see each other again.

"I love you both," Justine said. A kiss on the cheek was her final good-bye to her children before she walked out of the room.

Raven grabbed Morgan's hand and led her to the door. When she saw her mother step into the elevator with the agents, she eased out of the room. She jogged to the door that led to the stair well.

"Come on, Morgan, we have to get out of here," she signed urgently as they descended the steps. The burn on her hand began to throb, but she didn't have time to pay attention to the pain.

"Wait, Rae, what is going on?" she replied, moving her hands swiftly as she refused to move. Little Morgan wanted an explanation and Raven knew that she would have to tell her something so that thay could both get out of there.

"Mommy is in trouble . . . we have to get out of here. If we don't they are going to try to take us, too," she informed her. "Now let's go!" Raven grabbed her sister's hand and took off down the stairs. Morgan chased after her sister, following her down the twelve flights of stairs. Morgan's tiny feet couldn't keep up with Raven. "Come here, stank," Raven said as she picked her sister up and carried her down the rest of the stairs. Finally she reached the bottom floor and walked out of the hospital with her sister crying on her shoulders. She froze in shock and her heart broke when she saw her mother being escorted out of the hospital in handcuffs. Justine's head hung low on her chest and she was hunched over, her long hair hanging in her face.

"Raven, there's Mommy!" Morgan signed frantically and began to take off in Justine's direction, but Raven quickly grabbed her sister and picked her up, dragging her the other way. It took everything in her to keep moving. They walked six blocks before she stopped to call a cab.

"Where are we going?" Morgan signed in frustration, then folded her arms across her chest.

Raven sighed, knowing that Morgan wanted answers. She could only imagine how confused and lost her little sister felt. She had to remind herself to be patient. "We're going home. I need to get some stuff from the house," Raven signed. "Don't worry, Morgan. I'm gon' take care of everything."

The cab carried them to the suburbs. When they pulled into their neighborhood, they saw police cars everywhere.

"Don't stop, drive by that house slowly," Raven instructed as she slumped down in her seat and observed the government agents going in and out of the house. Everything was being seized from televisions to vehicles; nothing was accessible anymore. Raven watched in dismay as they hoisted her Lexus up onto a flatbed tow truck. All the things that her father had worked hard to provide were now being stripped away. She had the twenty thousand that Ethic had given her, but she was a minor. She would not be able to do anything on her own until she turned eighteen, and four weeks was a long time to be out on the street. She thought of calling Mizan and going back to his place, but she was still angry with him for hitting her. With his temper she never knew when he would fly off the handle, and she did not want to put her sister in the middle of their drama.

Ethic has to take us with him. We don't have any-where else to go, she thought. She told the cabbie to take her back to the hospital. Morgan was antisocial the entire way as she clung to Raven. "Everything is going to be okay, Morgan. I'ma take care of you," Raven assured her. The confidence behind her words waned and she hoped that she could live up to what she had just promised.

They finally arrived back at Hurley Medical Center and Raven gave the cabbie a hundred dollar bill. "I need you to wait right here. Keep the meter running. I'm going to leave my sister in the car with you. There is more where that came from if you keep an eye on her," Raven stated. She showed the black man the money inside the envelope as proof.

"I'll be right here, sista, do your thing," he said.

"I'll be right back, Morgan. I have to go find Ethic," Raven signed.

"No, Raven, I want to come with you," Morgan objected.

"I'll be back, stank, I swear on everything. Nobody is going to take me away from you, okay?" she said sincere-ly, not bothering to sign the words because she knew her sister could read her lips. Morgan nodded her head, but she choked on her own sadness as Raven peeled her sis-ter's small hands from around her waist. No matter how hard Morgan cried she could not take her back into the hospital. She was sure that the feds knew that they were missing and Child Services would no doubt be looking to take them in as wards of the State.

"Stay here, I'ma always come back for you," Raven said.

She closed the cab door and looked around nervously before making her way quickly inside the hospital. She ran to the trauma unit, and by the time she made it to the nurses' station she was out of breath.

"Can I help you with something?" the nurse behind the desk asked.

"I'm here to see Ethic . . . um . . ." Raven couldn't even finish her sentence. She realized she had no clue who Ethic really was. She couldn't even tell the lady his legal name. "My friend was caught in a car explosion. He was rushed here. I need to see him," Raven described quickly, trying to get to Ethic as fast as she could.

"Slow down, child. I didn't get anything you just said. Are you a family member?" the nurse asked.

A heavy whisper escaped her lips as she thought of her circumstances and grew impatient. "I am. It seems like he's the only family I have left."

The nurse noticed the sadness in Raven's voice and pointed down the hall. "Room 812."

"Thank you," Raven said appreciatively as she headed off in search of Ethic. Right now he was the only answer to her problems.

She stepped into the room and everything was cleared out. She paused in confusion as she looked at the crisp, white sheets and the empty bed. She rushed back to the nurse.

"There must be a mistake. Did he switch rooms? There is no one in there," Raven said.

"No, that's the room he was admitted to after his surgery," the nurse said with conviction as she arose from her desk. She walked with Raven back down the hall as if by her going, Ethic would suddenly appear. Discovering the same thing as Raven, a look of utter confusion spread across her face.

"I don't understand. He is supposed to be here. There have been no changes and he has not checked out. In his condition he could not have checked out. The doctors would have never allowed it," the stubby woman said. "I'm going to find out what is going on here."

Raven took that as her cue to leave. She didn't know what to think. *Did the feds come and arrest him to? People don't just disappear. Where is he?* she wondered as tears came to her eyes. The people around her were dropping like flies. Her back was against the wall and she only had one place to turn. Making her way back to the cab, she pulled out her cell phone. She went back and forth with her decision in her mind. The only person she could call on was the one who she was afraid may hurt her the most. He had her young heart in the palm of his hand. She only hoped he wouldn't break it.

She got back into the cab and told the driver to pull off before she slowly dialed Mizan's number. She wanted to teach Mizan a lesson and stay away from him for a while, but circumstances were pushing her to swallow her pride and go back home to her man.

Mizan sent Raven's call to voice mail, then smirked to himself when he saw her call him right back. As a master manipulator, he was going to turn the tables and make her feel wrong, as if she had started the fight. He didn't need Raven, but he wanted her. Having her by his side was an ego boost. She had no clue that she was sleeping with the enemy, and by the time she found out it would be too late to leave. On her third phone call he finally picked up the line.

"Yo', I got your shit packed. You need to come scoop them so we can go our separate ways," he said in a low, serious tone.

"Mizan don't do this . . . I need you now more than ever," she replied. He could hear the desperation in her voice. Her plea was more needy than an addict begging his pusher. Mizan was her drug and Raven needed him to survive. Right now he held all the cards in his hand.

"Nah, I don't think so, ma." Mizan's voice was dripping with sadness. "You're making me crazy, Rae. I can't do this with you. You make me do things that ain't me. I've never put my hands on a woman, but you just have no respect for your man, ma. You pushed me to the limit and you know how to press my buttons. You put everybody above me. I'm supposed to be your king. I love you and you shit on me," he said. He knew he was making her feel bad, evoking guilt and instilling unwavering loyalty in her at the same time. He sniffled to make the conversation more real.

With every word Mizan spoke, Raven's resolve softened. She began to replay in her head what had happened between them. She had been so sure that he was wrong, but now she was beginning to think that she had provoked the situation. "I do respect you, Mizan. You know I do. I'm just going through a lot right now and I spoke out of the side of my neck. I should have never asked you to come to the funeral. I apologize . . . just please don't leave me."

"Where are you?" Mizan asked, smiling to himself because he had her directly where he wanted her.

"I just pulled up outside." She grabbed Morgan's hand and exited the cab. After paying the man, she walked slowly up the driveway. Mizan came outside and stood on the porch. He watched her approach him unsurely until they were standing face to face, with Morgan standing by Raven's side.

"Your stuff is in the house," Mizan stated, avoiding her stare as he adjusted his fitted Detroit hat and folded his arms across his chest.

Raven's eyes spilled over. "Please," she whispered. "What about all the things you promised me? You said you would be here." She was so young and foolish as she begged Mizan to be with her. Her entire world centered around him.

"You said a lot of things, Raven. If you're not real, how you expect me to be?" Mizan asked, laying it on thick. "Then I hear about you riding around town, making me look like a fool. My man went to your people funeral and said you left with a nigga. What type of shit is that, Rae? I'm out here telling these mu'fuckas you my lady, and they see you hopping in cars with other dudes and shit . . . said you was extra friendly with the mu'fucka. You got niggas clowning me out here."

"That was nothing. It wasn't what you think!" Raven defended.

"You don't know how to act. I need a chick that can follow rules and hold me down."

"What about the baby, Mizan? I'm pregnant. My father is dead, my mother was arrested today. We have nowhere to go." Raven stepped closer to Mizan so that Morgan wouldn't be able to read her lips. She did not want her baby sister to know that they were homeless and desperate for a place to stay.

"I'll hit you off with some paper to take care of that little situation. You're not that far along. You can still get rid of it," Mizan stated. "The rest of it ain't my problem." His words were cold and carefully calculated. They broke Raven down to the ground and stung her naïve heart. She clutched her stomach as if he had punched her in it, and then held on to the porch railing for support.

Seeing her sister cry was tearing Morgan up, and tears began to slide down her young cheeks as she grasped Raven's hand tightly.

Mizan smirked. He had broken her. He had shattered her heart to the point that not even God himself could put the pieces back together. He had torn her down; now it was time to build her back up. It was his way of letting her know who was boss. She needed to understand that her happiness depended on him. She felt what he made her feel. Fuck everybody else. He needed to be the only one who mattered. Her world now revolved around him. He reached for her and she fell into his chest, sobbing hysterically.

"Why you doing this to me, Rae? You did this, ma," Mizan said soothingly. "You got your baby sister out here crying."

"I love you," she bawled.

"You love me?" he asked rhetorically. He rubbed her back gently. "I love you too, Rae. You got to act right, though, ma. You can't push me to the edge. You got to cater to your man, Rae. I'm your king, right?"

She lifted her eyes and nodded in agreement.

"You belong to me?" he asked.

"You know I do," Raven said. "You just hurt me, Mizan. You told me you would never do that and then you hit me. I know I made you do it, but I'm sorry."

Mizan's smoky eyes burned deeply into Raven's, then he put his hand on the small of her back and led her inside. *Mission accomplished*, he thought. "Unpack your stuff. Your sister can sleep in the second room," he said.

Just like that, Mizan had lured her right back. It wasn't the first time he had manipulated her young mind, and it definitely wouldn't be the last. Her father had birthed a diva and gave her all of the makings to become a hustler's wife. Unfortunately, she had fallen for the wrong type and he had no intentions of putting her on the throne next to his. Mizan was going to keep her beneath his feet. Her life as she knew it was about to change for the worse and would never be the same again.

Phase 2

Five Years Later

Chapter Twelve

"I can't do this," Raven whispered as she stared down at the body in front of her. Her hand shook nervously as she pointed the .45-caliber pistol toward the bed. "I can't," she reiterated as she put her hand over her mouth to stop herself from throwing up.

"Bitch, you can . . . you have to," Nikki urged. "It's the only way. You know what he will do to you if you don't take care of it now. It's never going to stop."

Raven closed her eyes and thought about all the bullshit that Mizan had taken her through. The black eyes, bloody lips, the unbelievable heartache. Her emotions were torn because at one time she had really loved him. He had rescued her and protected her from everything that had ever hurt her in this world, but one day that protection transformed into control. His love had turned to hate, and her love had turned into regret. Just pull the trigger, *she thought.* It'll all be over soon.

Raven's arm shook so badly that she couldn't get her aim right. Nikki stepped behind her and placed her hand over Raven's. "Just pull the trigger," she whispered.

Raven closed her eyes. Her finger wrapped tightly around the trigger and before she could talk herself out of it . . .

Bang! Bang! Bang! Bang!

The kickback of the gun caused Raven to drop it in fear, and her wide eyes filled with terror as she thought about what she had just done.

"There ain't no turning back now," Nikki whispered. "Let's just finish this and get out of here."

Raven retrieved the gun and picked up the cans of gasoline. Nervous energy filled her body and sweat poured down her face as she hurriedly doused the entire room. She poured gasoline on the sheets, on the body, all over the floor and walls.

"Go and get the other rooms. We have to make sure this house burns to the ground," Raven said, her voice distant, but her tone authoritative.

Nikki rushed out of the room and the pair made sure every surface of the house was covered in the flammable liquid.

They met at the door; Raven's bags were already packed. It was obvious that this murder had been a long time coming. It was planned carefully. Premeditated. Callous.

"You ready?" Raven asked.

Nikki nodded as she pulled a book of matches out of her back pocket. She struck one, igniting a tiny stick of flame.

Raven watched eagerly, anticipation filling her chest as Nikki tossed the match. The fire spread quickly, blazing a trail in every direction, while Raven stood in the doorway, hypnotized by the flame.

"This could've been me," she whispered. "All the shit I've let him do to me . . . that could have been me in there."

Nikki tugged at Raven's arm. "But it's not you, Raven. You made your move first. You're going to win. He has consumed your life ever since you were seventeen. It's payback time and karma's a bitch. Mizan deserves everything he's getting," Nikki urged.

Raven nodded reluctantly as she backed off the porch.

"Let's go!" Nikki yelled as they hopped into the car.

Raven slowly pulled away from the house. It was 3:00 A.M. so no neighbors were awake to see them make their exit; all they had to do was drive away. Raven looked into her rearview mirror as the flames engulfed the house and danced playfully against the pitch black sky.

"We did it!" Nikki screamed in excitement.

"We did it," Raven repeated as she focused her eyes on the road.

Raven sat up in her bed, her body covered in sweat as her eyes danced frantically around the room. Putting a sweaty palm to her breasts, she tried to gain composure of herself and calm her racing heart. The silhouette of Mizan's body lay next to her. He was very much alive and sleeping soundly as murderous thoughts commanded her mind. If he could read her thoughts he wouldn't be so placid. This same dream plagued her around the same time every year. It was the anniversary of the day she had given birth to a stillborn child. It was on that day that a great sadness took over her life. The constant beatings that Mizan had bestowed upon her had undoubtedly killed the baby that had grown inside of her stomach. "Trauma to the womb" was what the doctors had said. Ever since, her hatred for Mizan had only grown, but it was too late to leave. He had convinced her to pledge her allegiance to him when she was just a little girl. At seventeen, she had no clue what she was getting herself into, and now she was too involved to be set free.

Oddly, she still loved Mizan. He was all she knew, and on the days they were good, they were so good. He was the perfect man if she caught him on the perfect day and in the perfect mood. The only problem was that relationships are imperfect and no matter how hard Raven tried, she just was not able to please him all the time.

Financially he took care of her and provided the best for Morgan, but emotionally and mentally he was a tyrant. By giving him control over her early on, she had set the precedent and had given him permission to reign over her life. She was torn down the middle because a part of her hated him to the core, but the other half loved him without remorse. It was that part mixed with fear that forced her to stay. Those things acted as invisible chains and kept her enslaved to Mizan's manipulation. He had gotten so deep into her head that now only his thoughts remained. Her free will was nonexistent, and the only place where she had control of her life was in her dreams.

From the outside looking in having taken over her life was lovely. Mizan ran the city, over the late Benny Atkins' lucrative drug operation. He was filthy rich with plenty of money. He could have retired from the game by now, but the power was what kept Mizan going. He thrived on it, and he covered his abusive behavior toward Raven with shopping sprees and a lavish lifestyle. Many women had tried to take her spot. They wanted the four thousand-square-foot roof Mizan kept over Raven's head, but what they did not know was that it was simply a fancy version of a prison. Raven had learned the hard way that everything that glittered was not gold. She couldn't run if she tried. He kept her broke. She had no access to any real money. The money that she had gotten from Ethic all those years ago had quickly been spent on frivolous things, leaving her completely dependent on Mizan. Whatever she wanted he took her to purchase, and if he was too busy to accompany her on her many shopping trips, he sent one of his workers to make the transaction on his behalf. The only money she was allowed to handle was from the monthly pickups from his stash houses. But his dough was well accounted for and she did not dare lift a dollar of his monthly profit. She was trapped. Mentally he had her. Financially he owned her. Emotionally he commanded her. The mysterious allure of Mizan had faded away, and now the reality of her situation was almost too much for her to handle. At twenty-two, Raven was nothing like the vibrant and daring teenage girl she had been when they had first met. Now she was reserved, timid, and obedient. The thirst she had for the streets when she was younger was gone. She had seen all that it required to be wifey and now she resented the position. *How could I have been so stupid to ask for this life?* she asked herself.

Raven pulled back the covers and slowly eased out of the bed. Her feet sank into the plush carpet as she made her way out of the room. She peeked in on Morgan and found her resting soundly. Raven walked in silently, not wanting to interrupt her sister's peaceful slumber. She was envious because peace was so unfamiliar. She hadn't felt that in quite some time. As she observed the slight smile on Morgan's eleven-year-old face, she imagined the sweet dreams that came along with a naïve view of the world. *How nice it must be,* she thought. Raven's nights were restless and paranoid because she did not fully trust the man she lay next to. Raven pulled the covers up around Morgan's shoulders, then tightened her robe as she sat down in the corner rocking chair.

She could pinpoint the moment her life began to go into a downward spiral. Her hard head and grown attitude had led her to Mizan. If she had listened to her father all those years ago, her life would be so much different . . . so much better. She sat in that same spot all night, thinking of how she had chased the fast life, causing her to grow up way too quickly. She rocked back and forth, pondering her life until daylight crept through the venetian blinds.

The ringing phone caused Raven to jump out of her sleep. She rushed to the kitchen to answer it before it disturbed Mizan.

"Hello?" she answered quietly, keeping her eyes trained on her closed bedroom door.

"You have an automated call from, Justine," her mother's voice came through the phone announcing herself and then the digital voice continued. "This is a call from a prisoner at Huron Valley Correctional Facility. If you would like to accept this call, press pound. If this is a harassing call and you would like to block further correspondence from this prisoner . . . ."

Raven desperately wanted to accept the charges and hear her mother's voice. It had been too long since they had last spoken, but she knew that Mizan would have a fit if he saw the call on their monthly phone bill. He had forced her to cut all ties with her past life. At first she refused to let her mother go, but Mizan had forced her to. As long as she kept communicating with Justine, Mizan made her mother's time in prison hell. He refused to stock her commissary until finally Raven broke down and accepted his terms. As long as she didn't talk to her mother, he would keep the commissary full and reach out to his connections inside to make sure she was protected.

Raven hung up the phone. Justine had been trying to reach out to her more than usual, and Raven told herself that this was the last time she intended on ignoring her. She was determined to see her mother. "I have to see her," she whispered.

"See who?"

Raven jumped out of her skin at the sound of Mizan's voice behind her. "Oh . . . um . . . Nikki. I have to go see her and make sure she is doing okay," Raven lied quickly. Nikki was one of the few people Mizan allowed her to see.

"You wake baby girl up for school yet?" Mizan asked.

Raven cringed. "Please don't call her that. That is what my father used to call me." Her eyes shifted to the floor as memories of her dad flashed in her mind. She lifted her head, a fresh pool of tears threatening to fall.

Mizan scoffed, disregarding her request with a hard stare. "Baby girl!" he yelled while still looking at Raven. "Wake up, baby girl." He was mocking her.

Raven gripped the kitchen sink so tightly that her pale skin turned red. Sometimes he purposely tried to hurt her. She could deal with the physical punches. Those were only dished out in the heat of the moment. It was the emotional jabs he took at her daily that were unbearable. She could never understand his cruelty. She told herself that it had to stem from somewhere, but he never opened up enough with her to divulge the information.

She listened as Mizan woke up Morgan. Her baby sister adored Mizan and Raven fully understood why. With her, he was so charming, almost the same way he used to be with Raven when they had first met. Time had changed everything between them. Mizan became arrogant and more possessive with each passing day. It was his world and she was simply living in it.

He seems to forget that he didn't have shit when I first met him. If it weren't for me he would still be sticking niggas up. He came up off of my father, she thought snidely as she went to get herself dressed.

She had sacrificed her dignity all in the name of love, and as she looked in the mirror she could see the sadness in her face. Chicks envied her. They wanted to have the olive-colored Chanel pencil skirt and white ruffled blouse. They craved the Gucci stilettos on her feet and the Lexus tag on her key chain. They wanted it all and she would gladly give it up to regain her freedom or restore a piece of her old self. She grabbed her bag out of the closet, and as she was putting in her diamond stud earrings, Mizan came waltzing into the room.

"Going somewhere?" he asked.

"I told you I have to go see Nikki. After I drop Mo off at school, I'm going to do lunch with Nik," Raven explained. She broke her day down to him play by play, purposely leaving out the trip she planned to make to Ypsilanti to see her mother. It was only an hour drive. *He'll never know,* she thought as she looked into the mirror and added more makeup to cover an old bruise that had turned green.

"What about yo' man?" he asked. "Where do I fit in your plans today?"

Raven turned to face him. "I did not know you wanted to be with me. I barely see you some days. I thought you might be busy. Can we meet back up later tonight?"

Mizan's silence spoke volumes. He put her last on his priority list every day, but having her put him on the back burner aroused his suspicions.

"You getting real dressed up just to go see Nikki," Mizan said as he rubbed the bridge of his nose.

"I dress like this every day. You're just never home long enough to notice," she replied. "Everything in my closet is name-brand. Besides, I like this outfit."

Mizan stalked over to her and pinned her against the dresser, causing her things to spill to the floor. "I didn't ask you what you liked," Mizan seethed through clenched teeth. He gripped the sides of her face, causing her lips to form a pout. "Take this off and put on something old. If you're going to see Nikki it don't matter what the fuck you wearing."

"Okay . . . okay, babe," she whispered submissively as he used all of his weight to manhandle her, mushing her face against the mirror. This wasn't a big enough issue for her to fight, so she conceded in an attempt to calm him down and keep the peace. A small situation like that could easily blow up into a huge fight with him, and most times he won, leaving her with a new scar or bruise.

He didn't let her go until Morgan knocked at the door, snapping him out of his controlling trance. Her incessant knocking let Raven know that Morgan had felt the vibrations of their fight. She couldn't hear, but she knew when her sister was in trouble.

"She's ready for school," Raven sobbed as she scrambled to her closet to change clothes.

She felt Mizan behind her, but she didn't turn around. He threw a few hundred dollar bills at her and they fell onto the closet floor at her feet. "Go buy yourself something to wear tonight. We're going out," he said simply, his ignorant way of apologizing for his actions. She ignored him. "Oh, so you too good to pick up my money?" he antagonized. Raven sighed and got on her knees to pick up the cash. "What do you say?"

"Thank you," Raven whispered through clenched teeth.

She put on a Juicy Couture sweatsuit and turned to him to see if he approved. When he did not comment she assumed it was okay. She fixed her ruffled hair, pulling it back into a long ponytail, then hurried out of the house.

Morgan was lost in her daydreams as she stared out the passenger window, but Raven knew she was well aware of what had gone down. She always knew when Raven and Mizan fought. The tension in the house was always so thick that her senses picked up on it with ease. Raven wished that she could take Morgan and move away. It was not healthy for Morgan to grow up around all of the arguing and fighting. Her parents had not exposed them to an unhealthy male/female relationship, and she felt bad for presenting one to Morgan now that they were gone. She never wanted her little sister to think that it was acceptable for a man to put his hands on her.

She turned Morgan's chin toward her, forcing her to look her in the face. "I know you heard what happened back there, Morgan. I want you to know that Mizan is foul for the way he treats me. No woman deserves to be hit. Do you hear me?" she asked as she drove to Brownell Elementary School.

Morgan smiled and cut her eyes playfully at her sister. "No, I don't hear you. I'm deaf, remember?" she signed sarcastically. Raven smiled and shook her head.

"I'm serious, Morgan. Mizan is wrong for how he behaves," Raven signed.

"But you make him so mad all the time, Rae. Why don't you just stop doing stuff he doesn't like?" Morgan replied.

The fact that Morgan justified Mizan's actions broke her heart. *I have to get her away from there. She can't think this is okay. It'll only make her weak, and the next thing I know some nigga will be treating her the same way Mizan treats me.*

"It doesn't matter if I make him mad Morgan. He's an adult and that is not how adults solve problems. What he does is wrong and I want you to know that you deserve to feel safe. Never let a man beat you down. I'm down so low that I don't know how to begin climbing back to the top," Raven said softly, talking more to herself than to her sister. She rubbed her sister's head gently and put on a fake smile. "Go ahead, before you're late. I'll be here to pick you up after school. I love you," she said with a kiss to the cheek.

"I love you too, Rae," Morgan signed, and then ran off into the school. Before pulling off, Raven reached into her purse and pulled out a small sandwich bag full of cocaine. She stuck her pinky finger in and scooped some of the powder up with her acrylic French tip. She raised it to her nose and inhaled. She took a deep breath as the drug entered her system. It was the only way she knew to deal with her existence. She had gone from a social user to a full-time cocaine connoisseur. There wasn't a day that went by that she did not indulge. Stress had pushed her over the edge and it was the only coping mechanism she knew.

Raven sat nervously in a steel chair as she waited for her mother to come into the visiting room. She had already been waiting for half an hour and she was growing nervous, thinking that maybe her mother did not want to see her. She hadn't seen her face in so long, since the day that the judge sentenced her to twenty years for the role she had played in her husband's drug empire. Raven kept her eyes on the door until finally Justine came walking through it.

Dismal, weary, and worn, Justine exuded none of the qualities Raven had once admired. It was as if life behind bars had sucked the life out of her, leaving behind merely a shell of her former self. Her hair was in one long braid to the back, but her roots were horrendous, as if they had never been relaxed a day in her life. The heavy bags under her eyes expressed fatigue and the wrinkles on her face were permanently etched into her skin. There was nothing flawless, glamorous, or diva-like about the woman before Raven's eyes.

"Hey, Mommy," Raven whispered as she put on a fake smile. She did not want to be the one to tell her mother how badly she looked.

"My baby," Justine replied in disbelief. She had not had a visitor in so long, and she did not expect Raven to come, so this was a pleasant surprise. "Where is Morgan?"

"She had school, Mommy. I just wanted to come and see how you are. I know you've been calling, but Mizan . . ."

Justine put her hand up and shook her head to stop Raven's sentence. "I know he has you secluded from the world, Raven. It's a shame he doesn't even want you talking to your own mama, but I get it. He has the control and he doesn't want to share you. I'm just glad you're here right now."

"How are things coming with the lawyer?" Raven asked. "Is he working on your appeal? Because I paid him good money, Mommy. He should be working day and night to get you out of here."

"He's doing what he can, Raven, but I'm not counting on it. Save your money. What's done is done . . . ain't no rewinding time. I did what I did. Me and your father both knew that what he was doing couldn't last forever. Now I have to deal with the consequences," Justine stated. She sounded so hopeless, as if she had given up a long time ago.

"You don't deserve to be in here, Mommy," Raven said.

Justine scoffed as her shoulders fell a little lower. "Don't worry about it Rae. Your mama got everything under control. I've got a plan. I won't be in here too long. These crackers won't hold me for too long."

Raven laughed slightly, thinking that her mother sounded just like her father. She was a direct reflection of him. Her parents had been the Romeo and Juliet of the hood, a perfect pair.

"Do you need anything?" Raven asked.

"I need your father, Rae. Nothing seems the same without him. It's been five long years and it has not gotten any easier. I just want us to be together again," Justine said.

"You will be, Mommy. Daddy's waiting for you. When it's your time, you guys will be reunited," Raven said confidently. If she had never witnessed her mother and father's love she would not be able to tell that it was missing in her own relationship. Justine and Benny Atkins had a love that was talked about through the grapevine. Theirs was one for the history books.

Giving Raven a weak smile Justine replied, "I hope so Rae. Where is that grand baby of mine? I was hurt when you did not even send me a picture."

A dark cloud formed over Raven's head as sorrow over-cast her. "My baby was still-born, Mommy. I have tried to have a baby since then, but Mizan and I . . . we fight a lot. I can never bring a baby full term. I've had so many miscarriages it's hard to keep track."

Raven wiped the tear from her cheek and quickly put a bandage over that emotional scar. Her mother had picked the scab off of it, causing her to become emotional, but she had been down that road. Depression and regret mixed with thoughts of suicide had been her story many times. She was not going back down that road. She buried her emotions deep inside. It was easier for her not to think about it.

"Oh, baby. I'm so sorry. I did not know," Justine said as she reached across the table and took her daughter's hand. "Your father had a bad feeling about that boy from the first day he lay eyes on him. He knew that he was no good for you. It would break his heart to see you like this."

"I know, but he's the man I chose, right?" Raven stated, reiterating a lesson that Justine had once taught her. "I wish I had listened all those years ago. I miss Daddy so much. I have to sneak to his grave site just to spend time with him. I just want to tell him that I love him and I'm sorry."

"Sorry for what?" Justine asked.

"For everything, Mommy. For everything," she said as she shook her head.

"I'll let him know, baby . . . don't you worry about it," Justine replied. "But I need you to do me a favor, Raven. Don't waste your life on Mizan. The first chance you get, you leave him. A man like that can only make your life hell, and you deserve so much more."

Raven nodded, but there was a self-awareness inside of her that told her she was not going anywhere. Her allegiance was too strong, her determination too weak, and her heart too fragile to break free. She did not put her burden on her mother's heart though. Justine was dealing with enough and Raven did not want to be selfish by putting her own problems off on her mother. "I will, Mommy," she lied.

The guards indicated that the visiting time was over. They both were full of tears as they stared at one another, taking in all they could.

"Mommy, I'm going to contact that lawyer and I will try to come back when I can," Raven promised.

"No, you won't," Justine whispered as she hugged her daughter tightly. Her mother's embrace felt so good that Raven did not want to let go. They hugged and rocked from side to side. "I understand though, Raven. I really do, but get away from him, Rae. Don't be the moth that flies into the flame. You take your sister and you go somewhere safe, before it's too late. I love you, darling. I love you with all of my heart. Remember that."

Raven was bawling as she stepped back and held onto Justine's forearms. "I love you too, Mommy."

"Thank you for coming to visit. You made this so much easier for me. I wished you could have brought Morgan so that I could see her one last time. Please remind her that I love her every day, and you remember that too, baby girl."

The nickname sounded so soothing coming off of her mother's lips. She nodded as she watched Justine walk out of the room. Before she disappeared fully, Justine blew her a kiss. Raven waved good-bye knowing that it would be a long time before they crossed paths again.

Raven felt extreme guilt as she walked out of the prison. *She does not deserve to be in here,* she thought as she pulled away, headed back to Flint. She noticed that she had missed four calls, all from Mizan wanting to know her whereabouts. He was like her watchdog checking in with her every hour on the hour. At first she thought his concern was cute and she was flattered that he wanted to be around her all the time; now his over-bearing nature drove her crazy. She decided not to call him back right away as she hit I-75 and dialed her moth-er's lawyer. Unable to reach him, she left a message to return her call, and then threw her cell on the passen-ger seat. The hour-long drive gave her time to clear her head and gain her composure before she arrived at Nik-ki's house.

Raven knocked on the door lightly and smiled when her Aunt Gena answered. She remembered when the woman before her was so vibrant. A classic forty-some-thing woman who loved to party and bullshit, but when Nikki was shot her entire life changed. After that one fateful night her carefree lifestyle disappeared. Before her stood a tired, old woman. "Hi, Auntie G," she greet-ed her with a peck to the cheek.

"Hey, Raven. Come on in," she said as she stepped to the side. Gena used to be what kids would call the cool mama on the block. She dressed young, talked young, dated young men, and was the ghetto mother who did not care where her children were or what they were into as long as they were not in her way. One bullet had changed everything in the blink on an eye. Nikki would never be the same, and after almost losing her daugh-ter once, Gena had become overprotective, causing her many sleepless nights.

"Nik! Raven is here," Gena shouted as she went back to watching her soap operas. Wobbly, slow, and timid, Nikki attempted the staircase on her own. Raven trotted halfway up and took her best friend's hand.

"Thanks, Rae," Nikki said as she leaned against her for support. Nikki was lucky to be alive. After being shot at almost point blank range she had miraculously survived, but the bullet was so close to her spinal cord that the doctors could not remove it. So they let it remain and put her on medications to take the swelling down around her brain. Unfortunately the scar tissue that healed around the bullet damaged parts of her hippocampus. Her short-term memory was shot. Everything that occurred after the moment she was shot, she would never remember. Anyone who crossed her path from now on would be forgotten the very next day. Most days she was fine, but sometimes her energy was extremely low and she had a hard time standing for long periods of time. Raven's eyes misted as she helped Nikki to the kitchen and they took a seat. Her appearance was exactly the same. The scar on her temple was concealed by her long hair. Her face seemed a bit tight on the right side, but other than that her appearance was unaffected. She still looked the exact same way she always had.

"Mizan called here for you," Nikki said.

Raven's back stiffened in surprise. "What did you tell him?"

Nikki reached across the table and grabbed Raven's arm, giving it a light squeeze of reassurance. "Relax. I told him you went to the pharmacy to pick up some medicine for me," Nikki replied.

Raven sat with Nikki and reminisced about old times. It was the only thing that Nikki could really talk about. Their teenage years were the only true things that she could recall, and although the conversations became redundant, Raven obliged her every time, laughing at jokes she had heard a thousand times as if they were new. Her friendship with Nikki was important and had withstood a lot over the years. Raven loved Nikki and would do anything for her. She visited with her until it was time for her to pick Morgan up from school.

"You feel up to going out tonight?" Raven asked.

"Where are we going?"

"Probably to the Purple Moon. Mizan and his people are going. You know I don't like being the only chick in a group of niggas. You should come out. It'll be fun," Raven urged, trying to offer Nikki a sense of normalcy.

Nikki nodded. "Okay. You'll pick me up?"

"Of course, Nik. I'll be here around ten o'clock," Raven answered. She stood then embraced Nikki. "I love you, girl. I'll be back later tonight. I'm going to get you out of this house and show you a good time."

After much pleading, Raven finally convinced Mizan to let Nikki join them for the night. After leaving Morgan with Aunt Gena, they rolled to the club with a caravan of luxury vehicles behind them. The knock from the speaker beat through their chests as they pulled right up to the door at the popular night club.

They bypassed the crowd, the velvet ropes lifting instantly as the bouncers granted them access to the club.

Mizan and Rich led the way with Raven and Nikki behind them. The rest of Mizan's entourage brought up the back. They were ten deep. Mizan was the king and his round table of knights were right behind him, loyal and ready to pop off if need be. The girls walked arm in arm, both dressed as if they were attending a New York City fashion show. Raven was used to the jealous stares she got. The five-hundred-dollar pair of True Religion skinny leg jeans and Marc Jacobs one-shoulder blouse made her the envy of every female in the club. Her hair was swept to one side with big spirals cascading down her shoulder, and the diamonds in her ears and on her wrist were blinding. Nikki was equally stunning in a short Dolce & Gabbana shaker dress and Gucci peep toes, but despite her stunning appearance she was insecure. Raven could tell that Nikki was nervous. The vice grip that Nikki had on her arm gave her away. Everyone in the hood knew what had happened to her and they all showed her love as she made her way to VIP.

"See, your peoples missed you, hon," Raven whispered to her over the loud music. Nikki had not been out since she had been shot. Her life had slowed down drastically because of her recovery and it felt good to feel like a hood star again. "Just relax, we're here to have a good time."

Seeing the look of apprehension melt away from Nikki's face made Raven smile. They sat down and the waitresses immediately catered to their group, bringing the finest bottles of champagne and liquors over to them.

"Start a tab," Mizan told one of the waitresses. "You make sure everybody with me is good and at the end of the night I'll make sure you right, a'ight, ma?" He slipped her a hundred dollar bill. "That's for you, baby. There's more where that came from, but you got to work for it."

"Oh, I can work for that. I'll work all night if you need me to," the girl replied with seductive insinuation.

Mizan smiled, then whispered in the waitress' ear. She giggled loudly and then walked away, putting an extra switch in her step.

Raven rolled her eyes in disgust at Mizan's blatant flirting. *This nigga is so disrespectful,* she thought as she cocked her head to the side and raised an eyebrow in annoyance.

He smirked and nodded at her, challenging her to say something, but Raven didn't cause a scene. She simply grabbed a glass of Dom and sipped it slowly. The DJ kept the music live and the crowd was extra animated as everyone drank and had a good time. Liquor flowed freely and, for once, Raven felt like life was carefree. She and Nikki laughed and joked with one another. They had not been out together in such a long time, and it felt like the good old days. Raven noticed Rich eyeing Nikki, and she leaned over to put her girl up on game.

"Rich been staring at you all night, Nik. I think he's feeling you," Raven said.

Nikki discreetly looked in Rich's direction. Brown-skinned and attractive, Nikki smiled. "Who?" Nikki asked.

"You know Rich . . . Mizan's best friend," Raven said.

Nikki turned up her nose and shook her head. "Girl, please. Ain't nobody trying to fuck with him."

Raven smiled curtly and shook her head. "Why not, Nik? You need to get out and start dating again. You can't just live the rest of your life as a hermit inside of Aunt Gena's house. I'm not telling you to marry dude. Just give him some play. See what his conversation is like."

"He's cute, but I know how Mizan is, and birds of a feather flock together, you know? That nigga probably ain't no good," Nikki responded seriously. "I'm so not interested, so don't try to play matchmaker tonight, Rae. I'm just enjoying being out with my girl."

Before Raven could respond, Rich had switched places with one of his boys and positioned himself directly on her other side, putting her right in the middle. He couldn't really help himself. He had a dangerous attraction to Nikki. It was obvious that she was a fighter. He had shot her in the head himself and she had bounced back miraculously. He knew that he was taking a huge risk, but something in him was urging him to push up on her. He had always wanted to fuck with Nikki, but her arrogant persona had always deterred him from trying to get at her. He had not seen her in years, since the day that he and Mizan had secretly terrorized her, but he was about to make his move. He refused to be turned down again, and he was determined to get another sample of the jewels she kept on lock between her legs. This time he was going to use the good guy approach to see if it got him any closer to his prize.

"What's up with your girl?" he whispered in Raven's ear.

Raven shrugged. "I don't know. Why don't you ask her yourself? Get your grown man on," she joked as she switched seats with him.

Nikki gave Raven a stern look that said, *Bitch, I told you I wasn't interested,* but Raven turned her head, feigning ignorance. Nikki put on a friendly smile to avoid being rude. Raven moved next to Mizan, who had a presumptuous leer on his face, as if he knew a joke that no one else did. Little did Raven know, she had just urged her best friend to speak to the man who had almost killed her.

Nikki wanted to kill Raven for placing her in the uncomfortable situation. She went to reach for her drink.

"What's good? You look nice tonight, ma," he said loudly over the music.

"Thank you," she responded as she nursed her drink.

"You dance?"

"Oh, no . . . I don't dance. I used to, but I haven't in a long time. I was in an accident and it seems like after that I lost my rhythm," she said with a light smile.

"Aww, shit . . . now I'ma have to teach you," he said jokingly. Nikki froze when she heard him say that phrase. Something about it was too familiar.

Now I'ma have to teach you a lesson.

Now I'ma have to teach you a lesson.

Her body tightened instinctively as she replayed the phrase in her head again and again. They the last words she had heard before she had been shot, and as Rich spoke in her ear she realized it was the same voice who had taunted her so many years ago. Her breath caught in her throat. *It's him,* she thought in panic as her eyes watered. Her drink slipped out of her hand and spilled all over her dress. She could never forget the voice. She had replayed it over and over again in her mind for years.

Bitch . . . Now I'ma have to teach you a lesson.

Bitch . . . Now I'ma have to teach you a lesson.

Nikki stood up, upset and near tears as fear choked her. "Excuse me. I need to go to the ladies' room. I have to go." She put her hands out for balance. The liquor had her head spinning. "Rae!" she cried out. Raven immediately went to her side.

"Yo', you a'ight?" Rich asked.

"I'm fine," she said as she pulled away from him and grabbed onto Raven. "Get me out of here."

"Okay . . . okay, sweetie, hold on." Raven turned toward Mizan. "She's not feeling well. I'm gonna take a cab back to her place to make sure she makes it home safe. I'll just pick up Morgan and head home after that."

Mizan barely acknowledged her. His attention was on the waitress he had been hitting on all night.

"Mizan! We're leaving!" she yelled.

He threw up two fingers and dismissed her. Pissed beyond belief, Raven helped Nikki out of the club.

Nikki was silent as tears rolled down her face.

"Tell me what's wrong, Nik. What did he say to you that has you so upset?" Raven asked after they'd gotten into the car.

"It was him, Rae. He's the one who shot me." She looked out the window, her thoughts distant.

"What? Rich? Nik, you might just be confused. That doesn't make sense," Raven protested.

"Raven! It was him! I know his voice. I know I don't remember much but I remember that! He shot me," Nikki said with certainty.

Raven knew that Nikki was not the type of girl to make false accusations. For her to say something like that meant that she was a 100 percent positive.

"Why would he do that? I have to tell Mizan," Raven gasped in disbelief as she tried to figure things out in her head. *He could be trying to set Mizan up.*

Nikki looked at Raven with contempt. "Raven, when have you ever known anyone to outsmart Mizan? I'll put money on it that Mizan was behind the entire thing."

"No." Raven denied the accusation vehemently. "He wouldn't do that to me."

"He would do that to you, Raven! He fucks you up on a daily basis. Stop being so naïve. I know for sure that Rich and Mizan were behind what happened to us that night. I know it."

Raven's silence filled the car as she argued with herself in her mind. She wanted to take up for him. She wished that she had the confidence in her man to tell Nikki that she was wrong, but their jilted relationship gave her doubt. She wanted to be mad at Nikki for even accusing Mizan of the sinister act, but she could not. His track record and his treatment of her spoke volumes. The truth was, he was capable of anything. Insecurities began to creep into the back of her mind regarding his whereabouts on that night. The cab finally pulled up to Nikki's house and they walked inside.

Raven woke up her sister and prepared to leave. She stepped out onto the porch.

"Rae, be careful. I know you don't want it to be true, but I don't trust Mizan. I could have died, Raven," Nikki said.

"I know," Raven whispered as she lowered her head. She was ashamed. If she had not invited Mizan into her life, Nikki would have never been hurt.

"I don't want to sit around and watch something happen to you. He's grimy, Rae. He doesn't love you. Get away from him," she warned.

Raven nodded, took Morgan's hand, and reluctantly caught a cab back home, despite the protests going off in her head.

Raven rushed into the house, practically dragging Morgan behind her.

"What's wrong, Rae? Why are you acting weird?" Morgan inquired.

"I'm just thinking . . . Go and get in bed. It's late. I'll see you in the morning," she signed, then kissed her cheek and pushed her gently toward her bedroom.

Raven retired to her own room, burning holes in her hardwood floor as she paced back and forth in contemplation. All the people who mattered most to her had wanted her to leave Mizan, but still she stayed. *It just doesn't make sense,* she reasoned. *How could he do something like that and then look me in my face?*

Her suspicions arose as she thought back to that night. It was so long ago, but she remembered everything like it had occurred yesterday. *He said they ran in his house because he owed them some money. A hundred thousand,* she thought, trying to piece the puzzle together. She began to search around the room, opening drawers and pulling out old shoe boxes, to see if she could find anything that could give her answers. *This is stupid . . . Nikki is wrong.* She showered, but she could not shake the chill that had taken over her body. *But what if she isn't wrong?*

"Oh my God!" she whispered to herself. "What if she's right?" she asked herself. She hopped out of the shower and wrapped a towel around her body, then tapped on the wall that separated the master bedroom from Morgan's room. She knocked hard and frantically, knowing that Morgan would feel the vibration, and then raced to her bed and pulled out a suitcase from underneath it. She suddenly felt as if she was in danger and she did not know who to trust. She heard her bedroom door open and saw Morgan step into the room, wiping her sleepy eyes.

"What?" Morgan signed, frowning.

"Go and pack some clothes. We're going to stay with Aunt Gena and Nikki for a couple of days," Raven signed back. Raven's body language was panicked and urgent, so Morgan immediately knew that something was wrong. Morgan watched Raven's hands shake as she piled her clothes inside the bag. "Go pack!" Raven yelled. She threw on a pair of sweatpants and put her wet hair up into a ponytail, then headed for the door with her sister trailing behind her.

"Why are we leaving?" Morgan signed once they were in the car and pulling out of the driveway.

"We're just going to keep Nik company. She's not feeling too good," Raven said, not wanting to let Morgan know what was really happening. She looked at the clock on the dashboard. It was already 2:00 A.M. The club had just let out. She did not have much time.

When Raven arrived on Nikki's doorstep she was trembling at the thought of what she had just done. *I left him,* she thought in disbelief. *I finally found the courage to leave.*

Chapter Thirteen

"Where the fuck you at?" Mizan yelled through the phone.

"I'm leaving, Mizan . . . I can't do this anymore," she said, her courage diminishing as each second passed. Mizan was silent. He did not have to say a word to intimidate her. Just hearing his erratic breathing let her know that his temper was through the roof.

"Raven, you've got thirty minutes to carry your yellow ass back through this door, or I'ma come drag you up out of that house. Fuck you think? I wouldn't know where you went?" he asked.

"I have to ask you a question, Mizan," Raven said as her palms began to sweat. "Did you have anything to do with Nikki getting shot?"

Mizan thought back to that night and lied with ease. "Fuck is you talking about? I would not do no shit like that. Is that why you picked up and left? That stupid-ass bitch putting shit in your head?" he yelled.

"I just needed to know," Raven replied.

"Bitch, bring your stupid ass home!"

Click!

Raven stared at her cell phone and then slowly eased out of bed. Morgan lay asleep beside her. Raven shook her out of her dreams. Morgan sat up in confusion. "Morgan, wake up. It's time to go back home," Raven signed. She did not even bother waking Nikki because she would only try to convince her to stay.

Before those thirty minutes had passed, Raven was pulling back into her driveway. She could feel Mizan's eyes burning a hole through her as she stepped out of the car.

Morgan waved and smiled as she looked up at the house.

Raven followed her gaze, and sure enough Mizan was looking out of the master bedroom window. His facial expression showed his displeasure.

"Morgan, I want you to play outside for a little while. I'm gonna go make you something to eat. I'll come out and get you when I'm done," she instructed. It took everything in her to force a smile. Morgan nodded and went running off into the backyard.

Raven entered the house, expecting Mizan to meet her at the front door, but she had to go searching for him. She ascended the staircase wearily. It was too quiet. She had expected yelling and arguing, but the still of the house was killing her. When she got to her bedroom door, she paused and took a deep breath to prepare for the fight she was about to get into.

"Take off your clothes," Mizan instructed calmly as soon as she opened the door.

"Can we talk?" she asked.

He gave her a stern look and Raven lowered her head.

"You're only going to make it worse on yourself if I have to say it again," he warned as he pulled off his leather belt.

Raven's anxiety grew and her heart ached as she saw him fold the belt in half. She was terrified, but to her own surprise she felt an anger like never before. *Who the hell does he think he is? Nigga got the nerve to take a belt out! He's not my fucking daddy! That's what he doesn't understand!* Her rage transformed into courage and she wiped her tears away.

"No," she replied.

"What?" Mizan said. "I know I heard you wrong."

"No!" she repeated, sternly this time.

Her defiance sent Mizan into action. "Bitch! Who the fuck you telling no?" he asked as he swung the belt, grabbing one of her arms to keep her from running. It was as if he were beating a child. He disciplined her hard, causing large welts to form on her skin wherever the belt struck.

"No!" she screamed as she fought back for the first time. She punched the shit out of him, connecting her free fist to the top of his head, catching him by surprise.

"Oh, you gon' hit me?!" he raged, as he suddenly gained the strength of ten men.

"I hate you!" she hollered as she continued to punch him. She felt the sting of his belt as he beat her mercilessly, but she was so upset that she could not stop herself from swinging. She was trying to take his head off as she put all of her might behind her punches. Raven was well aware that she was not winning the fight, but she was making a point. Like Ike and Tina Turner, they brawled relentlessly as she desperately tried to prove to him that she was tired of being his punching bag. She was standing up for herself. She was tired of being run over by him. His definition of love was not what it was supposed to be like.

"Bitch, I'ma kill you," Mizan seethed. Sweat dripped down his forehead as he grabbed her by the neck. He picked her up with one hand and slammed her down so hard on the floor that he knocked the wind out of her chest.

"No! Let me go!" she screamed as she reached up to scratch at his face, aiming for his eyes. The more she fought back, the harder he choked her, until no air could get through her throat.

She kicked and contorted her body until his grip had loosened enough for her to get oxygen. She gulped in the air greedily as she climbed to her feet. Mizan was not used to her fighting back and was kneeled over, out of breath.

"Bitch, I'ma kill you tonight," he stated.

"Then let's go because every time you hit me, I'm hitting your bitch ass back! I'm tired of you! I'm tired of this!" she screamed.

"Too fucking bad, bitch, because the only way you're leaving up out of here is not breathing," he stated as he touched his bleeding face. She had scratched him so deeply that the flesh was showing.

"What happened to you?" she cried as her legs gave out and she flopped down onto the bed. "What happened to the man I fell in love with?"

Mizan approached her and loomed over her. He brought his hand back to smack her.

She stared him in the eye. "You can hit me all you want, but I'm not going to make this shit easy for you anymore. I'm not going to just let you abuse me, Mizan. So every time you ready to box, know that I'm fighting back now. I don't give a fuck. Your ass gon' be sweating and breathing hard every day because I'm done being your victim!"

Mizan lowered his hand and nodded as if she had just insulted him. "Okay. You tough now, bitch? I'ma break you down. I'ma humble your ass one way or another. You just wait and see," he threatened. He walked out of the room, slamming the door. Raven heard his tires burning rubber as he sped down the street.

As soon as she was sure he was gone, she broke down. She felt every spot that he had hit, and stood to examine herself in the mirror. Red marks covered her face and neck. They would undoubtedly bruise over. "Agh-hh!" she screamed in frustration as she hit the mirror with both of her fists. Glass shattered everywhere as her reflection cracked. Grabbing her candy box from her dresser, she sat on the floor, sobbing as she rocked back and forth. She poured a small pile of cocaine out onto a magazine. She divided the powder into two equal lines, working meticulously like a chemist, and without thinking twice she devoured them into her nose, sucking them up like a vacuum. She sniffed loudly as she grabbed the tip of her nose to make sure no residue remained. Her cries instantly subsided as the drug entered her system.

She went to her bathroom window and saw that Morgan was outside, jumping on her trampoline. She was glad that Morgan hadn't been inside the house to see what had gone down. *I can't keep her here. Mizan's not going to stop and she doesn't need to be around all of this,* she thought. Raven knew that she did not have the strength to leave yet, but in the meantime she would have to think about someone who would take Morgan in.

The house phone rang loudly, interrupting her thoughts. She thought that it was Mizan and she rushed to answer it.

"Hello?"

"Hello, this is Warden Christopher Hill at Huron Valley Women's Correctional Facility. I'm trying to reach the daughter of Justine Atkins . . . a Ms. Raven Atkins."

"Yeah, this is she," Raven responded. "What's going on? Is my mother in trouble?"

"No, miss. I regret to inform you that your mother committed suicide last night," he stated.

Raven dropped the phone, sending it crashing to the floor. *I was just there yesterday. Why would she do this?*

Overwhelmed with anguish, Raven could not take any more. She heard her sister run into the house.

"Rae, I'm hungry. Is the food done?" she sighed.

Raven's mouth felt like it was stuffed with cotton, and she couldn't form the words to respond. She gripped the wall to try to stop the room from spinning, but it was too late. She collapsed and the last thing she heard was her sister calling her name before the lights in her head went out.

Somber and in a state of shock, Raven stood in front of her mother's casket as it was lowered into the ground. She hid her devastation behind large Chloe sunglasses as she allowed her tears to fall. Mizan stood beside her quietly, checking his watch as if the funeral was a waste of his time. Raven could count on her hand the amount of people who had shown up. She shook her head in disgrace. *Where is everyone?* When her father was alive, Justine was loved by many. All of the people who had once worshipped the ground beneath her feet had gone on with their lives and forgotten all about the diva who was Justine Atkins. It was a prime example to Raven that the streets loved no one. The people who had watched her parents rise to the top were the same people who enjoyed watching them fall.

Raven put her hands on Morgan's shoulders and rubbed them gently as she listened to their pastor deliver the Lord's Prayer. *I just saw her . . . I can't believe she did this to herself,* she thought as she stepped up to throw her white lily into the grave. When the gravediggers began to shovel dirt on top of the casket, the few people who had attended began to disperse. They all offered their condolences as they left, but Raven could not make her feet move. She knew that when she walked away, her good-bye would be final.

"Come on, ma, let's get out of here." Mizan pulled her arm gently.

"No, not yet," she said. "Just give me a few more minutes. I can't leave her yet." As she looked up from the ground, her breath caught in her throat. She hadn't seen him in years, but she still recognized his stature and mannerisms from a mile away. *Ethic?* she thought. She quickly tore her eyes away before Mizan noticed that she was staring. She desperately wanted to run up and hug Ethic, but her feet were like roots in the ground. She was stuck, but her heart beat wildly inside of her chest, like a caged animal trying to break free. The feeling of anxiety overwhelmed her, because although he was many yards away, she would have sworn that he was looking directly at her. She could feel his energy. The pastor walked over to them.

"I'm very sorry for your loss," he said with sadness in his eyes. "You may be too young to remember this, but your parents helped me build my church. They were good people. If there is anything I can do for you and your sister please let me know," the old black man said as he held out his hand to Raven.

"I will, thank you," Raven replied as she shook it. She gasped when she felt a piece of paper that he slipped into her palm. She quickly put it in her clutch purse. She had a feeling that the letter was from Ethic.

Raven was silent the entire ride home. She expected to receive some type of sympathy from Mizan. If she had ever needed a shoulder to cry on, surely today would have been that day. It was the one time she wished they could put their differences aside. She wanted him to hold her, to comfort her, to be her man, but when he pulled up in front of their home and popped the locks she knew that even the death of her mother would not soften his ice-cold demeanor.

She got out of the car and opened the back door for Morgan. "Be ready tonight. I've got a business meeting in

Detroit at the Renaissance Center and my man is bringing his wife, so I need you on deck," Mizan said.

"Mizan, not tonight. I'm not in the mood to deal with anyone right now. My mother just died," she argued.

"And now the bitch is in the ground. I paid for the funeral and the whole nine. There ain't shit you can do for her now. I need you tonight. So be ready," he stated harshly.

Raven slammed the car door and glared at him through the window. If looks could kill Mizan would have been circled in chalk. He pulled away from the house with no remorse. As soon as he was out of sight, Raven ushered Morgan into the house. Once she was settled, Raven hurried to her bedroom and retrieved the note.

Meet me at my spot in Swartz Creek at three o'clock. There is something you need to know.

Raven grabbed the keys to her CLK, grabbed Morgan, and was out the door within minutes. She sped through the city streets as she rushed to Ethic's house.

"Why are you driving so fast?" Morgan signed. "Where are we going?" Raven was driving so frantically that she could barely look over to see what her sister was saying. She glanced again as she tried to interpret her sister's message.

"We're going to see Ethic," Raven said truthfully. "You can't tell Mizan though, Morgan. No matter what, okay?" she asked, sticking up her pinky finger.

Morgan squinted her eyes so that she could read Raven's lips from the side and once she understood, she nodded. She interlocked pinkies with Raven, promising that she wouldn't tell.

Raven raced toward Ethic like her life depended on it. She could not stop her foot from becoming heavy on the gas pedal. Ethic represented familiarity for Raven. He made her feel safe, and protection was something she had not felt in such a long time. When she saw his shiny new Dodge Challenger sitting in the driveway, she let out a sigh of relief. It seemed as if she had been holding in her fear for years, but the closer she got to him, the more she felt it melt away.

"Are you okay?" Morgan signed as she looked at Raven curiously.

"I will be," Raven responded as she pulled one of Morgan's pigtails playfully.

"I know when you and Mizan fight. I know he hits you. I hate him when he hurts you," Morgan signed.

The words were like a punch to the gut, because Raven had tried hard to keep Morgan from seeing too much. "I thought you liked Mizan." Raven said, trying to lighten the mood.

"I just pretend to like him so he won't start hurting me too," Morgan revealed.

Raven's chin trembled as she held on to the sob that was building in her throat. She reached over and grabbed her sister's hand. "I would never let that happen, Stank. I'm always going to protect you," she promised.

"But who is going to protect you?" Morgan signed.

"I don't know Stank . . . I don't know," she replied as she pulled into Ethic's driveway. They got out of the car and Raven kneeled down to face her sister.

"Morgan, I am so sorry for everything I have put you through. I never want you to be with someone like Mizan, and I haven't set a very good example for you. Don't be like me, Morgan. You grow up to be strong and independent. Don't fall for a hustler. This lifestyle is no good." Morgan was too young to truly comprehend what Raven was saying but she nodded anyway. Raven gripped her chin and kissed her cheek, then stood up. She inhaled deeply as she approached the front door. She knew that she looked a mess. She had been used as a punching bag for so long that her appearance looked ragged and worn. The stress of an abusive relationship had aged her, and her once vibrant eyes were mere pools of depression.

She shuffled uneasily from Giuseppe to Giuseppe as she rang the doorbell and waited impatiently for Ethic to answer. Finally he opened the door, and Raven gasped in shock. The handsome man she had crushed on when she was a young girl no longer existed. Before her stood a gruesome sight. Ethic's face was so badly scarred from the car fire that if she did not have his eyes etched in her memory, she may not have recognized him. While the left side of his face remained intact, the right side was damaged beyond repair. His skin tone was uneven, mixing shades of black and light where the flames had eaten through his flesh. Even his ear was burned and badly disfigured. On one side he was perfect, and on the other side he was hideous.

"Oh my God . . . Ethic," she whispered as she reached up to touch his face.

He stopped her, catching her wrists quickly, and turned his head to the side, out of her reach. "Don't," he said firmly. Then he stepped to the side and invited them in.

"Hey, Ethic!" Morgan greeted happily, ignoring his physical change. She rushed him and wrapped her arms around his waist, burying her head in his stomach.

"What's up, li'l bit?" he said with a half smile as he rubbed her back gently. The burnt side of his face seemed stiff and barely moved as he held out his hand for Morgan to slap him five. "Let me talk to your sister for a minute. There's a TV in the basement. We'll be down in a minute."

Morgan obediently raced out of the room and an awkward tension filled the room. Ethic stared at Raven for a long time. The same way she was examining his face, he was studying hers. The dark, healing bruises that covered her neck and the black eye that Mizan had given her caused his left temple to throb in anger.

"Why didn't you call me? When you lost control I would have come back," Ethic said.

"You left us here, Ethic. I haven't seen you in five years. I wasn't just going to call you out of the blue. I thought about it so many times, but I always hoped that things would get better. He was all I had." She stepped closer to him, closing the space between them. She reached up and touched his face as tears came to her eyes. "I'm so sorry," she whispered. He let her hands roam over his burns and inhaled deeply. "You look so different. Everything about you is . . ." She was at a loss of words as she stared at his ugly face. It seemed like a sin for a man who was once so fine to now be so damaged. "All I recognize are your eyes."

"I can say the same thing about you. You let him break you."

"I thought he loved me. I trusted him," Raven replied, her head hung low in embarrassment.

Ethic lifted her chin with one finger as his hand gently graced her face. "He used you, Raven. Mizan wanted to take your father's place and he got to him through you. You gave him the combo to your father's safe. He emptied it and left one brick. He was trying to set your pops up. That one brick would have been enough to send Benny away for a long time. He hit the silent alarm on the way out. Your father getting killed by the police was just icing on the cake for him. After that it was easy for him to take over. He knocked off your father's lieutenants one by one."

"He put the bomb underneath your limo?" Raven asked, already knowing the answer to the question.

Ethic nodded, and she doubled over, holding her stomach as guilty pains plagued her.

Raven grimaced as Ethic lay the truth out in front of her face. Inside she had known all along. She could feel Mizan using her, but the fact that he needed her for something made her feel worthy, as if she were doing what she had to do. The rules of the streets told her to hold her man down, to be the Bonnie to his Clyde, and she willingly obliged. But in the process, she had turned her back on everyone who truly cared for her. She put her hand over her mouth and closed her eyes.

"Your father loved you. Why would you betray him?" Ethic asked.

"Mizan made me think I had to," she whispered as she thought of Nikki. "Oh my God . . . she was right. He was behind it all. It was him. This entire time I have been sleeping with the man who is responsible for destroying my life. How could I be so stupid?" she asked herself as her nose began to run and she sniffed loudly. Whenever she felt stressed or overwhelmed she began to get jittery. Her body began to crave cocaine. She wiped her nose as she shook her head.

"You were young, and I can forgive you for the role you played in all of this. You were dumb back then, but now it's time for you to grow up," Ethic said.

"I just want my life back."

"I can give you that, but it's something you have to choose for yourself. If you're ready, I'll take you away from here," he assured her. "I can help you get on your feet. Set you and Morgan up in an apartment back in Missouri."

"Why can't we stay with you?"

"The lady in my life doesn't like to share," Ethic said with a small smile.

Raven nodded in understanding and wiped her face. She was tired of crying, tired of being weak. She wanted to start over and take care of her sister. Hatred filled her as she thought of how Mizan had deceived her. From the very beginning, he had been plotting against her.

"I just have one question. If you knew about Mizan all this time why didn't you handle it?"

"Because you were with him and I never wanted to hurt you," Ethic said.

Raven jumped to her feet. "But what about all the bricks he stole! What about the fire? You're just going to let him get away with all of that?"

Ethic took her hand and led her to one of the couches. "Let me explain something to you, Raven. This isn't a gangster movie or an episode of *The Sopranos*. I handle my beef and I don't have a problem with gunplay, but it's about the money first. That's what I'm in it for, to chase a dollar. I never worked for your father. . . . I supplied him."

"What?" Raven asked in disbelief. "My father was a boss . . . so you trying to take credit for what he built?"

"No, I would never do that, but he built his empire off of the work I supplied him. So when your little boyfriend decided to rob your father, he robbed me, but I knew that those bricks wouldn't last him forever. I put the word out that no one was to supply him because he owed me a debt. He went through every connect in the Midwest."

"Mizan's been getting money for years, Ethic. He cops his weight from some old woman. So you didn't stop anything. He still ended up on top," Raven said sadly. She had so many regrets that they were hard to count, but she knew one thing: all of the bad things that had occurred in her life had come from fucking with Mizan. He was a curse.

Ethic shook his head and replied, "That old woman is my Aunt Dot and she's taxing him. Mizan is paying double for the product. Over the years he has paid me back my money and then some. The only reason he is still breathing was because of you, and now that I know how he's been handling you, I'ma handle him."

Raven thought of how sweet revenge would be. After all of the degradation and humiliation that Mizan had taken her through, he deserved whatever death Ethic had intended for him. She wanted him to die, but the mustard seed of love that remained in her heart for him would not allow her to let it happen.

"Please, Ethic. I don't want you to hurt Mizan. I just want to get away from him. Karma is real and eventually he will pay for all the lives he has ruined, but I don't want that guilt on my shoulders. If I let you kill him, I will carry that burden with me for the rest of my life. That's giving him too much power. I just want to move on," she pleaded.

Ethic bit the side of his cheek in rage. He had waited a long time to deal Mizan a losing hand and now she was asking him to let bygones be. He sighed, knowing that nothing was going to stop him from settling this beef. "Okay," he said. "I'll let it rest."

As Raven looked in Ethic's eyes, she knew that he was lying.

"Ethic . . . please."

Ethic looked at the expression on her face. He could not believe she was begging for Mizan to be spared after all that he had done. It showed her level of absolution and made him look at her with a new perspective. She was much different than the seventeen-year-old princess he had met so long ago. She was now a grown woman who had been humbled by life's hardships, and he respected her for having such a good heart. He fully understood how in the wrong hands she had been manipulated. No matter how big of a front she put on, he knew that she was tender hearted.

"Okay," he said simply as he reached into his jacket pocket and removed three plane tickets. "We leave tonight at eight o'clock."

"I need to go back to get some of our things," Raven said as she stood up. Ethic grabbed her upper arm firmly.

"I can get you all new shit, Raven. Don't go back there," he demanded firmly.

"Some things can't be replaced, Ethic. I have to," she answered. "Keep Morgan with you. I'll meet you guys at the airport." She saw the look of doubt on his face. "I promise, Ethic. I'll be on that flight."

Ethic reluctantly handed her the plane ticket. "Be careful, Raven. Don't try to take dumb shit like shoes and clothes. Get only what you must and get out of that house as fast as you can. Whether you make it or not, I'm taking your sister somewhere safe."

She nodded, and grabbed the ticket from him.

Ethic watched her leave the house as his heart filled with anxiety. He wanted to follow her. Everything in him told him to run after her, but leaving Mizan had to be her choice. He could not force her. His gut told him that she wasn't going to show up, and he went back into the house to get Morgan so they could head out of town. By taking Morgan with him he was saving one of Benjamin's daughters. He felt he owed him that much. Now he hoped that Raven had enough courage to take him up on his offer and save herself.

Phase 3

Chapter Fourteen

When Raven pulled onto her street, she admired the immaculate house that sat in the cul-de-sac. She had chosen it herself, designed the interior to her liking, and customized every detail. Everything about the house appeared perfect, from the stone exterior to the manicured front lawn. It was her dream home, but if the walls could talk, they would reveal the ugly truth that dwelled inside.

She took in the opulence of it all as she exited her car and walked inside. She did not want to give it up. With every punch she had endured and every bruise she had tried to hide, she had earned this house. The materialistic side of her wanted to stay and enjoy all of her life's amenities, but the realistic side told her that if she did not leave, Mizan would eventually kill her.

She rushed into her room and went into her jewelry box to retrieve the only picture that she had left of her parents. Because of Mizan's sadistic nature, he had not wanted her to have anything to remind her of her father. He wanted her to worship only him, and she had obliged, putting all of her faith in him. She had depended on him to take care of her and to nurture her, but instead he had demeaned her and made her feel worthless. *I trusted him,* she thought miserably as she looked down at the photo of her parents. She covered her mouth and muffled her cry as she gripped her stomach in pain. *I helped him destroy my father . . . my family. He took away every single person I loved.* She wiped her runny nose on the sleeve of her shirt and forced herself to keep moving. *None of that matters anymore. Just get out of here,* she urged herself.

She tucked the photo inside of her Birkin Hobo bag and began to leave. As much as she thought she deserved everything inside the house, she took nothing else. She did not want anything that Mizan's dirty money had purchased. All she wanted was what she had come into the relationship with: her self-respect. As her feet graced the polished wooden floors, she felt a sense of accomplishment. She knew that once she walked out the front door she was never coming back. She laughed slightly as she thought of the new life ahead of her.

Freedom was within arm's reach as she descended the stairs, but all of that came to a screeching halt when she heard the lock to the front door click. Mizan came walking in. She could feel the invisible chains he had on her being clamped down.

No, she thought as her eyes widened and her pulse raced. She resembled a deer in headlights, helpless and afraid.

"Hey, w . . . what are you doing back so soon?" she asked. Mizan stared up at her, instantly picking up on her nervousness. She was jumpy and her eyes darted around the room. If she could have fallen into a hole and disappeared she would have, but this was real life and there was no escaping it.

"Where you going?" he asked as he nodded toward the car keys in her hand.

Raven thought quickly, knowing that she couldn't slip up now. She was too close to let Mizan stand in her way.

"I . . . I need to go to the salon so that I can be ready for tonight," she replied as she descended the rest of the steps. She was so glad that she had not packed any bags, because it would have been a dead giveaway of her plans to flee.

"Where's baby girl?" he asked.

"She's staying the night with one of her friends from school," she lied quickly.

"Friend from school, huh?" Mizan asked as he gave her his full attention. Raven wanted to bite her tongue off as soon as the words left her mouth. Mizan knew that she was lying. In all the years that they had been together, Raven had never let Morgan stay the night at a friend's house.

"I've got to go, my appointment is in fifteen minutes," she said as she tried to slide past him. Mizan grabbed her hand and squeezed it tightly until she dropped the keys on the floor.

"I'll drive you," he offered calmly, but behind his cool visage was a volcano of rage, threatening to erupt at any moment.

Fuck, what am I going to do? She checked her watch. She only had a few hours to make her flight, and with Mizan stuck to her like glue, there was no way she would be able to meet Ethic. She hesitated, stalling for time as she tried to figure out what to do.

"Don't you have an appointment to get to?" Mizan asked suspiciously.

Raven nodded and walked out the door, praying that her stylist happened to be at the salon so that she could play off the situation without arousing skepticism in Mizan.

I have to get away from him, she thought frantically as she got into the passenger side. Jittery butterflies filled her stomach, and she felt sick from the thought of Mizan figuring her out. *Please let this girl be working today . . .*

They pulled up to *Chic* hair studio and Raven hopped out of the car. Mizan was right behind her as she entered. Her eyes searched the room for her stylist, and when she finally located her, she smiled. The women approached each other and kissed each other once on each cheek. Mizan stood behind her like a hawk, carefully inspecting their interaction.

"Hey, Sasha, girl, thanks for squeezing me in on your books," Raven said as she looked her stylist directly in the eyes and raised her brow in a pleading way. *Please,* Raven mouthed desperately. *Help me.* Sasha frowned in confusion. "You are the best. I know my appointment was last minute, but I'm going out tonight and I need my shit lay. You know I'ma tip you nice for looking out for me," she said. Her back was to Mizan and she pleaded with Sasha with her eyes.

Sasha glanced in Mizan's direction. She could feel that something was not right, so she played along. "Oh . . . yeah . . . no problem, girl. You know you're my best client. I always have room for you in my chair," Sasha replied.

Thank you, Raven mouthed. Sasha winked and then pointed toward the waiting room. "You can wait for her out there. She might be awhile . . ."

"I'll wait," Mizan interrupted.

Sasha took Raven back to her booth, and once they were behind closed doors, Sasha began her interrogation. "What the fuck is going on?" she asked with wide eyes.

"I have to get out of here, Sasha. I need to shake him . . . like yesterday," Raven explained frantically. "I have to get away from him. I don't have that much time."

"Well, how the hell do you expect to do that?" Sasha asked. She poked her head out of her styling room and saw Mizan sitting with his arms crossed over his chest. "The nigga is posted like he's your bodyguard or something."

Raven paced back and forth as the rusty wheels in her head began to work again. It had been so long since she had thought for herself that she almost could not function.

"What do I do, Sash? Please, you have to get me out of here," she whispered.

"Raven, why are you running from that man?" Sasha responded as she put her hand on her hip. "If you want to get up and walk out of here then just do it! He's not your damn daddy."

"It's not that easy," Raven replied.

"The only person who is making it hard is you," Sasha answered. "Now, there is only one way in and one way out of here and that's through the front door, because the back is blocked by that damn dumpster in the alley. So unless you plan on standing up for yourself, you might as well sit back and let me do your hair."

Raven's soul was weary as she closed her eyes. Sasha leaned her back in the shampoo bowl.

"I'm trapped with him," she whispered.

"Look, Rae. I know how a nigga can get. Trust me, I've been where you are. The only way you are ever going to break free is if you choose to. Sneaking and running away is not going to solve your problems, because a man like Mizan ain't gon' do nothing but drag you back. He has your head, Raven, and as long as he has that, you are never going to get rid of him."

Raven tuned Sasha out and sat silently while she was primped into perfection. Her hopes of leaving with Ethic slowly faded away.

Like a porcelain doll, Raven sat at the dinner table with Mizan and his guests as they discussed their business. Her appearance was flawless, her bruises hidden behind cosmetics, and a Band-Aid stuck on her bleeding heart. She truly did make Mizan look good, but she was tired of playing a role. She was fed up. Being his trophy was no longer enough.

She was wasting the best years of her life on Mizan. It was time for her to move on. She stood up. Mizan reached across the table to grab her wrist.

"Where you going, ma?" he asked nicely, but the menacing look he gave her told her to take a seat.

She smiled curtly as all the attention became focused on her.

"I'll be back. I'm just going to the ladies' room," Raven responded. She hurried away from the table until she was out of sight. When she saw a pay phone posted next to the bathroom door she sighed in relief. *This is the only way,* she thought as she picked up the phone. Feeling like a traitor, she hesitantly dialed 911.

"Nine-one-one, what's your emergency?" the operator asked.

She could see Mizan looking around the restaurant for her. She had a perfect view of him, but he could not see her. A lump formed in her throat as she opened her mouth to speak, but when she saw Mizan rise out of his chair she quickly found her voice.

"Yes, I am at the Renaissance Center in the waterfront room on the top floor. There is a drug deal going down right now at one of the tables. Please send the police right away," Raven whispered. She hung up the phone and rounded the corner. She smiled when she saw Mizan.

"Everything a'ight?" he asked.

"Yeah, I'm good," she replied.

"Then go do your job and stop being so fucking anti-social. This is the first connect I have been able to get in touch with in over two years. I *need* to plug that in." He put his hand on the small of her back and pushed her forward with such force that she almost broke the heel on her stiletto.

She straightened herself up and rejoined the table as her eyes watched the clock. She hoped that the operator had not pegged her as a prank caller. Her leg bounced anxiously as she waited for them to arrive. *I only have an hour to get to the airport,* she thought.

Twenty minutes passed, and she smiled when she noticed the detective walk into the crowded dining room. She stood up.

"Where you going now?" Mizan asked.

"I'm leaving you," she stated honestly as she watched the police officers approach.

Mizan's nostrils flared as he stood and grabbed her elbow. He was oblivious to his impending arrest, and all he could focus on was that she had chumped him in public. Such a flagrant display of disrespect made him look like he was inferior.

"Mizan, if you cannot control your woman how am I to know you can handle my product?" the connect asked, laughing.

Mizan smacked Raven across her face, causing her to turn crimson. She held her jaw as she slowly turned her head back so that she was staring him in the eyes. She kissed his cheek and whispered in his ear.

"You deserve everything that's coming to you," she said. She lifted his wallet with ease as she pulled away from him, knowing that she would need money to catch a cab back to Flint. Just as he moved to go after her, the police stepped closer to their table and drew their weapons.

"Get down on the ground right now!" the officers yelled, causing chaos to erupt throughout the crowded room. Raven slipped into the frenzied crowd as they apprehended Mizan. His eyes followed Raven out of the dining room, and when she was at the door she turned around to look at him one last time. She could see the hatred and wrath on his face. A smile graced her face, and she could not help but antagonize him more by sticking up her middle finger. For the past five years he had defeated her and terrorized her life. Finally she was winning, and she only had two words to say to him as she left. "Fuck you," she mouthed.

She took the elevator to the bottom floor and ran to the street to flag down a cab. As she stepped into the car she pulled out a neat stack of hundred dollar bills. "This entire thing is yours if you get me to Bishop Airport as fast as you can."

"At this time, we are calling the final boarding of Northwest flight 810 headed for Kansas City, Missouri. All passengers who have not boarded yet are asked to please board the aircraft."

"She's not coming, is she?" Morgan signed as she looked up at Ethic. Ethic had no answers for her. He kept hoping that Raven would miraculously appear. Even if she did not want to save herself, he knew that her little sister needed her.

"Sir, I'm sorry but you are going to have to board the plane now," the ticket attendant said. Ethic nodded and swallowed the hard lump that had formed in his throat. *She is not coming. She don't want to leave him. I gave her a way out . . . she didn't take it. Now it's out of my hands.* He gave the woman the boarding passes and he got on the plane with Morgan.

Raven ran into the airport and disregarded the long line, going directly up to the ticket counter.

"Excuse me, miss, you have to get in line," the white woman said politely as she pointed to the line of travelers.

"Please, my flight takes off in five minutes. Can you just check me in?" Raven asked as she checked her watch and looked around the airport nervously.

"I'm sorry. You have to be checked in at least half an hour earlier than your scheduled departure," the woman replied.

Raven's eyes watered over as her head hung low. She was so tired of everyone standing in her way, and was too close to turn back. "Please . . . I just need to get out of this city. You don't know what I had to do to get here. If I'm not on that plane my life might as well be over. My boyfriend is going to kill me. Everything that I have is on that plane," she whispered desperately as tears clouded her eyes and she gripped the woman's hand in sheer terror. "Please," she begged brokenly. Her tears came down and slowly washed some of her makeup away, revealing the green and black bruises underneath. They washed away the visage of a perfectly kept wifey and revealed the truth: a beaten and frightened little girl who had done too much too soon. All she wanted was to escape. She looked so defeated and the sadness on her face told the story of a woman who had been neglected. The bruises instantly made the white woman feel sympathy for Raven. "I can't let that plane leave without me."

The woman nodded and picked up a phone. "Okay . . . I'll see what I can do."

After putting an emergency call in to the control tower, Raven was escorted through the security check point. When she saw her gate, she ran full speed as tears ran down her face. *You're almost there,* she coached herself. She handed her ticket to the boarding agent. "Thank you so much," she whispered as she smiled and wiped tears from her face. "Thank you, God," she choked out as she covered her mouth to stifle her cries of joy.

Ethic closed his eyes and leaned his head against the headrest to relieve the stress he felt. He imagined what

Raven would endure by choosing to stay in Flint. It was a ghost town with nothing but dead souls inhabiting it, and when he had looked in her eyes he had noticed that she was slowly dying as well. He inhaled a deep breath as he tried to convince himself that he had done all he could to help her. *I should have never let her go back,* he thought.

Raven stepped onto the plane and smiled brightly when she saw Ethic and Morgan sitting in the front of the coach section. Morgan smiled and Raven put her finger to her lips, telling her to be quiet. She walked down the aisle until she was standing directly over Ethic. She leaned over and whispered into his ear, "You didn't think I was going to make it, did you?"

Ethic's eyes shot open in surprise. He stood up and extended his arm, motioning for her to take the middle seat next to him, as Morgan scooted down to the window seat. Relief washed over him as he sat back down. "Now, what was so important that you had to go back one last time?" he asked.

She removed the picture from her handbag and handed it to him. "This is all I have left of them," she replied. "I couldn't leave it behind."

Ethic nodded and leaned back; instinctively, he grabbed her hand. It was almost like he felt that if he wasn't touching her, she would vanish. The intention of the gesture was purely innocent, but Raven's heart fluttered as she held onto him tightly. She reached over with her free hand and held on to Morgan as the plane took them into the sky, heading for a new life.

Chapter Fifteen

By the time they arrived in Kansas City, the moon had taken over the sky. Exhausted from the flight, Morgan slept soundly in Ethic's arms as they walked to the parking lot.

"Ain't she too big for you to be carrying?" Raven asked with a smile as she took note of how Ethic still treated Morgan like the six year old he had met all those years ago.

Ethic smiled and then replied, "I guess she is . . . it's just so crazy how much time has passed. I still think she's that snaggled-toothed baby girl who used to sit on my lap." Although he said the words, he did not put her down. Raven was silent as she got into Ethic's Benz. She watched the city streets pass by. It was weird to be in such an unfamiliar setting. Flint was all she knew, and as they headed into the suburbs, Raven absorbed all of her surroundings. She welcomed the change. The pace of the city seemed to be completely different than that of her hometown. Death and destruction did not dwell on every corner.

She rubbed her bare arms as they pulled into Ethic's driveway. The home was beautiful. It wasn't overly large or tackily decorated with all of the fixings of the average hustler. Tasteful and just the right size, it was the most comfortable-looking house she had ever lay eyes on. The landscape was gorgeous, and Raven automatically assumed that the flower garden had been planted by his girlfriend. A short jealous streak raced through her, but she quickly shook it away. She had come to realize over the years that Ethic would never be hers. She did not expect to come to town and steal him away from another woman. All she could do was be grateful to him for helping her. The four-bedroom, three-bathroom, ranch-style home sat on two acres of land and sat back a quarter mile from the road. When Ethic hit the button to open his five-car, double-deck garage Raven's mouth dropped in awe as five luxury vehicles sparkled flawlessly. *Wow, he really is the bird man,* she thought, impressed. It was quiet and serene as she stepped out of the car.

"I love this house," she said as she got out and looked around.

"You and Morgan can stay here tonight. Tomorrow morning we'll start shopping for a condo for the two of you," he said.

"You could have dropped me off at a hotel Ethic. I don't want to invade your girlfriend's space. I know I would not like it if my man took in some random girl," Raven said.

Ethic smirked as he awoke Morgan. "Wake up, Morgan . . . We're here," he said as he nudged her gently.

Raven and her sister followed Ethic inside. Raven immediately felt uncomfortable when she saw a beautiful Hispanic girl lying on the couch, flipping through channels on the TV.

"Hey, baby," she greeted happily as she stood up. "How was your trip?" she asked. She wrapped her arms around Ethic's neck and pecked him on the cheek. "I missed you, papi." Her golden skin was flawless. She was undeniably stunning, and Raven turned up her nose in disgust. She couldn't help it. She was green with envy and the hater in her came out instantly.

"It went well," Ethic replied as he removed her arms from around his neck. "Dolce, I want you to meet my friend, Raven, and her sister, Morgan."

Dolce's eyes scanned Raven from head to toe and she frowned. Raven's eyebrows rose in defense as she cocked her head to the side and glared right back at Dolce. "Hey," Dolce finally greeted dryly.

There was obvious hostility in her tone, but Raven couldn't give two fucks if Ethic's girlfriend liked her. She crossed her arms and turned to Ethic. "Where are we sleeping?"

"They're staying here?" Dolce asked in displeasure.

"Oh, don't worry about it, Dolce. Morgan and I always stay with Ethic when he comes to Flint. We go *way* back," Raven responded deviously, knowing that she was getting under the girl's skin.

"Oh, really?" Dolce turned to Ethic and stared a hole through him.

"Really," Raven confirmed with a smirk. "We're *real* close friends."

Ethic cleared his throat and stared firmly at Raven. "Chill out," he whispered. He focused on Dolce. "Don't trip. She's only staying for one night."

"You won't even let me stay over for a night Ethic," Dolce shot back.

Ethic gave her a stern look that told her he wasn't going to continue to explain himself. "How did everything go here?" he asked, changing the subject.

"Everything went fine. It always does." She picked up her purse and stalked over to the door.

Ethic pulled out a knot of money from his pocket, all big faces. He placed half the stack in her palm, knowing that money would pacify her.

"Thank you, ma. You're the best. I appreciate you taking care of everything," Ethic said as he walked Dolce to the door. Raven frowned as she made her way to the couch. She watched Dolce leave.

"Your little girlfriend doesn't live with you?" Raven asked as soon as Ethic walked back into the room. She was unable to contain her jealousy.

Ethic smirked. "Retract your claws, ma. Because of that slick mouth of yours I'm going to have to spend a small fortune to get back in her good graces. She's good people. She helps take care of my little girl when I have business to attend to."

"Your little girl?" Raven exclaimed in surprise. "You have a daughter?"

Ethic nodded. "Come on," he said as he led the way down the hall. He took Morgan to a guest room and she immediately allowed her sleepiness to take her away to her dreams. Raven kissed her forehead, and she and Ethic walked out of the room.

He stopped in front of a closed door. There were pink wooden letters attached to the door that spelled out "Bella." He opened the door and invited Raven inside. A chocolate little girl lay peacefully in her bed, and Raven smiled when she saw how much she resembled Ethic.

"How old is she?" Raven whispered.

"Seven," Ethic replied.

"She's beautiful," Raven complimented as she watched Ethic lean over the bed and kiss her.

"Thank you," he responded as they exited the room.

Raven followed him back into the kitchen and watched as he began to pull out food to cook.

"Where is her mother?" Raven asked.

"Melanie died. I met her when she was dating this dude named Guy. He used to beat her up, degrade her," Ethic said. "When I was a little nigga moving ounces I met her. I used to cop my weight from Guy. One day he beat her up when we were all out at a night club. He asked me to take her home."

"And you stole his girl," Raven added with a smile.

Ethic laughed as he began to prepare a meal and nodded his head. "I wouldn't say that. More like borrowing his chick. I was only sixteen. Guy was older than me. He was in his twenties. I was a young'un in the game. He was already a boss. I couldn't compete with his pockets. I could only give her me, you know?"

"So how did she die?"

"I got her pregnant and all of a sudden I wasn't enough for her. She got scared because I wasn't established. We were in love but we were living poor out of a room where I paid rent weekly. She wanted to live lavish, and she wasn't patient enough to wait for me to come into my own. So she went back to dude. Right after she gave birth to my baby girl, they got into a fight . . . Shit went bad and he killed her," Ethic revealed, a distant look of agony taking over his face.

"What happened to Guy?" Raven asked.

"I killed him. I took all the bricks out of his house and I took my daughter," Ethic stated bluntly, without remorse.

"I'm so sorry," Raven said.

"It was a long time ago. I had left all that behind until I met you. Melanie's story sounds familiar, don't it?" he asked.

Raven nodded, knowing that she had been going down the same path as the mother of his child had. "Is that why you were never interested in me? Because I remind you of her?" Raven asked.

Ethic pondered the question for a long time as he continued to move around the kitchen like a professional chef. "You are different then she was. You were smart enough to leave," he said.

Hearing Ethic's story took some of the mystery away from him. He had always been such a big puzzle to Raven, but now that she knew what he had come from, she understood how he ticked. The five years that had gone by had given her time to experience life. She had matured and so had he. Now she knew why he acted the way he did, why it was so hard to get him to open up. She knew that the worry lines around his eyes had come from the heartache of losing his child's mother. She understood that he was so focused because he had to raise his daughter alone.

"So why don't you have Dolce living here with you? To help you take care of Bella?" she asked. She felt like she was interrogating him, but she was eager to learn all there was to know about him. She had never had such an honest discussion with Ethic before. In the past, he had never seen her as worthy enough to even hold a decent conversation with, and now that he was spilling so many details of his life, she was intrigued and eager for him to open up to her. She didn't want to miss one thing that he said. He was such a mysterious man, and she wanted to learn all there was to know about him. She felt special just from him giving her access to his personal life.

"Set the table," he said. He told her what to do, not in a demeaning way, but in a way that a man was supposed to, with authority and kindness all in the same breath. Raven hopped up without thought. She went through his cabinets until she located the dishes.

"Don't avoid the question," she teased. "Why won't you let Dolce stay the night?"

"Because she doesn't need to get used to staying here. She is not the type of person I want raising my little girl. Bella is the only lady in my life. She's selfish with my heart and I don't have time to deal with a woman who wants to compete with my daughter. Women aren't built like they used to be. They see a child as a threat. I will never put Bella in a situation where she feels like my attention is somewhere else," Ethic explained.

"So Dolce's good enough to fuck, but not to be around your daughter," Raven concluded bluntly.

Ethic laughed and shook his head. "You still got that foul mouth on you," he commented with a smile. "We spend time together when I'm free, but no, she is not good enough to raise my daughter. Her mother is not here, but if I'm going to replace her, I owe it to her to at least find Bella someone who can compare. My standards have to be high for the sake of my daughter."

Raven looked at Ethic in amazement. He was only twenty-seven, but he had the wisdom of a man twice his age. She smiled in admiration. He put his child first and no one above her. He possessed qualities that would endear any woman to him. She averted his gaze so that he would not see how taken aback she was by him.

"What?" he asked.

She shrugged and smiled. "Nothing. I just respect how you raise your daughter. It reminds me of my daddy," she admitted as she fanned her eyes with both hands to avoid becoming emotional.

"He was a great man. He loved you and Morgan as much as I love my daughter," Ethic said. "That's why when I heard that your mother had passed, I felt responsible for making sure you and your sister were straight."

"What makes you so loyal to my father? If he worked for you, why do you feel like it's your duty to keep his loose ends tied?" Raven asked seriously. She could not understand Ethic. He seemed to be so perfect. She had never met a man with as much character as he possessed. He was absolutely marvelous and admirable. A true gentleman in every sense of the word.

"I have a daughter, and if something happened to me I would want the niggas I fucked with to look out for her. Loyalty transcends life and death. Just because your father is not here does not mean that I don't still admire him. And, trust me, just because he copped his work from me doesn't mean he was beneath me. I looked up to him. He had a lot of years in this game and had a lot of wisdom to share," Ethic stated.

Hearing him speak so respectfully about her father weakened her, and Raven had to turn away again. She walked back over to the cabinet to grab two wine glasses, and she broke down. She felt responsible for everything that had led her to this point. If she had never invited Mizan into her heart, then her father would have never died and her mother would not have gone to jail. Mizan set off a sequence of events that had left her deserted. She gripped the countertop and tried to gain composure over herself, but the tears would not stop. Ethic turned to her and stepped close.

"This is all my fault," she sobbed into his chest. "I was so stupid."

Ethic rubbed her back soothingly. "Let it out, ma. I knew you were going to crack sooner or later."

She cried harder than she ever had in her entire life and Ethic never moved from her side. When she finally stopped, her face was flushed from embarrassment.

"It's okay," Ethic assured. "You needed that. You've been through a lot."

Her eyes were red as she excused herself to go to the bathroom. When she looked in the mirror she realized she looked a hot mess. "Great," she mumbled as she touched her blackened eye. "I look like shit."

She bent over the sink to splash water on her face. When she stood back up, she saw Ethic behind her and she jumped in fear. She didn't like to have men behind her. Mizan had snuck up behind her plenty of times and attacked her when she was unable to fight back. She wanted to be able to see her opposition coming at all times, and with Ethic looming over her, she immediately tensed up.

"Oh my God . . . you scared the shit out of me. Don't do that! Don't sneak up on me," she exclaimed in exasperation as she put her hand near her breast, inhaling deeply. She suddenly felt as if she couldn't breathe as the fear of Mizan coming after her settled into her shaken bones. She closed her eyes, but quickly popped them back open when she saw Mizan behind her lids. The more she thought about what he would do if he found her, the harder it was to breathe. She began to hyperventilate as she leaned over the sink.

"I can't breathe, Ethic. What if he comes after me. He's going to kill me," she whispered as she reached out and gripped his wrist. Her hand was so ice cold that she caused goose bumps to rise on Ethic's forearm. He grew angry as he finally realized why Raven had not called him to come to her aid. She was deathly afraid of Mizan. He had her head so twisted and detached that the only way she knew to survive was to do as Mizan said.

"Relax, ma. No one is going to hurt you here," he said genuinely, the tone of his voice assuring her of her safety. He stood behind her, rubbing her back and massaging her shoulders tenderly, caringly.

"I've been through a lot, Ethic. He hurt me. Every day he found a new way to break my spirit. Fear has been all I've known for so long. Just please don't sneak up on me. My mind knows you are nothing like him, but I have to get used to being treated like a human being again. You have to handle me with kid gloves, otherwise, I might break. It's been so long since a man has been genuine with me that I don't remember what it feels like. I haven't had that since my father," she said.

"I got you," he said. No other words needed to be spoken for Raven to believe him. He took her hand and led her back out to the dining room, where he had grilled chicken, vegetables, and wine set up on the table.

As they ate dinner they talked, and this time Ethic wasn't short or rude to her, but open and honest. She loved every minute of it, but she could not help but sneak peeks at his scarred face. Everything else about him was the same. The way he walked and talked were exactly as she remembered, but his face did not match her perfect memory of him. As her eyes roamed his face she felt tears building in her eyes. Inadvertently, she had done this to him. Ethic noticed her watching.

"You can look. I won't get offended," Ethic said.

Raven dropped her eyes to her plate and shook her head in shame. "I'm sorry, Ethic. That was rude. I don't mean to stare. You just . . . Your face, it's . . ."

Ethic put down his wine glass and sat back in his chair. "Come here," he said. She placed her dinner napkin on the table and walked toward him. She was slightly tipsy. They both were on the second bottle of wine and she could feel herself becoming intoxicated. The antsy feeling that Ethic usually gave her was masked by the liquid courage, making her comfortable around him, and him more trusting of her.

He pulled her down onto his lap and took her hands in his. A shiver went up her spine as she felt his hands on hers. It felt reassuring, and she instantly felt a sense of security that had been lacking in her life. Nervous butterflies filled her stomach. She had never felt so close to Ethic, and she hoped that the moment could last forever, but time doesn't stand still for anyone. When Ethic spoke she came back down to reality.

"Go ahead," he said as he placed her hands on his face. "Touch me. Look at me. Do whatever you have to do to get used to it. I know how I look now, Raven. This is who I am, but when I talk to you I don't want you to feel uncomfortable. I want you to be able to look me in the eyes. So go ahead."

Raven's hands roamed his face tenderly. Her left hand touched nothing but baby soft skin, while her right one felt rough, sandpaper, like scars. He stared her in the eyes to see what her reaction would be. He knew Raven well and thought that her shallow attraction to him was nothing more than a childhood crush that had followed her into adulthood. He was expecting her to be disgusted by his appearance. He suspected that her infatuation with him was purely superficial, but as they stared unflinchingly at one another, all he saw was sincerity in her eyes. He kept waiting for her emotions to change to contempt, but to his surprise they never strayed. She was stuck and lost in his stare. All that dwelled in her eyes was the love she had always harbored for him. Her eyes turned as dark as onyx as a look of sadness crossed her face.

"You're perfect," she whispered in awe.

Ethic felt the emotion pouring from her. He could not deny that she had grown up beautifully as he placed his hand on her chest. He could feel her apprehensive heart pounding furiously as she breathed in and out. His hand traveled up her neck as he pulled her face to his. He kissed the spots on her face that were battered, and kissed away each tear that fell gracefully from her eyes.

She had wanted this moment to happen for so long. She had dreamt of it and imagined it in her mind so many times, but nothing compared to the real thing. To have Ethic, the man she had loved from the first moment she saw him, kissing her softly, was simply amazing. It was rare like a full moon, a beautiful sunset, and she cherished it like an exquisite diamond. The memory that they were making in this moment was more valuable to her than gold. *This is what love is supposed to feel like,* she thought as she realized she had never in her life felt that way. She waited in anticipation for his lips to cover hers as her love box thumped wildly, soaking her satin panties. She wanted to grind on him. She wanted him to make love to her on his living room floor. At humanity's most complex level she loved him, and at its simplest level she wanted him to ravage her. She closed her eyes and waited for him to take it to the next step, but when she felt his body tense up she knew that their moment had passed. The look of uncertainty in his eyes spoke volumes.

He doesn't trust me, Raven thought desolately.

"Wait, this isn't right, ma. You're my man's daughter. This can't happen," he whispered as he rested his forehead against hers.

"Is this really about my father, Ethic? Or is it about something else?" she asked with hurt feelings.

"It don't matter what it's about, ma. This just can't happen," he stated firmly.

"It can happen, Ethic. You just won't let it," she responded with disappointment as she climbed out of his lap.

Ethic watched her walk out of the room and he rubbed his Caesar haircut in frustration. *Fuck,* he swore to himself, beating himself up for allowing himself to lead Raven on. He knew that he had messed up, because although having her in his arms had felt so right, he wasn't sure about her yet. Raven's past decisions had caused a lot of good people to be hurt and he could not put himself or his daughter at risk, not for her or anyone else. He looked at the bottle of Chardonnay that they had been sipping and poured himself another glass, then retired to his room. Frustrated and full of uncertainty, he forced himself to walk past the guest room that Raven was staying in. *Get your head together. That's not something you need in your life right now. First thing in the morning, I need to find her a crib. I don't want to get used to having her around. She has been the downfall of plenty of men . . . I can't let her be the downfall of me.*

The next morning Raven lay in bed for hours staring at the ceiling. She could hear Ethic, Morgan, and Bella in the living room, but she refused to show her face. She was mortified that Ethic had turned her down once again. *How could I have been so stupid?* she asked herself. *He has never wanted to fuck with me before. So why would I expect him to now?* She felt foolish for allowing Ethic to shut her down the way he had. He had humiliated her, and she could not run away or shut him out as she had done in the past because she needed him. She was stuck in an unfamiliar city with him and he was all she had. *I should have stayed my ass in Flint,* she thought stubbornly.

The door cracked open and she saw Ethic's little girl peek into the room. Pretty in lilac and plum, she bounced happily into the room. "Are you Raven?" she asked sweetly.

"Yes, I'm Raven," she replied. "And who might you be?"

"Bella."

"It's nice to meet you Bella," Raven stated.

"My daddy told me to tell you to quit hiding out in here." She put her hands over her mouth and with big eyes she whispered, "He really wants you to do my hair because he doesn't know what he's doing." She pointed to the curly mess on top of her head.

"I see that. He definitely does not know what he is doing," she replied with a bright smile and vibrant laugh. She pulled back the covers. "Tell your daddy I will be out when I'm dressed," she said. "Then I'll hook you up."

"Thank you, Raven!" Bella said as she raced out of the room.

An hour later, Raven walked into the living room. The BCBG maxi dress she wore and the spiral curls all over her head made her look angelic. She had covered her bruises with M•A•C foundation and highlighted her face with Bronzer to make her skin shine radiantly, as if she had been personally kissed by the sun.

"Ohhh! I want my hair like yours," Bella said excitedly. "You're so pretty. I want to look just like you when I grow up."

"Oh-no. Bella, you're gorgeous just the way you are. You don't need to look like me to be a princess. You already are one," she said. She purposely walked past Ethic without speaking.

"Raven, can we talk?" he asked.

"No," she replied simply as she sat on the couch with Morgan and Bella. It was evident to her that the two girls had become fast friends.

"How did you sleep?" Raven signed to Morgan as she completely ignored Ethic. She could feel him staring a hole through her, but she refused to look his way.

"Good," Morgan signed back as she pulled out barrettes and bows for her own hair. "I like it here."

Raven put spiral curls in both girls' hair. She talked and interacted with Bella with such ease that Ethic was dumbfounded. Bella had never taken to anyone as quickly as she had taken to Raven. As he sat back and watched them laugh, his heart swelled with emotion. His daughter did not have a motherly figure in her life. He desperately wanted that for her, but he knew that Raven could not be it. He erased all thoughts of keeping her in his life and cleared his throat.

"We better get going. I made an appointment with a Realtor. We're going to look at condos for you and Morgan today," he said. "After we're done we'll go to the dealership to get you a whip."

Raven nodded and rallied up the girls. Bella clung to Raven's side. Raven was flattered by the little girl's fascination with her. They all climbed into Ethic's Escalade and for the first time since she had left home, Raven felt like she had a family.

Raven rode in complete silence and stared out the passenger window to avoid looking at Ethic. It was obvious that the vibes from the previous night were long gone. Their interaction had gone from natural to unnatural in mere hours, and now an awkward fog filled Ethic's vehicle as he drove through the city.

Ethic wanted to say something to Raven, but he was at a loss for words. For some reason he felt himself growing interested in her. As he glanced over at her in his passenger seat, he admired her features. There was something about the way the light hit her face that made her irresistible. He had never noticed her before, but now he could not help but acknowledge her. Maybe it was her maturity, or her wisdom, or maybe it was because she needed him that had him thinking differently about her. He knew his emotions were reckless, which was why he simply wanted to find Raven and Morgan a place to stay as quickly as possible. If she wasn't around, he could go back to doing him without worry of falling into her trap. He needed her out of sight and out of mind. Raven came with too much baggage. He had rescued her from Flint now it was up to her to get the rest of her life in order.

They met the Realtor at a downtown condominium and Raven got out of the car. She smiled as she looked up at the two-story row of condos that rested in the middle of the city. At first she had thought Ethic would put her in a low-budget apartment, but she was pleased that he planned on maintaining a comfortable lifestyle for her.

"Ms. Donnelly, thank you for taking time out of your schedule to show me a few places today." Ethic walked around his truck and shook the older black woman's hand.

"Not a problem, Ethic. Anything for you, darling." She spoke with sophistication and arrogance. Raven could tell that she was old money just by the ivory two-piece Versace suit she wore. "You must be Raven."

"I am," Raven said as she shook her hand.

"Well, Raven, I have a fabulous place to show you!" Ms. Donnelly exclaimed.

"Lead the way," Raven said with excitement as they followed her.

All it took was for Raven to step inside of the 2,500-square foot space for her to know that she was home. The fully furnished, loft-style condo was beautiful with its red, black, and white modern décor. It seemed to be pulled straight out of the pages of *Better Homes and Gardens*.

"I love it," Raven whispered. "I want it." Bella and Morgan went racing upstairs to look at the master bedroom.

"Are you sure, ma? You don't want to look at other places?" Ethic asked.

Raven shook her head. "No, this is so me. I can see Morgan and me being comfortable here."

"So shall we draw up an offer?" the Realtor asked. She set down her briefcase. "They are asking $250,000 for this place."

Ethic shook his head and replied, "Tell them I will pay $175,000 cash and that I'm ready to purchase. We want the keys today."

"That's significantly lower than the asking price . . . ."

"Make it happen," he said calmly. "The less I pay for this place, the bigger your thank-you commission will be." He winked charmingly at the old woman. The realtor did not know how she was going to pull it off, but she could not tell her best client no. She had to make it happen and within the hour she was handing Ethic the key and the deed.

Raven was elated as she stood back at stared at her new home. She could not believe that it was all hers. She had never had a spot of her own. She had always depended on other people to put a roof over her head. She was tired of leaning on others, especially on men who did not truly want her. All these years she had been searching for independence, but she had hindered herself by allowing men to take control over her life. First Mizan, now Ethic . . . and although Ethic's intentions were good, she still *needed* him to survive. After she had weathered the storm, she now knew that the only person she could truly depend on was herself.

I have to learn to stand on my own two feet, she thought. As the girls ran around the house playing and going in and out of every room, Raven stood in the middle of the living room thinking of how she had to get her life in order. She had escaped the belly of the beast when she had left Mizan, and now she had to be a new woman. She had to be strong and she had to build a new life for herself in Kansas City.

Ethic remained quiet as he watched Raven soak in her new surroundings. He wanted to do all that he could to make sure that she was comfortable. He never wanted her to contemplate going back to Mizan. Even though Ethic did not want her, he did not want Mizan to have her either. Mizan did not deserve her. He was the one who had corrupted her and Ethic would do all that was in his power to make sure she never went back.

"You ready to go pick out your whip?" he asked. "This place is yours. You don't have to keep looking at it, it'll be here when you get back."

"No, you've done enough, Ethic. You don't have to buy me a car. I'm tired of being given things. Mizan gave me all of this and more, but in the end there was a price to pay. I don't know what you want from me, but I don't want to feel like I'm indebted to you," Raven explained.

"I would never make you feel like you owe me anything, Raven. I'm doing this for you because I want to. I don't expect anything in return," Ethic stated truthfully.

"And what happens when you stop wanting to, or when Little Miss Dolce decides that you can't do for me any-more?" Raven questioned. "My sister and I are out on our asses with nothing? I got to make a change. I can't put myself right back in the same position, because in the end the only person who I can really count on is me. The only person that Morgan can count on is me."

Ethic turned and began to walk toward the door. His hands were tucked in the pants of his casual black Ferragamo slacks. "Bella, Morgan, let's go!" he called out. The girls raced into the room and Ethic opened the door for them to go outside.

"I hear all that Miss Independent stuff you talking and I respect it, but a car is being purchased today. Now, you can come and pick it out, or I can do it for you, but either way there will be one sitting in your driveway tomorrow morning."

"Ethic. . . ." Raven protested.

"Raven," he interrupted firmly. "Let's go."

Raven cut her eyes and stalked over to him, her long maxi dress swaying sexily with the direction of her hips. Before she passed him, he grabbed her arm.

"I'm not Mizan. I would never hurt you and I would never put you and Morgan out," he whispered.

Raven raised her eyebrows and asked, "Oh, really? Well, tell me, Ethic, whose name did you put on the papers to this condo?"

Ethic did not respond.

"I thought so," Raven replied. "It doesn't matter if you let me live here for free. It doesn't belong to me and at any moment I can be put out. I know you are not Mizan, but you're still a man and men like to control. I'm tired of being controlled. And as far as you not hurting me . . . ." She scoffed and shook her head before she looked him dead in the eye. "You did that a long time ago when you crushed my heart as a little girl. I was never good enough for you, and last night you reminded me of that."

By the time they were done shopping, Ethic had not only purchased Raven a new car, but had fully refurbished her and Morgan's closet. He filled their refrigerator with food and then dropped them back off at the condo. Morgan and Bella were so exhausted that they had fallen asleep in the backseat of Ethic's truck.

Conversation between Raven and Ethic had been nonexistent the entire day. They were both holding back for their own reasons. Raven was too afraid to be embarrassed and look stupid. She was tired of being rejected by Ethic, so to save face she only spoke to him if he directly asked her a question.

Ethic, on the other hand, felt his growing attraction to Raven, but he did not trust her. He was fighting with himself to keep things appropriate between them, but the more time he spent around her, the more he wanted to make her his. He knew that she was vulnerable from her abusive relationship, and he was also well aware of her questionable loyalties. This is what held him back from pursuing her. His feelings for Raven surprised him, because before he had seen her at her mother's funeral he had barely noticed her. He had viewed her as a spoiled and ungrateful diva who would do anything to get what she wanted. Now he wasn't sure what he thought of her, but he knew that the fast teenage girl had transformed into a beautiful woman, and if he could groom her the way he wanted to, she would be perfect for him.

"Someone from the dealership will drop the car off tomorrow morning," Ethic said. He got out of the car and picked Morgan up. Her sleepy head draped over his shoulder as he followed Raven into the house. He put her down in her bedroom and then came back out to find Raven sitting on the couch.

"Thank you," Raven said sincerely. "I'm going to pay you back for everything that you're doing," she insisted.

Ethic would never accept it, but to make her feel better about taking the handout he nodded. "Call me if you need anything."

"I will," she said as she watched him head for the door. As he walked out, Raven followed him.

He looked at his car to make sure that Bella was still sleeping inside and then turned back to face Raven. "You good? Everything a'ight?" he asked.

Raven rubbed her bare arms and nodded with a weak smile. "I'm fine. It just feels weird. I have never had a place of my own. I just have to get used to it."

"I'll be by to check on you tomorrow," Ethic said.

"No, don't start coming over here every day. I'm not your girl so you don't have to act like this is more than what it is. I appreciate you getting me out of Flint and away from Mizan. I'll see you around," she said before closing the door in his face.

She leaned back against the door and closed her eyes as she thought about the drastic decision she had made by fleeing her hometown. Now that she was on her own she had to learn how to do everything for herself. She no longer had to report to anyone or be afraid to make decisions on her own. She set the deadbolt on the door and walked into her house. Her cell phone vibrated in her pocket and she pulled it out quickly, expecting to see Ethic's name on her caller ID, but instead UNKNOWN appeared.

"Hello?" she answered.

"That was some real slick shit you pulled, Rae. That's fucked up, but don't worry because I'ma make sure I see you, bitch," Mizan threatened.

Raven's heartbeat sped up and the trance he had over her instantly kicked back in. Her breathing became labored and she felt as if she would throw up. *Don't let him do this to you, Raven,* she coached. *He's locked up. He can't hurt you from behind bars. He doesn't even know where you are.*

As she listened to Mizan threaten and berate her through the phone, her fear of him slowly left her body.

"You grimy bitch. On everything I love, I'ma see you. I'm gon' find you and when I do, I'm going to smack fire from your stupid ass."

"Mizan, let me explain," she began, but was silenced quickly by Mizan's tirade.

"Fuck you, bitch, it ain't shit to explain. There were only four people in the world that knew about that meeting, and since you the only one left standing, that tells me all I need to know. You set me up! Fuck you," Mizan screamed at her.

"Fuck me?" Raven replied as she began to laugh in disbelief. "No, fuck you, nigga!" she shot back. "Yeah, I called the police and told them what was about to go down. You damn right I set you up. You've been setting me up from the beginning and payback is a bitch! You can stop with all your little threats and temper tantrums because you can't do shit to me from where you going. You bitch-ass nigga. Fight on them niggas in prison, since you like to hit on mu'fuckas. See what it feels like to hit someone who is just as big as you! Or do you only know how to hit on women?"

"Bitch, you must've lost your fucking mind," Mizan spewed. She could hear him foaming at the mouth in rage.

"No, you lost your mind when you started thinking I was your punching bag! I got your bitch . . . You know what, Mizan? Don't call my phone anymore because we're done. You need to hope you don't drop the soap!" Raven slammed her cell phone shut and held it tightly in her hand as adrenaline pumped through her. She had never stood up for herself when it came to Mizan and when she played back the conversation in her head, she laughed loudly as she imagined the look on his face. She was so amped that she did not want the feeling to leave. She loved the fact that she had the upper hand. Finally,

Mizan knew what it felt like to be played by the person he trusted most.

"Yo', dial that bitch back!" Mizan yelled to Rich when they heard Raven hang up the phone. Mizan's ego was crushed because Rich had placed the three-way call to Raven on Mizan's behalf. His boy had heard all of the disrespect that Raven had dished out.

When Rich tried to call Raven back, the call was sent to voicemail. "She gave me the 'fuck you' button," Rich said, stating the obvious.

Mizan was so heated that a light sweat began to break out on his forehead. "Find out where that bitch is and drag her ass back home. And get my lawyer down here ASAP! I don't give a fuck what I got to do to get out of here, just make it happen. Me and Raven got some unfinished business to settle, n'ah mean?"

"I got you, fam. I'm on it," Rich responded.

Mizan slammed the phone down so hard that he almost tore it from the wall. "Bitch wanna get cute," he mumbled to himself as he made his way back to his tier. He did not know where Raven's sudden backbone had come from, but he was more determined than ever to break her back down. "I got you, bitch. As soon as I'm out of here, I'ma see you," he said to himself as he imagined all of the tortuous things he was going to do when he finally caught up to her.

Chapter Sixteen

Determined to make it on her own without any further help from Ethic, the first thing Raven did was take her GED test so that she could enroll in the local community college. She had always regretted dropping out of school. She had become so wrapped up in Mizan as a kid that her entire world had revolved around him, but now she was all grown up and she wanted to make a better life for herself. Without their parents, all she and Morgan had were each other. She wanted to be a woman her little sister could look up to. *I never want her to make the same mistakes that I did. Trusting the wrong man ruined my life,* Raven thought.

As she sat in class she looked around at the other students and immediately felt a level of discomfort. She stuck out like a sore thumb. She felt inferior to the eager students around her. Her designer clothes and bourgeois attitude were a far cry from her fellow classmates. She felt like an airhead compared to everyone around her; it was obvious that she did not belong. She was out of her element, but she was committed to becoming a better Raven and no matter how hard it got she would stick with it until she finished. By enrolling Morgan in school, her days were free. She could take her classes and still be home by the time Morgan's school bus dropped her off.

She had not heard from Mizan since their phone altercation and she hoped that he would not try to contact her again. She was moving on, and she hoped that he would do the same. There were many occasions when Ethic crossed her mind, but he had hurt her pride one too many times for her to even entertain the thought of them ever being together. Although she knew he would never put his hands on her, he had a way of hurting her more than Mizan ever could. The physical pain from Mizan she could endure, it was the emotional pain of not being acceptable in Ethic's eyes that was too much for her. He just did not know that if he would have chosen her when she was seventeen, she would have never given Mizan the time of day. Ethic was the prince she had dreamt about when she was a little girl. In a perfect world he would have been her man, but in reality he wasn't even a friend. He was someone who felt he owed her father something. Nothing more, nothing less, and the two of them together just did not make sense. He knew too much about her and she knew too little about him. Even the loneliness of a new environment did not force her to pick up the phone to call him. She was doing just fine without his help. She was paying for her own schooling through the help of the student loan program, and with the reimbursement package that she had signed up for she was able to send Ethic money every month for rent. It was not much, and he had not asked for it, but she felt that she needed to pay her own way.

After class, as Raven made her way to her car, one of the guys in her class stopped her.

"Yo', Raven, right?" he greeted her with a smile. She recognized him from one of her classes. His schoolboy image didn't appeal to her. She was used to hood fellas with hood swaggers and the guy in front of her was the exact opposite.

"Yeah?" she responded shortly.

"I just wanted to introduce myself. I'm Jacob. We're in the same—"

"Philosophy class," Raven finished for him. "I know. Did you want something?" she asked.

The dude smiled and rubbed his clean-shaven face. "Yeah, I wanted to see if you wanted to get together sometime. I know you're not from around here so I thought I could take you to dinner, show you the town. . . ."

"I can't. I'm not really into dating right now. I'm just trying to stay focused and do me," she said.

"Okay, well, the invitation stands for whenever you want to take me up on it," he insisted.

She laughed at his persistence, and nodded. "Nice meeting you, Jacob," she replied as he opened her car door for her. She got inside and turned her key, but the ignition stalled. She frowned in confusion until she looked up and saw that her interior light had been on all day. "Fuck," she whispered as she rolled her eyes.

"Do you need a ride?" he asked, quickly jumping on the opportunity to assist her.

She hesitated and thought of calling AAA, but she knew that she needed to be home when Morgan arrived. *Triple-A is gon' take forever to get here,* she thought. *I don't even know this nigga though.* She debated the pros and cons in her head. Jacob could see the uncertainty on her face and he leaned down to look through her window.

"I'm not gon' kill you, ma. Let me take you home," he said.

"Straight home," she stated seriously with a pointed finger in his face.

He nodded and opened the door for her as she stepped out of the car.

While Raven kept herself occupied with school to avoid Ethic, he could not find enough to do to keep her off of his mind. Surprisingly, he found himself wondering about her and worrying about her well-being even though he knew it wasn't his place. It had been a full month since he had set her up in the condo and she had not called him since. Even when Ethic was making moves in the street he could not stop thinking about her, and when he saw Dolce he found himself wishing that it was Raven on his arm instead. When she was chasing him he had not been interested, but now that he was open to the possibility of getting to know her, she had shut him out. It seemed that she did not want anything to do with him. After becoming acquainted with the grown-ass woman Raven had become, she had more than his attention; but because of her past he forced himself to keep his life in perspective. He knew that if he ever invited Raven into his life, trouble would soon follow. She was disloyal, whether she meant to be or not. Like a black widow, she was poisonous, and Ethic could not afford to be bitten, which was why he did not make an effort to reach out to Raven. He respected her for trying to put her life back on track and if he did not have a daughter he would probably have been willing to take the risk of pursuing Raven. However, his life was not his own to live. He breathed for Bella and he would do anything to keep her secure. Although Raven and Ethic's thoughts brought them together many times in the course of a day, their pride, mixed with the cold sting of reality, kept them apart.

Ethic had not had a relationship with a woman he cherished since the death of his child's mother. Most of the chicks he met only wanted him because of his status in the streets, including Dolce. It was no secret that he ran the most lucrative and notorious drug empire in the city. He was smart, and had a chain of funeral homes as front businesses to avert attention from the police. After the fire had ruined his face, he could tell that his money was the only thing that attracted most women, and he steered clear of gold diggers. Raven had proved completely different, however, when he had looked into her eyes. She was the one woman in quite some time who had actually looked at him and saw him for who he really was. He attributed Raven's infatuation to the Ethic she used to know, but he had changed with the times. He was pushing thirty and looking to go completely legit. He had survived in a game where many had fallen and he did not need someone like Raven coming into his life creating chaos. *She's no good,* he thought. Ethic was jarred out of his thoughts by a knock at the door. He answered it, and a mailman stood in front of him with a certified letter. Ethic signed for the letter and opened it to find a check from Raven.

She's on that bullshit with this shit? he thought, slighted. He understood what she was trying to do, but by being self-sufficient, she was insulting him. He picked up the keys to his Dodge Challenger and headed out the door.

"Thank you so much. I really appreciate this," Raven said as she hopped out of Jacob's car. It was a far cry from the luxury vehicles she was used to riding in, but for some reason she welcomed the change. Jacob was not a thug or a hustler. He was just a regular guy trying to make something of himself. She could respect that, because even though he wasn't the type to make it rain in clubs and switch whips like he did underwear, she recognized that he would eventually become the type to have IRA accounts and life insurance. He was the smart choice.

"So have I earned the right to call you?" he asked as he stepped out and walked her to the entrance of her condo.

"Yeah, you can call me," she gave in as she pulled out a pen and wrote her number on his hand.

"Cool. So what I got to do to get you to say yes to dinner?" he asked.

Before she could fix her lips to respond, she saw Ethic's car pull into the driveway. Ethic exited the car clad in jeans and a Ralph Lauren sweater. The Piguet on his wrist shined effortlessly as the sun played hide-and-seek in the diamonds.

"E—Ethic, what are you doing here?" Raven asked, stuttering. A guilty feeling overcame her, as if she had just been caught cheating.

Ethic didn't respond. Instead his focus was on Jacob. Like a territorial lion he stared him down intensely until Raven cleared her throat.

"Umm, Ethic, this is—"

"We need to talk," Ethic interrupted, skipping the introductions. "I'll be waiting in the house while you tell your company bye."

Raven's face turned beet red. She had never seen Ethic be so rude. She turned to Jacob.

"I'm so sorry," she apologized. "Thank you for the ride. I will see you tomorrow in class, okay?"

"Yeah, a'ight. I'll see you around," he stated with a bit of salt in his tone.

Raven checked her watch and saw that she still had an hour and a half before Morgan made it home from school. *I'ma need every minute because I'm about to check Ethic's ass. Who the fuck do he think he is?* She stormed into the house to see Ethic sitting calmly on her couch as if he was the king of her castle, his leg propped up on her coffee table.

"What was that all about?" she asked in irritation. She stormed over to him and knocked his foot off of her table, she put her hand on her hip, awaiting a response.

"Who is he?" Ethic questioned as he put his feet back up. He was surprised at the amount of jealousy he felt and he could not help but demand answers. Raven was who he wanted, but could not allow himself to have. She was like a guilty pleasure, and although he refused to indulge in her, he was not going to sit back and allow another man to do it instead.

"Why?" she asked. "You need to get yourself some business and keep your fucking feet off my table." She was beyond irritated as she folded her arms across her chest and glared at him. "Coming around here asking questions."

"Don't play games with me, Raven. Who is that nigga that you had all in my crib?" Ethic asked. He never raised his voice at her. He did not need to intimidate Raven in order to get a response from her. She heard the seriousness of his tone.

"Oh, so now it's your crib?" she questioned as her neck snaked in anger. "What happened to all that good shit you was popping the other day, Ethic, about all of this being mine?"

Ethic had to bite his inner cheek to stop himself from checking Raven as she got indignant with him. She raised her eyebrows and put one hand on her hip while she raised the other one near her ear. "Huh? I don't hear none of that shit now, Ethic. I know you *bought* this condo, but I do remember sending you checks to cover *my* rent! So as long as I'm paying to live here, I don't have to explain myself to you. I've been there and done that. I'm tired of reporting my every move to a nigga."

Ethic leaned forward on the couch and put his hands together. She was trying his patience and she knew it. She could practically see the steam coming out of his ears, but she did not care. *He has no right to tell me who I can and cannot see,* she thought stubbornly.

"Who is he?" Ethic repeated calmly. He didn't give a fuck about how much shit she talked. She was going to answer his question.

"Huh!" Raven screamed in agitation. "Just some guy from the college, damn. My car battery died. He gave me a ride home."

"School?" Ethic stated in surprise. "You enrolled in college?"

"Yeah, I took my GED and then applied to the community college. I started last week," she replied.

Ethic smirked and shook his head. He was impressed at how quickly she was piecing her life back together and he found her determination intriguing. Her strength astounded him. There was definitely more to Raven than met the eye, and he was discovering that she was not the person he had labeled her to be.

"So you mean to tell me you got a brain up there?" he asked sarcastically.

Raven smirked, rolled her eyes, and stuck up her middle finger. She was aggravated with Ethic.

"I don't appreciate how you came up over here regulating. If you think I'm never going to go out with a dude just because I'm living here, you got me fucked up," Raven stated.

"Don't bring a nigga into my house," Ethic said sternly.

"Why, Ethic?" she asked as she scrunched her brow in confusion. She walked up to him and stood between his legs as she cocked her hip to the side. Her neck began to work at full speed as she went off. "You used to get this same little funky-ass attitude back in the day when I first met Mizan. Why can't I date a guy without you looking down on me? Why does it bother you so much?"

As she screamed at him, Ethic leaned back on the couch and relaxed as he listened to her rant.

"Why is it wrong for me to want to have a man?"

"You choose a man and I might respect him. You bring home these bitch-ass niggas that go upside your head or that can't afford to buy you a meal," Ethic responded simply.

"So what, Ethic? If that's who I choose then that's on me. What, I'm supposed to live by your rules just because you purchased this place? What if I want to have company? What if I want to go on a date?" Raven leaned over him and spoke directly in his face. "What if I want to be *fucked,* Ethic?"

Before either of them knew what was happening, the tension in the room exploded as Ethic pulled her down on top of him and absorbed her rants into his mouth, kissing her passionately. Their tongues performed a delicate dance and Raven closed her eyes as she melted into his embrace.

"Hmm," she moaned as she tugged at his sweater. Every muscle on Ethic's torso was so well defined that it felt like her fingers were gracing one of Michelangelo's stunning sculptures. He picked her up effortlessly and carried her up the stairs to the master bedroom. They had both waited years to know what a kiss between them would feel like, and they took advantage of every second, never breaking their connection. All of their disguised anger was really their chemistry rising to its boiling point. Items of clothing flew all around the room as they scrambled to undress one another. Ethic took both of her breasts in his hand and pushed them together, licking her areolas into erection. He sucked on them, blew on them, and bit them gently as she moaned softly in his ear. The tent in his boxers let Raven know that she would not be disappointed. She grabbed hold of his length and stroked it slowly, then propped her leg up on the bed so that she could rub his mushroom-shaped head into the gushy entrance of her love box. She could feel his passion as the heat from his body warmed her opening. She desperately wanted him to fill her up, but he didn't even knock on her door. He pulled away as his mouth found hers. He introduced his lips to every part of her body as he traveled south. Her neatly shaven lips stared him in the face as he pulled them back to reveal her throbbing clit. It resembled a juicy oyster, and he treated it as such as he sucked it into his mouth and applied pressure to it with his full lips. "Aghh!" she screamed in pleasure as he brought her to orgasm with torpedo flicks of his wet tongue.

He wiped his mouth and sat on the edge of the bed, then pulled her down on top of him. His thick girth parted her opening and her body tried to resist his size. She gasped as she arched her back and her walls allowed him in.

For every down stroke she put on him, he matched her, as his hands gripped her voluptuous backside. The only sounds that could be heard were their labored breathing and the sounds of their juices as skin slapped skin. Fuck noises filled the room and tears involuntarily filled Raven's eyes. Sex had never felt this good. She was experiencing things that she had never felt before. Her heart felt weak as she rocked her hips to the rhythm of her headboard hitting the wall. Her head fell back in ecstasy and Ethic put his hand behind her neck, forcing her to look up at him. Tears fell down her cheeks as she rode him and stared into his eyes. She continued to work him slowly as she brought her hands up to his face. She touched his burns and kissed every scar as they kept eye contact. There was no doubt about it. This thing between them was more than just a casual fuck. Something was happening, and neither of them knew if they were prepared to handle it.

"Ethic," she whispered as she felt her pussy muscles contract around his shaft. Her mouth fell open in pure bliss as she sped up. Slow grinds turned into full winds as her body began to move like a belly dancer. She bounced down onto him hard, and with every stroke his grip on her backside grew tighter. The feeling of him vibrating inside of her told her that he was about to climax. His guttural grunts echoed off the walls until he finally exploded. He held on to her so tightly that she did not know where he ended and she began; they were one. The feeling of him spilling inside of her caused her to cum, and she closed her eyes and rode the wave as if it were the best feeling she had ever felt in her life. She collapsed onto his chest and he wrapped his arms around her. They did not jump up or try to pretend that it had not happened. For this one moment, they did not speak. He moved her hair out of her face and kissed her forehead. He noticed the rhythm of her heart matched his own. All of the things that had occurred to lead up to this moment did not matter. The death, the destruction, the disloyalty . . . all of it was erased from his mind temporarily as he held onto her tenderly, loving the way she fit perfectly in his arms. He pulled the covers over their bodies and she lay on top of him, enjoying the feeling of his hands as he rubbed her back.

Before Raven knew it, she had drifted off to sleep. It wasn't until she felt Morgan flop down on her bed that she woke up.

Morgan shook her shoulder over and over again until she was finally awake.

Raven jumped up and clutched the covers against her breasts, thinking that she and Ethic had just been busted. Her heart sank into the pit of her stomach when she realized that he was no longer lying next to her.

"Hey, Morgan," she signed with a half smile as she looked around in confusion. "Let me get dressed. I'll be right out so that you can tell me all about your day at school."

When Morgan left the room, Raven shook her head and closed her eyes. She didn't know what to think. *May-*

be he regrets it, she thought. *I should have never let this happen. What was I thinking? He doesn't want me . . . It was just sex for him.* She did not know how she would face him the next time they saw each other. She stood and walked over to her dresser to retrieve some clothes, when she noticed a manila envelope sitting on top of it. When she opened it she put her hand over her mouth in shock.

Oh my God. He put everything in my name.

Inside of the folder was the deed to the condo, the title to the car, and also papers to a bank account that Ethic had opened up for her. He had put all of the checks that she had sent him for rent into an account for Morgan and had put $50,000 in a separate account for Raven. She smiled as she closed the folder and flopped down on her bed. So many things were running through her mind that she could not think straight. Sleeping with Ethic had just complicated her life. She was not naïve enough to think that sex was the same thing as love, but it sure had felt like it. The rational side of her told her not to get her hopes up. *He's never been into you,* she told herself, but her heart was forcing something completely different. *What does all this mean? And where the hell do I go from here?*

Chapter Seventeen

As Ethic put his daughter down to bed that night, he thought of Raven. He could not believe he had slipped up and had sex with her. The last thing he wanted to do was play with her emotions. After everything she had been through, he was not trying to bring her pain, but he had to be honest with himself. He was not sure if he was ready to welcome her into his life. There was no doubt about it that he wanted to. His life was lonely. His heart too guarded. His soul unflinchingly cold. But when he had held Raven in his arms he knew that she was what was missing in both his life and in Bella's. He had always found Raven attractive. Physically her beauty was undeniable, but her air-headed mentality made her easily influenced. If the wrong person put the wrong ideas in her head, she could easily switch teams on him and lead him down the road to his own demise, the same way she had done with her father.

"I can't afford that," Ethic said aloud as he watched his daughter sleep soundly. He was proud of the fact that she could sleep comfortably under a roof he had provided for her. He couldn't let Hurricane Raven blow through their lives and destroy everything he had worked so hard to build.

Mizan sat back in the cold metal chair with a mean mug on his face. He had been locked up for over a month and his patience was on "E".

"Look, I don't give a fuck what you got to do, but I want to be up out of here like yesterday," Mizan stated. "I mean, what's up? My man dropping the paper off to you, right?" he asked the balding attorney seated across from him.

"Yes, I have received payment for your case. . . ."

Mizan hit his hand against the table, causing a loud bang to echo off the walls. He leaned across and stared his attorney down. "Then why the fuck am I still in this bitch?" he asked angrily. The shabby five o'clock shadow that had grown on his face gave him a grimy look and revealed his true nature. His attorney could barely look him in the eyes. Even he had heard the stories of Mizan's wrath and he was scared shitless. If the money weren't so good, he probably would have never taken on the infamous gangster's case.

"There is only so much that I can do," the attorney defended himself. He pushed his wire-rimmed glasses onto his face nervously. "Unless you are willing to talk then I have to be honest with you . . . this doesn't look good for you."

Mizan looked around the room and then lowered his voice. "Tell them pigs I'll tell them whatever they want to know," he stated, fulfilling the prediction that Benny Atkins had placed on him years ago. Mizan was a snake. He did not stay true to the game. Now that his back was against the wall, he was looking to snitch his way out. "I want to walk away from this. If they can guarantee me that on paper, I'll talk."

He stood up, knocking the chair over as he called for the C.O. to let him out of the room. He was itching to get out of prison. Being confined behind the steel bars and brick walls was slowly driving him insane. He had a score to settle with the woman who put him there: Raven.

There was something about a woman's betrayal that drove an incarcerated man to his breaking point. Mizan did not think of all of the bullshit he had taken Raven through or any of the moments that had provoked her to set him up. All he could think of was the look on her face as they were taking him into custody. Every day, he was stuck behind bars, his resentment toward her grew, and when he was finally able to let it out he planned on punishing her hard. Her biggest sin against him was the disrespect she had dished out to him over the phone. Raven was out of pocket and he was determined to get out of jail so that he could personally put her back in place.

Three weeks had passed since Raven's rendezvous with Ethic and she could not get him off of her mind. Although they avoided each other, Raven had been sick to her stomach wondering about him. She had picked up the phone to call him so many times, but her ego always forced her to hang up. *If he wanted to talk to you he would call,* she convinced herself. *He doesn't want you.* The attraction that she had for him was ridiculous. Her emotions for Ethic were not something that she could sweep under the rug. She wanted him in the worst way. Making love to him was simply a teaser. She desperately wanted to feel what it was like to be his lady, but in reality she knew that she was not enough. No matter how hard she tried or how much she changed, she would never be on the same level as Ethic. The throne he sat on was too high, and his expectations of her unrealistic. Despite knowing all of these things, Raven still could not stop her heart from fein'n for Ethic. Her connection to him was magnetic. Her love ran deeper than he could ever comprehend. Ethic was her father figure, her brother, her friend, her potential lover, all wrapped up in one. He had so many charming qualities that she admired and his demeanor was exactly like her father's. She had always been a daddy's girl and since she did not have one, she wanted him to fill that void. She wanted him to be that and so much more. If she could turn back the hands of time and change his perception of her, she would. The first impression that he had gotten of her was that of a selfish, self-absorbed, spoiled young woman. But time, as it always does, had changed things . . . it had changed her. She was trying to do better, but those lasting notions of her had stuck with him, and no matter what she did he would always judge her for what she had done in the past.

As she sat in her morning class, her foot bounced busily against the floor as she chewed on the tip of her pen. Ethic had her distracted, anxious, and off her square. Her focus was all off because there was no room in her head for any thought that did not revolve around him.

"Where's your head at, ma?" Jacob asked, noticing the starry look in her eyes as he slid next to her, taking the chair right beside her.

She smiled at him slightly and shook her head. "I just got a lot on my mind," she replied.

"Maybe you need to relax and have a little fun," he said as he slid a small plastic baggie filled with powder over to her. Raven immediately recognized what it was. She had been fighting the urge to get blasted ever since she had come to Kansas City. Every day she told herself that she wanted it and it took everything in her to stay away from the addictive drug, but now that the temptation was staring her in the face, her mouth began to water. She was struggling with what she should do and what she wanted to do.

"I don't get down like that," she lied as she looked around to make sure none of the other students were watching.

"Come on," he whispered as he grabbed the coke and walked out of the room.

Raven didn't move as she closed her eyes. *Don't go . . . You don't need that shit anymore. Life is better now . . . You've changed,* she tried to convince herself, but all the while her mouth was watering in anticipation of the drug. Unable to resist, she stood up and balled her fists. Her inner turmoil was unbearable and the devil on her shoulder was telling her to go for it . . . that it would make her feel good. She sat back down abruptly, causing some of her classmates to turn around and observe her weird behavior. "I'm sorry," she said as she stood again. "Excuse me, I've got to go," she said as she clumsily knocked into people, gathering her possessions. Raven followed Jacob out of the room. She could not help but go along. She was stressing and she knew that the powder in Jacob's hand would give her the relief she was craving. *One more time won't hurt anything,* she thought. She looked around as he took her hand and pulled her into the bathroom.

"No, not here," she whispered as she pulled away from him.

"Relax . . . nobody's coming in here. Just hit one line. We'll go back to your place to finish," he responded as he sat down on the toilet seat and put a book over his lap. He poured the coke onto the cover and began to separate the coke in four equal lines. Raven's eyes bulged in anticipation. She had not realized how much she had missed her high until she got on her knees and leaned over the book. All of the stress left her body as soon as the drug went up her nose. She didn't save any for Jacob. Selfishly she consumed all four lines. On her knees with her head between Jacob's legs, she smiled lazily as she looked up at him.

He began to smile mischievously. "I thought you didn't get down like that?" he asked. "Look to me like you've done this before, baby."

The cocaine was like the quick fix to all of her problems. All of a sudden Ethic's rejection did not matter, and the stresses of her everyday life melted away. She felt carefree as she closed her eyes and enjoyed the rush. Now that she had wet her tongue again, her palette yearned for more. She licked her finger, picked up the cocaine residue that remained on the book, and then put her finger in her mouth. Her tongue numbed immediately from the potency of the drug. She wanted the cocaine to numb her heart and put her life on pause. At that moment she did not care about anyone but herself. No one seemed to know her pain or acknowledge her hurt. She was the one who had been deceived, had her young heart stolen, beaten, and betrayed. *What about me?* she thought.

"You got some more?" she asked.

Jacob nodded. "I got all you need, but let's go back to your crib," he said.

Raven smiled as she stood. Her body felt shaky, but she was alert, as if she had just been thrown into a pool of cold water.

"You a'ight?" Jacob asked. Her red eyes indicated that she was blown. He knew that the good-girl visage she put on was an act, and he eagerly led her to the parking lot, thinking that their get-high session would lead to sex.

She hopped behind the wheel of her car and peeled out of the parking lot with Jacob in her passenger seat. The rush of the wind in her hair and the coke in her system made Raven feel more alive than she ever had before as she pushed the car to the limit. She didn't care that she was on a city street. The speed only intensified her thrill. She turned on her radio and lifted her hands in the air, snapping her fingers as Keyshia Cole sang a song about love.

"Wow, ma, chill out. Put your hands on the wheel," Jacob stated with laughter as he watched her groove to the song. "You wild'n."

Raven put her hands on the wheel and glanced over to Jacob. It was obvious that he was attracted to her and at the moment his attention was much needed. For years she had felt like she was not good enough. Both Ethic and Mizan had a way of shitting on her. Jacob, on the other hand, boosted her ego, and the cocaine hindered her judgment as he placed a hand on her thigh. Her nipples poked through her shirt as his hand crept up her skirt. A tear slid down her face as she thought of what she was doing. She felt cheap. She called herself stupid. She was reverting to the old Raven, who made dimwitted decisions. She was trying to mask her feelings for Ethic and push him out of her mind by indulging in the only man who was willing to give her attention. *Don't do this,* she told herself as she felt Jacob's hand slide further up her skirt until he played with the silky hairs of her womanhood. The cocaine made her clit swell in anticipation. *You're better than this,* she lectured. *You have worked so hard to get your shit together.*

She wiped the tear away and found the courage to speak up. "Don't," she whispered as she pushed his hand away.

"What you mean don't?" he asked. "You know you want to." He ignored her request and leaned over to kiss her neck.

"I'm serious," she said as she moved her head and shook him off of her neck. "Come on, Jacob, stop."

Jacob's grip on her thigh grew firm and Raven tried to pry his fingers off. He held on to her so tightly that the shape of his hand was left on her leg.

"What the fuck is wrong with you?" she asked as she wrestled him off of her while driving. Raven never even felt the car veer to the left; all she heard was the sound of car horns, but by the time she looked up it was too late. At seventy miles per hour, she crossed the center lane and collided into oncoming traffic.

Chapter Eighteen

Mizan loosened his tie as he walked out of the District Attorney's office a free man. After turning state's evidence he was a free man. He had told the police all he knew and had turned snitch on every hustler in the city he knew of; nobody was out of bounds. He figured that he was killing two birds with one stone by getting rid of the competition and negotiating his freedom. In return for the valuable information, he was given his life back. The D.A. publically dropped the charges against Mizan for lack of evidence. He would be the new hood star for beating the case, but in actuality he was a rat.

Rich waited outside the county courthouse. When Mizan emerged they slapped hands and embraced slightly.

"Welcome home, baby boy," Rich stated.

"Get me out of here, fam," Mizan replied as they sped away. As soon as Mizan made it home he made his way to the kitchen and pulled a Corona out of the refrigerator. The flashing message button on his phone was blinking furiously and he pressed play as he began to walk out of the room. He paused when he heard a woman's voice.

"Hi, I'm trying to reach Mizan Simmons. My name is Donna Herring and I am a nurse at Concentra Medical Center. A Ms. Raven Atkins has been in a car accident and we are trying to reach her loved ones. I found your information in her cell phone. She is badly hurt and we wanted to make sure that her family was informed of her condition. Please give me a call back when you receive this message. I can be reached at 816-891-0000."

Mizan smiled when the message ended. "You hear that?" he asked.

Rich nodded. "What do you want to do? You want me to take care of her?"

"Nah, I want her alive. Find out what city has the area code 816 and get to that hospital. Take one of the li'l niggas that ain't afraid to make some paper. Tell them I got a job for 'em."

"Fuck I need to take a soldier with me for? I can handle it," Rich assured him.

Mizan shook his head in protest. "I don't doubt that you can, but if Raven sees your face around her way, she'll run. Take someone with you that she doesn't know and make sure she comes back here in one piece. I want to see the look on her face when she sees that I'm out." *She thought she could get away from me. She doesn't leave unless I let her . . . and I'm not letting go until she's in the dirt.*

Beep! Beep! Beep!

The sounds of the hospital machines filled the room as Ethic sat at Raven's bedside. When Morgan's school called him and informed him that she had not been picked up after classes had ended, he knew that something was wrong. He had ordered all of his lieutenants to hit the city until they found her. When he became aware of her condition he rushed to the hospital and he had not left her side since. Red eyes and stress lines revealed his worry as he leaned over with his face buried in the palm of his hands.

"Don't you think you should go and get some rest? You've been here for three days," one of the nurses said as she injected morphine into Raven's system.

"I want to be here when she wakes up," Ethic stated. "How is she?"

"She's still in critical condition. We're doing all we can for her. She probably just needs time to heal. Her injuries are quite extensive. It's probably better that she is sleeping, because the pain would be unbearable for her at this point," the nurse revealed honestly. "Is there anyone else that we should call? Any family? We tried reaching some of the contacts in her cell phone before you showed up, but no one has called us back."

Ethic shook his head. "No, there is no one. I'm all she has," Ethic stated. He had left his daughter and Morgan with Dolce. She had been calling him day and night, but he never answered. He knew that she would urge him to come home, and he did not know how to explain why it was so important to him that he stay. All he wanted was for Raven to wake up. If anything happened to her he would never forgive himself. To know that she had been under the influence of drugs disappointed him, but he knew that none of that would have happened if he had kept her close. He had brought her to Kansas City and then tried to keep her at a distance. She was his responsibility, and as he watched her fight for her life, he realized that she was his heart, as well. He had fought his feelings for her because he felt that he could not trust her, but he was slowly beginning to think that it was he who could not be trusted. He had played with her emotions and drew her in, then closed her out without explanation. He prayed that he had the chance to make things right with her. Ethic had never feared anything a day in his life, but when he looked at all the machines Raven was connected to, he knew that his greatest fear was losing her.

Ethic felt another presence in the room and he looked up to find Jacob standing in the doorway. Ethic straightened his posture and glared in Jacob's direction. Here Raven was lay up in a hospital and Jacob had walked away from the crash with just a few scratches and stitches. Ethic also didn't appreciate the hand print that was left on her leg. Jacob had left his mark on her when he grabbed her leg and it took everything in Ethic to keep his cool.

"Did you give her the coke?" Ethic asked directly.

Jacob knew of Ethic's reputation and he was hesitant to answer. He didn't want to see Ethic. A confrontation with him would prove deadly.

Ethic smirked and shook his head. "I know she's a grown woman and she did what she wanted to do, but I don't want to see you around again. If I see you even look in her direction then things could get real bad for you, n'ah mean?" he asked.

Jacob nodded and backed out of the room while Ethic turned his attention back to Raven.

All of a sudden the monitor beside her bed went haywire and began beeping loudly, causing the nurse to rush back into the room.

"What's happening? Is she okay?" Ethic asked as the room began to fill with hospital staff.

"Her blood pressure's dropping! Her heartbeat is irregular!" Ethic heard the nurses call out.

"Yo', what's happening to her?" he asked again as he was pushed out of the room. He struggled against the tiny woman who was holding him back.

"Sir, you have to let us work," the nurse said. "I will keep you updated."

Ethic rubbed the top of his head frantically as he began to pace back and forth, looking through the tiny window on the door to her room every few seconds.

They wheeled Raven out of the room and the pit of Ethic's stomach felt hollow. He sat down in the waiting room and prayed. Before Raven's accident, he had not spoken to God in so long, and it did not feel right calling in favors from him now. But eventually every knee shall bow and every tongue shall confess, and it was Ethic's turn to turn over his earthly power. There was nothing that he could do to make Raven better. He had to put his life in God's hands. *Help that woman in there God . . . my woman. You just brought her to me. Don't take her away so soon. Don't do this to me again.* Uncertainty lingered in the air and hours passed before a resolution calmed his nerves.

When he saw the nurse wheeling Raven back into the room, he sighed in relief. He did not like this type of love. He had not felt this much pain since the death of Bella's mother, but out of nowhere Raven had opened Pandora's Box. She made him weak.

Ethic reentered the room and waited for the nurse to give him an explanation.

"Her blood pressure dipped dangerously low and we couldn't figure out why her heartbeat was irregular," the nurse stated. "We ran a couple, tests on her to find out why and we discovered that she is pregnant. We were picking up the baby's heartbeat and we have stabilized her blood pressure so that it is not a risk factor for her or the baby."

"Pregnant?" he stated in disbelief. "How far along is she?" he asked, trying to determine if the child was his or Mizan's.

"She's very early in her first trimester. Not even four weeks in yet," the nurse said. "This is the most dangerous time in a pregnancy, however. She is very lucky that she did not miscarry as a result of the car accident."

"Pregnant," he whispered as his eyes became glassy with emotion. His heart swelled as he wondered if Raven would have told him. If someone would have asked him five years ago where he and Raven would be, he would have answered, "On two different coasts." Today, however, she meant more to him than he could have ever anticipated. He moved his chair closer to the hospital bed.

Reaching over to grab her hand, he felt connected to her in a new way.

"Hmm . . . hmm."

The sound came from behind him, and he turned around to find Dolce standing in the doorway with Morgan and Bella behind her. She raised her eyebrows in disapproval. Her irritation was evident on her face.

"I need to talk to you," she said as she stalked out of the room, her high heels stabbing the floor with every angry step.

Ethic sighed as he stood and ushered the two girls out of the room.

"Daddy, is Raven okay?" Bella asked.

"She's resting, baby girl," he replied. He grabbed Bella's hand and led the way to the waiting area. He kissed the top of her head and then approached Dolce.

"What is up with you?" Dolce asked with crossed arms. "You've been here with that bitch for days like you're feeling her or something."

"Hey, watch your mouth," Ethic warned seriously. He wanted to handle the situation like an adult, but she was real close to him hurting her feelings.

"See! That's what I'm talking about! You're taking up for her like she's your girl. When she came here you told me she was just a friend, Ethic, but ever since she showed up you have been treating me differently. Just be real. Are you in love with her?" Dolce asked. She was irate. She desperately hoped that the answer was no, but the guilty look on his face said it all. "You love her?" she asked again, outraged.

"I don't know, Dolce. I have never lied to you so I won't start now," Ethic said. "Something is happening between me and Raven. I care for her."

"You care for her?" Dolce repeated dramatically.

"I do," he repeated. "I'm sorry, ma. None of this was supposed to happen. I would never purposely hurt you."

"You know what, Ethic? You're full of shit," she growled. "You got me sitting at home playing babysitter to those fucking brats while you're waiting for your little girl-friend to wake up. I've been putting in my time with you and this bitch comes along and all of sudden Dolce don't exist, huh?"

Ethic's eyes turned cold at the negative reference to his daughter, and he stepped close to her. What he had to tell her was for her ears only. "Look, ma, I'ma let that slick shit you popping slide because I realize that I'm wrong, but I want you to look at those little girls sitting over there," he stated as he took her chin in his hands and turned her head in their direction. He held her face firmly and continued, "Let that be the last time some stupid shit fly out of your mouth about them. I don't take kindly to my daughter being disrespected. Do we understand each other?" he asked.

Dolce had tears in her eyes as she snatched her chin away from him. "Yeah, we understand each other, Ethic. I'm done! I don't have to take this shit. Ain't nobody want your ugly ass anyway. You were a meal ticket, nigga. Fuck you," Dolce seethed, showing her true colors.

Ethic nodded as if everything was finally becoming clear. Unaffected by her words, he calmly said, "That's why you couldn't compete with her."

"Excuse me?" Dolce snapped.

"You wanted to know what changed when Raven came to town. I run through classless women. Fuck 'em and leave 'em then push 'em out the door with the same shit they came in with: nothing. You're nothing to me, Dolce. She's everything. You could never compete with her."

Dolce stormed off and Ethic watched her walk away. He hoped that he was making the right decision. No, he was not in love with her, but Dolce had been dependable. She was loyal, respectable, and trustworthy, or at least she had pretended to be. Raven was the exact opposite, but his heart dwelled with her, and now that he knew she was pregnant with his child, he owed it to himself to see if they could work. He walked back over to Bella and Morgan, unsure of what he was going to do with them now that Dolce was gone. Together they went back into Raven's room and sat by her side. With Bella in his lap and Morgan sitting beside him, they fell asleep as they waited for Raven to pull through.

Chapter Nineteen

Raven opened her eyes a week later. She was disoriented. She didn't know where she was and she tried to force her sight to adjust to the darkened room. She felt as if she would die from all of the pain she was going through. She could feel every throb, every ache, and every stitch on her body as she lay helplessly in the bed, but she was grateful because she knew that after what she had been through she was lucky to be alive. The only light in the room came from the rectangular opening on the doorway and she noticed Ethic's silhouette sitting to her right.

She opened her mouth to call his name. "E . . . Ethic . . . ." Her dry, raspy throat could barely choke out the word.

Ethic heard her stir and he quickly put a sleeping Bella down next to Morgan to rush to her side.

"Hey," he greeted her as he looked down at her and rubbed her long hair gently. She could hear the relief in his voice. "Welcome back."

She remembered everything that had happened. She could still hear the car horns blaring in her head. "How long have I been out?" she asked.

"A while . . . ."

"I was so stupid. I don't know what the fuck I was thinking. I just wanted to escape . . . get high and fly away. Where is Morgan?" she asked frantically. "Is she all right?"

"She's here and she's fine. She is sleeping. You can see her in the morning. Don't worry about Morgan. You just rest," he replied.

Raven held on to his hand tightly as she closed her eyes. "Are you leaving?" she asked.

"Nah, I'm not going anywhere, ma. I'ma be here whenever you need me. I promise," he stated. "Why didn't you tell me you were pregnant?" he asked.

"What?" she said in disbelief. "Pregnant?" Ethic chuckled softly because her reaction was identical to the one he had given the nurse. "Is it yours?" she asked.

"You tell me," he said seriously. "You're only a couple weeks along, so unless you've been with someone else . . . ."

Raven smacked her lips and rolled her eyes. "See that's exactly why this shit will never work. You think you know so much about me, but you don't. I'm not a ho, Ethic. I haven't had sex with anyone else in Kansas City." She shook her head as tears graced her cheeks. "Oh my God. I can't keep this baby. This was a mistake."

"Was it?" Ethic asked. "Because we both knew what could happen. I never go raw with anyone, but with you I didn't even think about it."

"And I was too caught up to ask," she whispered as she touched her stomach.

"What if I asked you to keep the baby?" Ethic asked as he placed his hand over hers. "What would you say?"

"I don't even know your real name, Ethic. Think about it? You know everything about me, but I don't know shit about you," she said.

"Ezra . . . my real name is Ezra," he informed her.

Raven was dumbfounded. She didn't even know what to say. "I've been in love with you since I was seventeen and you played me repeatedly . . . ."

Before she could finish her objection Ethic leaned over and kissed her lips gently. "I know, but when I found out

you had been hurt, my fucking world went grey, Raven.
I don't know what it means or how I came to feel that
strongly for you . . . but I'm feeling you, ma."

"You're feeling me?" she repeated sarcastically.

Ethic sighed and scratched the top of his head in frustration. "You gon' make me work for this, ain't you?"

Raven smiled. She wanted to make him kiss her toes
and jump through hoops but she knew that she would
only be fronting. She shook her head. "No," she responded with a gracious smile. "Come here."

She kissed Ethic sensually as he placed a hand on her
stomach. "You gon' keep my seed, ma?" he asked.

She nodded and wrapped her arms around his neck
tightly. She pulled back to kiss him, but he put his finger
over her lips, halting her.

"You gon' do one more thing for me?" he asked with a
slight grin.

"Anything," she repeated.

"We got to get you to the sink so you can brush your
teeth. You doing a lot of kissing with a stink mouth," he
stated jokingly. Her face flushed red in embarrassment,
but she couldn't help but to crack up in laughter. She
covered her face in mortification, but Ethic ignored her
stinky breath and kissed her over and over again. It was
so unreal, but she did not want to let go.

"Wait a minute . . . what about Dolce? I'm not for the
drama, Ethic. I don't want to have to fuck your bitch up. I
will put it on that bitch Flint style."

Ethic laughed at her frankness. "I don't think that will
be necessary, ma. She has already been given her walking
papers."

Raven gave Ethic a look that told him he better not be
playing games, and he reassured her with a kiss.

"No more drugs, ma. I can't have you around Bella if
you're going to be into that shit. I need you to take care

of her and the child that's growing inside of you. I got to have a strong woman behind me. So that when I'm down you can help build me back up, okay?"

Raven nodded and Ethic's heart swelled as he held her face in his hands. He knew that their relationship would not be perfect, but he was willing to work at it. He was going all in with Raven. He knew they had a lot to talk about, but it could wait until she was better. He sighed gratefully as he sat back down. The hard part was over. She had pulled through and opened her eyes. Now he could nurse her back to health and they could move on with their lives . . . together.

The doctors held Raven for three weeks, running tests and monitoring her pregnancy, before they finally let her go. As Raven watched Ethic talk with the doctor she realized how grateful she was to have him in her life. She loved the way that he treated her and accepted Morgan into his life. It was like after all this time she had finally found home and a new family to call her own. She could tell that Ethic's feelings were genuine toward her. Every day they grew closer to one another and she admired the way he included Morgan in their lives. He treated Bella and Morgan exactly the same. When he yelled at one he yelled at the other. When he tucked his daughter in at night he made sure that he kissed Morgan good night as well. He was her father figure and he stepped up without having to be asked because he knew that Morgan needed it. That reason alone was enough for Raven to love him. He was just as perfect as she had always dreamt him to be. She admired his confidence. Despite the burns on his face he still carried the same swagger he always had. He was gangster without being malicious, confident without displaying arrogance, and caring without being soft. Ethic had the perfect combination of qualities that endeared him to Raven. Now that she had Ethic she was slowly realizing that what she had experienced with Mizan had not been love. With Ethic she was better.

As she prepared to leave, Morgan and Bella rushed to her side to help her off of the bed. Besides having a leg full of stitches and deep bruising all over her body she had recovered fully. She was extremely sore, but she welcomed life's pain. All of the hurt that had led her to this moment in her life was worth it, because if she had not been through the fire she would not know what true happiness felt like.

"I see I got my own little personal nurses, huh?" she asked playfully as Morgan and Bella walked her over to a wheelchair.

"Yep! We decorated the house for you and everything. We are going to be your servants until you get better," Bella said excitedly as she displayed a gap-toothed smile.

"Oh, wow," Raven exclaimed as she pulled Bella into her lap. She held onto Morgan's hand and kissed the back of it. "I love you, Stank," she signed, meaning it from the bottom of her heart. Morgan had loved her unconditionally throughout the years and was the only piece of her family that she had left.

"I love you too," Morgan signed back. Being around Ethic and Bella had made her feel whole again. She felt like she had a new family and although it was not as good as her old one, she loved them and appreciated them so much because of what she had been through.

"What about me?" Bella asked. "Do you love me too?"

Ethic stopped speaking to the doctor as he looked back at Raven and Bella. He didn't want to put Raven in an awkward situation where she felt obligated to respond. Raven looked Bella directly in her eyes and lifted her hand to rub her unruly curly hair. "I love you very much, sweetie."

Hearing those words and seeing Bella wrap her arms around Raven's neck filled Ethic with great pride. There was nothing left for Raven to prove to him. She loved his daughter and that was all he could ask of her.

"I'm not trying to be a mushy nigga or nothing, but I love you, ma . . . on everything you mean the world to me," Ethic whispered in her ear as he wheeled her to his car. After hearing him say those words she felt her life was perfect. She had no idea that her past was just waiting for the right time to sneak up on her. No matter how hard she tried she would never be able to run from her past; sooner than later she was going to have to face it, including the hefty fines that she was going to have to pay and the court appearances for driving while impaired. But with Ethic by her side she felt like she could conquer anything.

Rich sat in the ambulance with a goon by his side, watching every move that Raven made. They had been waiting patiently for her to emerge from the hospital and finally after three days of staking out the entrance, she had appeared.

"That's her?" the goon asked as he watched her get into Ethic's car.

"Yeah, that's her," Rich confirmed.

"Damn, she bad as hell," the dude commented. "That's Mizan's bitch?"

"Don't let a pretty face fool you, my nigga. That snake-ass bitch is the one who got Mizan locked up," Rich stated. He pulled out his cell phone and snapped a quick photo of Raven with Ethic. "She out here playing wifey to that nigga Ethic who used to run with her daddy . . . Mizan is definitely gon' wanna see this."

When Mizan received the text, his hatred for Raven shot through the roof. He had always suspected her of having a thing for Ethic, but to see her kissing him confirmed his suspicions. He began to think of all the times he had had minor run-ins with Ethic. *She had me looking like a fucking fool,* he thought.

Before seeing this there had still been a part of him that thought of Raven as his girl, but now he was certain that he was going to murder her . . . even if it was the last thing he did.

Chapter Twenty

Playing mother to Bella and taking care of her sister made Raven fall in love with the idea of being a mother. She had even begun teaching Bella sign language so that she could interact better with Morgan. She had finally stepped into the life she had always wanted. Yes, she was the queen of the streets, but Ethic's reign over Kansas City was completely different than her father's had been. Ethic didn't stay away from home at night, and although he had all of the rewarding possessions of being a king-pin, she never saw him put in work. He kept her out of harm's way at all times. His reach was so far that he had people who he could call on to do his dirty work. Ethic had not touched cocaine in years. He had long transcended the positions in the game that risked his freedom. He was a business man and he conducted himself as such. When he was home, he left the streets on their front doorstep. There were no raised voices, slammed doors, or threatening atmospheres behind the four walls of Ethic's home. He did not try to prove his manhood by asserting dominance over her. He was a real man, her man, and he taught Raven how to be a real woman. If they did happen to disagree he made sure that they talked about it. He slowly made her feel comfortable in his world. Mizan had trained Raven to fear him, now Ethic was teaching her to love him fearlessly.

Raven tucked both of the girls into their beds and waited for them to fall asleep before she snuck out of the room. She rushed into the kitchen to check on the dinner she was preparing for Ethic. She never wanted to give him a reason to leave, so she made sure that she stepped up her game and did everything in her power to make him comfortable. She cooked and cleaned like a Stepford wife and was willing to do anything to please him. What she did not realize was that she did not have to work so hard because Ethic was already smitten. She picked up the phone and dialed his number as she stood over the stove. She smiled when she heard him answer because he was always so available to her. The women in his life came first above all circumstances.

"Hey, you," she greeted him seductively.

"What up, Rae?" he replied. "I'm on my way to you."

"Okay, well, when you get here come straight to the bedroom. I have a surprise for you," she replied.

"Straight up?" he inquired. She had piqued his interest and he wanted to hear more.

"Straight up," she confirmed as she turned the oven on low and made her way into the master bedroom. She turned on the shower, then began to undress.

"How far away are you?" she asked.

"I'm close," he replied.

"Okay, I'll see you when you get here. Don't take too long," she cooed sexily as she ended the call. She turned, put her Maxwell CD into the player and turned it on low before she stepped underneath the stream of hot water.

She washed her body gently as she swayed to the beat of the music. When she heard the volume increase slightly on her stereo she smiled, knowing that Ethic was home.

"I'm in here," she called out. "Why don't you come join me?"

She closed her eyes and put her face under the water as the bathroom door squeaked open.

Her back was facing Ethic and she bent over enticingly, pretending to wash her legs as she shook her hips from side to side to give him a good view. She heard the shower door open and turned around to greet her man, but she found herself looking into the eyes of a stranger. She fixed her mouth to scream, but a strong hand silenced her.

"Bitch, if you want to live then shut the fuck up," he threatened as he held a .45-caliber pistol near her face, tracing her cheek with it as his body weight pinned her against the shower wall.

She cried as his hands roamed between her legs. She shook as his hands invaded her. The goon had been sent there by Mizan, and although he had specific instructions to bring her back without a hair out of place, he had taken it upon himself to see what all the fuss was about.

Raven panicked as he violated her. She could see his ill intentions in his eyes but she knew that she couldn't fight back. Morgan and Bella were asleep in the other room, and she didn't want them to wake up to find her being raped. *Ethic is on his way,* she thought frantically. *I have to stall for time.*

"Please don't do this," she whispered.

He stopped groping her for a second as a wicked leer crossed his face. His hand wrapped around her throat. He pulled her out of the shower with so much force that she thought her neck would break under the pressure of his grasp. She hit the vanity hard, causing the mirror to shatter as she fell to the floor.

"No!" she grunted in defiance and pain as he grabbed at her kicking feet. He straddled her and grabbed her arms, pinning them above her head as he parted her naked legs roughly.

Raven tried not to scream as terror built in her throat. She wanted to call out for help, but she was afraid to put Morgan and Bella in direct harm.

"Bitch, quit all that fucking squirming," he barked as he brought one of his hands up to slap her across the face. He hurriedly pulled down his pants, exposing himself as he mounted her. With one of her hands free she quickly reached for one of the broken shards of glass on the floor. She stretched her arm as far as it would go as she felt him entering. As he thrust inside of her she cried sorrowfully. She jerked her body to the left and finally her hand wrapped around the jagged edges of the glass. She gripped it tightly. She didn't care that it cut into her skin like a razor, causing blood to flow down her arm.

"Aghh!" she hissed angrily as she jabbed it into the intruder's neck with all of her might. The man grabbed at his neck as his eyes grew wide and he pulled himself out of her in a panic. Blood gushed out of his neck like lava from a volcano as he stumbled around the room. Raven stood and ran for the door as he grabbed at her desperately. She raced into Bella and Morgan's room.

"Bella, get up!" she screamed in distress as she rushed to scoop Bella up in her arms. She then shook Morgan out of her sleep.

"What's wrong?" Morgan signed with big eyes as she looked at the blood on her sister's naked body. Raven was so distraught that she did not even realize that she didn't have on any clothes. She could hear the intruder stumbling around in her bedroom and the only thing on her mind was getting out of the house safely.

She carried Bella and grabbed Morgan's hand as she raced out of the house and into the yard, screaming for help.

"Oh, shit," Rich mumbled as he watched Raven run out of the house. He didn't know exactly what had happened inside, but he knew that the snatch had gone bad. *Fuck, this nigga was supposed to be in and out,* Rich thought as he reached underneath his seat for his snub .380. He started up the car and began to roll slowly toward Raven. *I'ma just snatch the bitch and go,* he thought as he crept closer to the scene. His plans were thwarted when he saw Ethic pull into the driveway. He quickly picked up speed as to not arouse suspicion as he drove by.

Ethic ran out of his car, barely parking before he jumped out to aid Raven.

"What happened?" he yelled as he examined her body, trying to figure out where the blood was coming from. "Where are you hurt?" he asked.

Raven was distraught as she sobbed and attempted to explain, but she was shaking and her words came out a jumbled mess. She pointed to the house as she wept. Her hysterics caused both Bella and Morgan to break out into frightened cries as well. He picked Raven up and ushered the girls into his car.

"Don't open these doors for anybody but me," he instructed as he removed his gun from his waistline and cautiously walked through the front door.

He could hear the shower running as he crept through the house going in and out of every room, his gun leading the way. When he reached his bedroom he immediately saw the pool of blood that had seeped into his carpet. He followed the stream into the master bath where Raven's attacker lay on his stomach; dead eyes open in a room full of steam.

Ethic lowered his gun and unmasked the dead man. He didn't recognize him, but anger surged through him as he stood and hit the bathroom door.

"Fuck!" he yelled as his fist cracked the wooden frame. He had avoided this type of setup for years and now as

he was trying to exit the game, complications were beginning to arise. He knew that it could not be a coincidence.
He thought of how bad the situation could have ended. It
could have been Raven lying in the pool of blood or, even
worse, Morgan or Bella. He pulled out his BlackBerry
and called his clean-up crew. It would not be hard to get
rid of the body. Owning a chain of funeral homes came in
handy when it was time to put in work.

One phone call was enough to erase the dude lying on
the floor, but Ethic knew that it wasn't enough to keep his
family safe. He had to get to whoever had given the order,
and since dead men don't talk, he had no idea where
to start.

Chapter Twenty-one

Raven stared blankly at her bloody hands as she listened to Ethic settle Morgan and Bella's fears in the next room. She was glad that she had kept her condo because it would be awhile before she was able to step foot back inside Ethic's house. She would never feel safe there after what had happened. Ethic came into the bedroom and scooped her up in to his arms. She rested her head on his chest as he carried her into the bathroom and placed her inside the antique porcelain tub. He filled the tub with water and washed her gently, but Raven still saw the blood on her hands. She grabbed the soap and scrubbed herself until her skin was raw. She didn't want to tell Ethic all that had happened. Afraid that he would look at her differently, she did not reveal that she had been raped.

"Did I kill him?" she asked.

Not wanting to put the burden of murder on her heart, Ethic shook his head. "No, he was still alive when I walked in. I took care of it," he answered.

She nodded. "Good," she replied.

She stood and Ethic carried her into the bedroom. He catered to her every need as he lotioned her down and massaged her back.

"I'm sorry that I wasn't there," he whispered sincerely. "I made that mistake with Melanie. I wasn't there for her. I loved her and I let her die. It won't happen again. I should have been there for you, Raven . . . No one should be able to touch you," he stated.

Raven put her hand on the side of Ethic's face. "It's okay, Ethic. You can't control everything . . . This wasn't your fault. You didn't know," she responded, assuring him with a tender kiss.

Raven lay down on her side and turned away from Ethic. A bone, chilling aura swept over her and she could not quite place her finger on it, but she felt it in her soul that something was not right.

Ethic put the locks on Raven and didn't allow her out of the house alone under any circumstances. If he wasn't by her side then she didn't go, and the same went for Morgan and Bella. He even went as far as pulling them out of school until he could figure out what was going on. Ethic arcked his mind as he tried to think of people who would want to bring harm to him. There were only two things that could cause another man to beef with him so hard: pussy and money. But Ethic didn't borrow either. Any chick he smashed belonged to him and at the moment his only focus was Raven. He put word out to all of his workers: if anyone even spoke his name in a derogatory way he wanted to know about it. *I'm about to start making examples out of niggas.*

Mizan's obsession with getting Raven back had pushed him into the realm of insanity. After viewing the picture of her and Ethic together he wanted to be the one to personally destroy her life. He drove to Kansas City and had been staking out her every move. As he sat shotgun in Rich's car they observed the condo that Raven was hiding out in. Steam emanated from him as he watched her like a hawk. Her growing belly told the story of her betrayal. She had moved on with her life, but he refused to follow suit. After having her under his influence for so long there was no way she was going to have her happy ending without him. He was infatuated with her, and even Rich was getting tired of playing the cat and mouse game.

"Yo', fam . . . we've been on this bitch like a hawk for two months. We just going to sit and watch her or we gon' do what we came here to do?" Rich asked in irritation as he noticed the crazed look in Mizan's eyes.

"We've got to wait for that nigga to slip up. He's with her twenty-four-seven," Mizan stated as he watched Ethic help Raven into the house. "One of these days he gon' get comfortable and that's when I'ma show my face. Once she sees me, it's a wrap. She'll be back home to Daddy."

"What the fuck is up with you and this girl?" Rich asked, wondering why Mizan was not willing to let her go. "The pussy that good?" he joked.

Mizan's eyes never left Raven. She was his prized possession and a sadistic, crazed look overtook his face. "The bitch belongs to me. She doesn't leave until I tell her it's okay for her to go. She's mine . . . she'll always be mine . . . bitch better get that shit through her skull. It don't matter how far she run. I'm never giving her life back."

Raven rushed around the condo, her big belly leading the way as she searched for her car keys. "I can't wait to get this fat baby boy out of me. I never knew that pregnancy would be so uncomfortable," she huffed as she wobbled around the living room, breaking a light sweat. It seemed like the baby was sucking all the energy out of her and even the most minute tasks exhausted her. She couldn't even touch her own toes or tie her own shoes anymore. Although she loved that she was pregnant she was tired of this stage. She was ready to experience motherhood and be past the pregnant part. She finally found her keys underneath the couch cushions and made her way into the bedroom where Ethic was sleeping.

"Get up, babe . . . I swear you sleep more than I do and I'm the one carrying this baby around," she stated with laughter.

"Come here, lay down with me, ma," he replied as he grabbed her arm and pulled her onto the bed. "I promised Bella I would take her to put flowers on Melanie's grave today. It's her birthday."

Raven looked up at him. "I have to go to the doctor's today. You aren't coming?" she asked.

"Fuck, I forgot about your appointment," Ethic stated. "Can you reschedule it? Bella would really like it if you came. She invited Morgan and she keeps asking me when you're going to come meet her mother."

Raven raised an eyebrow and replied, "No, I can't cancel it, Ethic. I have the best doctor in town. If I cancel I just have to wait until my next check up to go in and I don't want to do that. I'm not trying to sit by your dead love's grave all day."

Ethic could hear the jealousy in her tone. He knew that it bothered Raven that he cared for Bella's mother.

"Don't be like that, ma . . . I love you and only you, but I need to remind Bella that her mother loved her too. Melanie is always going to be a part of my life because of Bella," Ethic stated.

Raven rolled her eyes and felt herself becoming emotional. It was more the hormones than anything, but she hated to hear Ethic talk about another woman in such a sincere way. She was selfish with his love, wanting it all for herself, only willing to make an exception for Bella and Morgan. "I just don't know how I'm supposed to compete with a ghost," she whispered as she dropped her head.

Ethic pulled her close to him and kissed the bridge of her nose. "You don't have to compete with anyone. You're my number one, ma, and I know Melanie would love you for taking care of Bella the way that you do. You want me to take Bella another day?"

Raven shook her head and wiped her eyes. "Nooooo," she replied like a spoiled little girl. She knew that she was being unreasonable. "I can go alone." She headed for the door.

"You know you're not going out of here by yourself," Ethic protested as he stood up and grabbed her arm to pull her back to him. He wrapped his hands around her waist and buried his head in the back of her neck, inhaling the scent of her Dior perfume.

She turned around and put her hands on her chest as she looked up at him with adoring eyes. "Ethic it's been months since that guy ran in your house. I think it's safe for me to go to the doctor by myself."

"I just want to keep you safe, ma," Ethic said. "The only way I know to do that is to keep you close."

She smiled as she touched his face. "I don't want to feel like a bird in a cage, Ethic. I felt like that with Mizan and I refuse to live like that again. I can't be afraid for the rest of my life. I'll call you and check in with you."

She could see the worry lines forming in Ethic's forehead and it warmed her heart. *This man really loves me,* she thought as she kissed his lips. "I'll be fine."

When Mizan saw Raven leave the house alone he rubbed his hands together in anticipation. He knew that if he waited long enough, his chance at catching her alone would come. He called Rich at the motel and told him that it was time, and as she pulled out of the driveway, Mizan slowly eased behind her. He followed her until they were miles away from her home before he decided to let his presence be known.

Raven eased to a stop at the red light and heard a horn honk to her right. When she looked over to the car beside her the blood drained from her face as if she had seen a ghost. Urine saturated her car seat as her bladder gave out on her and her worst fear came true. Mizan had found her and all of the rebuilding of self-esteem that Ethic had done for her was demolished with one look at her former abuser. All of the fear that he had instilled in her were like invisible chains and only he had the key.

"Pull over," Mizan stated ominously.

Raven froze momentarily and felt herself beginning to hyperventilate as she stared into the face of the devil. She didn't know what to do, but her instincts told her to drive. She pressed her foot down on the gas pedal and the screeching of her tires sounded throughout the streets as she sped through the red light.

"No . . . no . . . this is not happening," she whispered frantically as she checked her rearview mirror to see that Mizan was right on her tail. Terror traveled up her spine as she reached into her purse to grab her cell phone, but her hands were trembling so badly that she dropped it on the floor between her feet. She saw Mizan getting closer and closer up on her car until she felt him ram into her bumper.

"Aghh!" she screamed frightfully. She knew that he would not stop. He was going to chase her until he caught her. In frustration she pulled over into a parking lot, conceding. He parked his car in front of hers so that she could not get out, and when he emerged from the car she closed her eyes, knowing that her day of judgment had come. Her baby went wild inside of her stomach as if it sensed her trepidation right along with her. She could barely breathe and she kept her eyes closed as she began to pray.

He walked over to her calmly and opened up the driver door.

"Get the fuck out of the car," he stated as he ice grilled her.

When she didn't move Mizan grabbed her by her hair. "Agh," she squealed as he dragged her from the vehicle and forced her to face him.

As he looked at her bulging belly he gripped the bridge of his nose to stop the tears from coming to his eyes. It was the first time he had allowed himself to feel something for another person since he was a child.

"You got me out here chasing you across the fucking country," he stated harshly. "You pregnant with that nigga Ethic's baby?"

He kicked her car in anger and Raven flinched, thinking that she would be next.

He grabbed her by the elbow and dragged her toward his car.

"No . . ." She pulled away from him and tried to scramble back to the safety of her own car.

"Get in the car!" he yelled as his grip tightened and he opened the door, forcing her inside. Once he slammed the door Raven quickly hit the locks. "Open the door, Raven." Mizan's voice was low and threatening as he peered into the window. Raven shook her head. Her distress was mounting and making her sick to her stomach. She was trapped and there was nothing that she could do to get away. Mizan pulled out his burner and tapped the steel against the window pane, aiming it directly at her.

She sobbed as she reached over and unlocked his door. "How did you find me?" she asked through her tears.

He smirked as he looked over at her. "I'ma always find you. You can't run from me, bitch."

"You don't even want me, Mizan . . . just let me go," she pleaded. "Please."

Mizan wrapped his hand around her neck and pushed her head against the passenger window so hard that it cracked, making a spider web of splintering glass form behind her head. He stuck his gun directly in the middle of her forehead as she closed her eyes and sobbed, waiting for the shot.

"You want me to let you go, Raven? Huh, bitch?" he grilled. "Because the only way I'm letting you go is when I put you in the ground. You want me to let you go?"

Raven didn't respond and Mizan bashed her head against the window pane again. "Huh?" Raven could feel her blood pressure rising as he baby began to do back flips in her stomach, and the pressure Mizan had on her neck became unbearable.

"No!" she finally yelled back as he released her neck.

He kept his pistol trained on her as he picked up his cell phone and shoved it in her face. "Let me show you something," Mizan stated, going from enraged to calm in the blink of an eye. Raven looked at the screen and saw a picture of Ethic, Morgan, and Bella standing at the cemetary.

"You call that nigga and tell him you're not fucking with him anymore. Tell him it's over and that you're coming back home to Flint," Mizan stated.

"I'm not doing that," she replied. "I won't . . . You're gonna have to kill me," Raven stated defiantly.

"Oh, it's not you I'm going to kill," Mizan stated as he pointed to the cell phone picture. He pressed the call button on his phone and put it on speaker.

"Yo'?" Rich answered.

"Yo', Rich, you ready to put in that work?" Mizan asked.

"Yeah, I'm looking at the nigga right now," Rich replied. "You want me to pop him?"

"No . . . Mizan, please," Raven sobbed.

"Yeah, kill him," Mizan instructed.

"Okay . . . I'll do it!" she screamed. "I'll make the call."

"I'ma call you back, fam. Keep watching the nigga. If I don't call you back in five minutes . . . kill him," Mizan stated.

"What about the girls?" Rich asked.

"Them too," Mizan instructed heartlessly, then hung up.

"Why are you doing this?" she cried.

Mizan ignored her question. "What's his number?" he asked. It was important for him to get Ethic out of the picture. Once she made the call he would not have to worry about Ethic trying to come to her aid. He knew that without Ethic, Raven was helpless. She wasn't strong enough to fight him on her own.

Raven felt like her back was against the wall. He really had her paralyzed with fear and she knew that if she did not do as he said then Mizan would follow through with his threats. He was psychotic and a killer with no remorse. She knew that he would not hesitate to murder Ethic, even if only to hurt her. With a heavy heart and much regret, Raven told him the number. She closed her eyes as he activated the speaker phone and placed the phone near her mouth. He held the phone with one hand and jammed his gun hard into her stomach with the other. Her face was like a waterfall of sorrow as she opened her mouth to speak.

"Ethic," she whimpered.

"Raven . . . what's wrong, baby girl? Did something happen to the baby?" he asked. His voice was so full of concern that Raven wept loudly. Mizan pulled back the hammer on his pistol and ice grilled her to keep her in line.

"I can't do this anymore, Ethic. I'm not feeling this," she whispered as she forced herself to stop crying.

"What? Raven where are you? Fuck is going on?"

"I'm going back to Flint . . . back to Mizan. I tried, Ethic . . . but I love him and I want to give him another chance," Raven mumbled. Every word tore through her heart as she heard silence fill the phone. Her lip quivered and her nose ran as she waited for his response.

"Don't do this to me, Raven . . . after everything that nigga took you through how could you even think of going back? Don't take me through this again," he retorted coldly.

"I'm tired of being your substitute for Melanie," Raven cried, knowing that she was rubbing salt in Ethic's wounded heart. "I don't want this life with you. I was not raised to be second best."

"You're not taking my baby back to live with that nigga . . . I don't give a fuck about what you do, but you're not . . . ."

"It's not your son!" Raven screamed out. "I was fucking Jacob," she lied.

Ethic's silence spoke volumes. She could hear his heart breaking through the phone as she sobbed.

"I'm not sending Morgan back to that city, Raven, and if you walk away now don't think of coming back. I can't save you if you don't want to save yourself," Ethic stated. She could hear him cutting her off. She could hear his hatred toward her building. As each second passed he withdrew from her. The love that he had for her transformed into resentment and contempt.

Raven closed her eyes and inhaled deeply. Her life was not her own to live. She had sold her soul to the devil a long time ago when she had trusted Mizan, and now he was coming to collect. Mizan was determined to have her and she knew that as long as he was alive he would never set her free. She could feel him consuming her . . . he was going to be the death of her. "Take care of her, Ethic. I'm sorry," she whispered just before Mizan disconnected the line.

She stared at Mizan with hateful eyes and said, "I did what you asked . . . now call Rich and tell him not to hurt them."

"Nah, I might still let him pop that nigga Ethic," Mizan stated with nonchalance. Raven exploded and threw fists his way as she screamed at him.

"I hate you . . . I fucking hate you!" she yelled as she scratched and clawed at him.

"Bitch, calm your ass the fuck down!" he hollered as he hit her with the butt of the gun, dizzying her and causing blood to flow from her busted nose.

"Call him!" Raven pleaded. "Please, Mizan."

"Who do you belong to?" Mizan asked egotistically.

"You . . . just please make the call. I belong to you," she whispered as she panted for air and held her throbbing nose.

Mizan placed the call and called off the hit as he started his car. "Sit your ass back and shut the fuck up. I see you done forgot who Daddy is," Mizan stated. "Don't worry, I'ma remind you, bitch. All you need is some discipline."

Ethic threw his phone to the ground, causing Morgan and Bella to jump in alarm. He swung at the air, taking his frustrations out on an invisible opponent as he felt the familiar sting of betrayal. For the second time under the exact same circumstances he was losing a woman that he loved. First Melanie and now Raven. They both had gone back to their abusive relationships and taken pieces of his heart with them.

"Daddy, what's wrong?" Bella asked as he picked her up in his arms. He bit his inner cheek so hard that he drew blood as he fought back his emotions. He kissed her cheeks as she wiped the tears from his eyes with her tiny hands. "You're sad. What's wrong?" she asked.

"Nothing's wrong, sweetheart," he lied as he covered her with kisses, trying to absorb as much love from her in an attempt to fill his bleeding heart. He put her down and then kneeled down in front of Morgan, then pulled them both close to him. "I need to talk to you two about Raven," he said. He could barely choke out the words without breaking down, but he put on a strong visage for the sake of Morgan and Bella.

"What's wrong with Raven?" Morgan signed in panic.

"Nothing, baby girl . . . nothing's wrong with her. She's just going back to Flint for a little while . . ." Ethic signed back, trying his hardest to display a smile to calm her nerves.

Morgan's eyes filled with fear. "She can't go back there. You can't let her go back to Flint. Mizan is crazy, Ethic. He is going to hurt her," Morgan signed, jumping up from the ground to get him to understand how serious she was.

Ethic could see that she had seen more pain than her young eyes should have ever been exposed to. He rubbed her hair. "Nah, li'l bit . . . I won't let that happen. You two go finish eating . . . I've got a couple phone calls to make."

As he stood, he looked at Melanie's tombstone. There was no way he was going to let Raven end up the same way. There was no doubt in his mind that he was done fucking with her. After what she had revealed he would never look at her the same way, but he was not going to let her go back to the same nigga who had torn her down. He flipped up his cell phone and put in the order to have Mizan hit without a second thought. It seemed that no matter how hard he tried to pull away from the streets they called him back in, but this situation needed to be handled. It was long overdue. With a $50,000 ticket on his head, Mizan wouldn't be breathing for long. Ethic knew that as long as Mizan was living that Raven would be drawn to him. He could not understand her logic and because she had chosen another man over him, Ethic could never take her back . . . but he could make sure that she did not fall into the clutches of Mizan. Ethic had spared Mizan's life before simply because he had not wanted to hurt Raven, but this time he was going to take it because of all the hurt that Mizan had caused.

Chapter Twenty-two

Raven shivered as she lay on the basement floor, chained to a foundation pole in the middle of the room. She had been down there for a week and she felt as if she was losing her mind. He fed her as if she were a dog, bringing bowls of food down for her along with a bowl of water. At first she was too proud to eat the food and would curse him out every time he opened the basement door, but as the days passed and her baby began to feel the starvation she gave in. She ate with her hands and licked the bowls clean she was so hungry.

"Mizan!" she screamed at the top of her lungs as she limped to the bottom of the steps. She pulled at the heavy chain around her ankle and banged it against the concrete ground to get his attention. She knew that he heard her. He was torturing her and his cruelty toward her only made her hate him more. She called his name until her voice went hoarse and then collapsed onto the ground, sobbing her heart out. All of the windows were covered and she didn't know if it was day or night. It felt as if she had been down there forever and she did everything in her power not to lose her mind. She thought of Ethic, Morgan, and Bella to help maintain her sanity. She promised God that if she ever made it out of that basement alive, the first opportunity that she got to leave Mizan she would . . . this time for good.

When Mizan finally opened the door she sat up weakly. With the light from the upstairs silhouetting his body as he descended the stairs he looked like her savior, but he had no intentions of coming to her rescue. He held two small puppies, one under each arm as he descended the steps.

"Mizan, please let me come upstairs," she begged shamelessly. "I'm pregnant Mizan. Please!"

Mizan placed the pit bull puppies on the ground and they instantly began to bark and jump on Raven.

"I got two more bitches that I have to train. They are much easier to train than you, though, Raven. These bitches right here are loyal. Once I break them in they never stray . . . You strayed, that's why I'm retraining you," Mizan stated cruelly.

"I loved you," she cried as the tiny pit bulls began to bite at her clothes. "What did I do to deserve this?"

"You let another nigga have what belongs to me," he replied. He spat on the ground in front of her and turned around to ascend the steps. He ignored her cries and left her to fight off the dogs alone in the basement.

For three tormenting weeks Raven was treated like an animal. She didn't eat unless he chose to feed her and she was forced to relieve herself in a corner of the room. The pit bulls had taken to her and made her the leader of their pack, which only demeaned her further, making her feel inhumane. Raven knew that the conditions were not good for her baby, but when she felt the sharp pain in her abdomen and a gush of water flow between her legs, terror seized her.

"Aww," she cried out softly as she felt her uterus contract. "No . . . no . . . not like this," she cried as she held her stomach, but despite her protests her baby was coming. She was about to give birth on the damp, cold, dirty basement floor.

"Mizan! Please! Help me!" she screamed as her hysterics caused the pit bull puppies to begin barking. "Aghh!" she hollered as pain ripped through her.

Her body temperature rose as she tried to hold in her urge to push. Sweat dripped from her body as the dogs began to circle her and bark furiously.

"Aghhh!"

The pain was too great for her to bear. She could feel every rip as her vaginal opening dilated to allow her baby access into the world.

"Mizan!" she cried. "Please help me . . . I need you!" she hollered. She felt that something was wrong. She had never expected childbirth to hurt this much. She tried to hold it in as long as she possibly could, but it felt like her baby was kicking at her opening. The urge to push was too much and she found herself straining as she pushed with all her might.

"Aghhhhh!" she screamed.

She gripped the pole and breathed erratically as she desperately sucked in the air. She felt her body reacting as she prepared herself to push again. She held her scream in this time as the dogs went wild around her. She bit her bottom lip and closed her eyes as she pushed aggressively.

"Oh God," she cried. "Please help me . . . God, please. I can't do this."

This was not how she pictured this day to be. No one was by her side. She had never felt lonelier than she did at that moment, and when she felt the urge to push again she didn't stop until she heard the sounds of tiny cries.

"Ohhh," she moaned as she shook violently as a gushy wailing mess lay between her legs. The dogs circled her, barking at her baby and she reached down to scoop him up in her arms as she sobbed uncontrollably. Fatigue raped her body so much that her shaky hands could barely hold onto her child. She found a pair of rusty yard sheers and cut the umbilical cord, as she tried her best to clean him off. His lungs worked overtime as his wails haunted her, filling the dirty basement, and reminding her of how horrible of a mother she was to allow him to be born into such a dire environment. "I know," she whispered. "I'm so sorry," she cried as she nestled him to her chest. When she heard the front door slam upstairs she began to scream for dear life.

"Mizan!" she cried. "Please help me!"

He appeared at the top of the steps and strolled down casually, but when he finally caught sight of what had occurred while he was gone he stopped abruptly. Even someone with a heart as cold as his could not stomach the bloody sight in front of him.

"Please . . . I need a doctor," she whispered, totally defeated.

"Are you trained?" he asked.

She nodded obediently as she stared up desperately at him. "Yes . . . yes, I'm trained."

"You know you're not keeping that nigga's baby, right?" Mizan stated callously.

"It's not his, it's yours," she stated quickly. She knew that it was a lie, but she was determined to convince him.

"Bitch, do I look like boo-boo the fucking fool to you?" he asked growing angry.

"I'm not lying to you, Mizan. I found out I was pregnant before I left Flint. Why do you think I decided to leave in the first place? I was afraid that you would hit me while I was pregnant. I didn't want anything to happen to our baby. I was just trying to keep him safe," she said through her tears, laying it on thick. Mizan began to pace the floor unsurely as he stared down at her.

"Why the fuck you just now telling me this shit, Raven?! I had you down here punishing you for being pregnant with that nigga's seed!" he yelled. "Fuck!"

"Mizan, please . . . just help me. We need a doctor," she whispered, knowing that she had turned the tables and made him feel a bit of guilt. She could see a tiny spark in his heart. Now all she had to do was fuel the flame and make him feel. *Come on, you bastard. I know you can't be this evil.* "Please, Mizan. He's your son. Help us," she pleaded.

Mizan picked her up from the floor and she cradled her crying baby in her arms as he carried her up the stairs. She was so weak that she could barely lift her head and she used all of her energy to keep her baby secure in her arms. "I'm getting a paternity test done," he informed her. "If you're lying I'm going to kill you this time."

"I'm not lying," she whispered.

He refused to take her to the hospital, but he hired a nurse to come in and make sure that she and the baby were okay. Raven named her son Benjamin Ezra Atkins, after her father and, unbeknownst to Mizan, after Ethic as well. Mizan resented the baby at first, but the more time he spent around the child the more he began to come around to the idea of keeping him around. Raven was so afraid of Mizan that she went along with the charade, but she knew that she would have to escape before Mizan found out the truth.

"How long are you going to keep me prisoner here?" she asked, her depression worsening. Ever since she had given birth to her baby she had felt lost. Maybe it was the constant isolation from the outside world or her yearning to be back with Ethic that had her going crazy. She didn't know, but whatever it was she could not shake the funk off that surrounded her life. She had thought of committing suicide numerous times, but the thought of leaving her son to be raised by a monster like Mizan always stopped her. She needed a way out, but she knew that running would be pointless because he would just find her and drag her back like he had done so many times before.

"Ain't nobody keeping your ass cooped up . . . take your yellow ass on somewhere," Mizan stated as he picked up baby Benjamin. "I'ma smack the shit out of yo' mama if she keep looking at me all sideways," he said to the baby as he blew on the infant's stomach. The sight of him touching her child disgusted Raven, but there was nothing that she could do about it. *I have to find a way out of here.*

"Why don't you go see Nikki or some shit?" he said. "Get the fuck from around me with all that depressing shit."

Raven looked up at him in surprise and hopped up to begin preparing a diaper bag for her son. Now was the perfect opportunity for her to get ghost. She didn't care that she had no money. All she wanted was to put as much distance between herself and Mizan as possible.

"Fuck you packing his shit up for? He's not going with you," Mizan stated.

"I just want to show Nikki her nephew, Mizan. I haven't even spoken to her since I left. She doesn't even know I have a son," she stated as tears came to her eyes.

"Too fucking bad, bitch, cuz he's not going with you. As a matter of fact if you take this li'l nigga out of my house I'ma bust your fucking ass, n'ah mean?" he stated.

"I won't take him out," she replied submissively as her stomach turned at the sight of them interacting. She did not want Benjamin to know someone as evil as Mizan, but it was out of her hands. As she turned to leave Mizan added, "Stop by my trap houses, too. It's the first of the month. That's money day, baby boy," Mizan said as he spoke to the baby and lifted him in the air. Raven could see that Mizan really loved Benjamin, but as soon as he found out that it wasn't his son all of that love would become deadly hate and Raven did not want to be around to see that day.

Raven nodded and reluctantly left the house. She knew what Mizan was trying to pull. He knew that she would never leave town without her son so he made sure that when she left the house the baby stayed. He knew that she wasn't running away without her child and that kept her rooted.

She found herself on Nikki's doorstep crying furiously as she banged it off its hinges. Finally Nikki opened the door.

"Oh my God . . . Raven!" Nikki exclaimed as she hugged her tightly. "Where the hell have you been?"

"He has my son . . . ." Raven sobbed.

"Your son?" Nikki said in shock. She could see that Raven was in bad shape and she ushered her to the couch. Raven confided in Nikki, confessing to her all that had happened since they had last spoken and even though Raven knew that Nikki would not remember it the next day it was cleansing to talk to another person about it. Nikki's mouth hung wide open by the time Raven finished telling the story of her torture.

"You have to call Ethic," Nikki stated. "He can help you. You can't go back there."

Raven nodded her head and replied, "I know . . . but what do I say to him, Nik? I played him. I know he probably hates me and I can't just leave my baby there with Mizan. The nigga is crazy. He kept me chained up like an animal. What type of person does that? How could he make me give birth on his basement floor?" Raven asked sadly.

"Call Ethic," Nikki urged as she passed her the phone.

Raven reluctantly dialed Ethic's number and impatience took over her as she waited for him to answer.

"Hello?"

The sound of his voice was like music to her ears and she began to cry. If only life could be simple . . . their love could have been so great.

"Ethic . . . please come and get me," she whispered.

"Raven?" he responded. The phone grew silent and then he spoke gently. "I'm not going through this with you, ma. You made your choice. I told you where I stood. You walked out on me. Had me thinking you were carrying my son."

"Please, Ethic . . . I can explain. I will explain everything when I see you. Just please come and get me." The desperation in her voice was immeasurable. She was broken. Since the day she had met Mizan her life had been nothing but strife. Trying to be grown she had walked down an irreversible path of pain and insecurity, now she was trapped and the only escape she knew was on the other end of the phone.

Ethic sighed deeply because he was about to go against everything that he stood for. Raven had disrespected him and he knew that she deserved to be cut off. But he loved her deeply and could not leave her on stuck.

"Where are you?" he asked.

"I'm at Nikki's. I really need you, Ethic. I know I fucked up but—"

"Save that shit, Rae. I'll be there next week. You get your shit in order by then and you can meet me at Mott Park by the bridge. This is the last time I'm coming for you, Raven. If you don't show, don't call me again. I can't keep doing this with you," Ethic stated. "I have two little girls to think about."

"I'll be there, Ethic. I swear to God . . . don't leave Flint without me," she said.

"Six o'clock, Raven," he stated.

"I'll be there," she replied gratefully. "Ethic?"

"What up?"

"I love you," she said.

Without responding Ethic hung up the phone and Raven turned to her friend. Her pale face was flushed in red as she put her face in her hands. "He doesn't love me anymore."

Nikki wrapped her arms around Raven and allowed her to cry on her shoulder. "Is he coming?" she asked.

Raven sniffled and nodded.

"Then he still loves you. I don't know a nigga in the world that would put up with your baggage if he did not care," Nikki said with a small smile as she lifted Raven's chin and winked.

"How am I going to get my baby out of that house?" Raven asked hopelessly. "Mizan will never let me take him out."

Nikki's eyebrows raised as a light bulb went off in her head, and she grabbed Raven's hand, leading her upstairs to the medicine cabinet. "I've got an idea," she stated, and Raven was all ears. She was willing to do anything to get away from Mizan once and for all.

Chapter Twenty-three

Raven prepared the candlelit dinner for Mizan and was waiting in lingerie when he walked through the door. The sexual ambiance was high in the room as she gave him an enticing smile and bit her bottom lip as she beckoned him closer with her index finger.

"Fuck is all this?" he asked suspiciously as he walked into the kitchen.

"This is me proving to you that I'm trained, Daddy, and me saying I'm sorry for disrespecting you. I love you, Mizan. I just want us to be right again . . . like we used to be back in the day," she said convincingly as she reached up and kissed his lips.

"Where's the baby?" Mizan asked.

"I fed him and he's asleep. We have a couple hours to do what we do before he wakes up and spoils the night," she replied with a seductive smile. "I made you food. Sit down," she stated as she catered to his every need, pulling off his shoes for him.

Mizan smiled as his eyes followed her ample behind as she walked back into the kitchen. "What you cook?"

"I made soul food, baby . . . I know what you like," she replied. She was doing and saying all of the right things to get his guard down. As she fixed his plate she also poured two glasses of red wine. She opened the sleeping capsules that Nikki had given her. She was only supposed to use one, but she emptied four inside the glass hoping that it would work like a charm. She knew how he thought and she placed the spiked glass of wine near her dinner plate; then handed him the unaffected drink.

"Taste it," she said as she lifted the glass to his lips. Just as she suspected, he moved his head to the side and motioned for her to sit down.

"You taste it," he said calmly but with authority.

She sipped the wine until half of the glass was empty and his suspicions melted away as he sat down in the seat with the spiked wine. He ate and drank like a king. Each time she refilled his glass she added more sleeping pills to it. By the time he was ready to stand up from the table he could barely keep his balance.

"You grimy bitch, what the fuck did you give me?" he asked.

She stood up once she saw that he was discombobulated and leaned over the table as she glared at him. "Maybe you just don't know how to handle your liquor," she stated with a devilish smirk. He reached for her but before he could make it to her he collapsed onto the floor.

"Nik, you can come out now!" Raven screamed as she sprang into action and grabbed her pre-packed bag out of the front closet. She slipped on a pair of jeans and grabbed her baby from Nikki. She already had him strapped in his car seat and ready to go, but she couldn't seem to find her keys.

"Fuck! Where are my keys?" she yelled as she ran around the house searching for the keys.

"You don't have time for this, Raven. I don't know how long those pills will last. Just get Mizan's keys and let's go," Nikki urged. Raven cautiously reached into his pockets and retrieved the keys to his black Audi and they darted out of the house.

Raven floored her engine toward Mott Park as her heartbeat sped up. She hoped and prayed that Ethic would be at the park waiting for her. She knew that they could never go back to the happy little family that they had once been. Mizan would come looking for her and if he ever found her with Ethic he would undoubtedly kill him. Raven would have to start a new life and leave behind the love that she had shared with Ethic, but she could not take his son away from him. She wanted Ethic to have a piece of her with him always and she knew that he would take care of their child. He was the perfect man to teach her little boy all he needed to know about manhood. She had not done many good things in her life. In fact, she had fucked it up along with the lives of many others, but as she glanced back at her child she felt accomplished. He was the one thing that she had gotten right. *Now I have to keep him safe,* she thought as she sped to her destination with a heavy heart and determined soul.

Ethic checked his presidential as he leaned against his car. He couldn't believe that he had driven all the way to Flint to meet Raven. He was skeptical that she would show up. He had already offered her an escape and she had crushed his heart under her stiletto when she walked away from him to go back to Mizan. As he looked up and down the deserted street he shook his head with impatience, feeling as though he was setting himself up for failure for a second time.

"When is she coming?" Morgan signed as she popped her head out of the back seat.

"I don't know," he replied as his temple throbbed from anxiety. "I don't know."

He opened the door and ushered Morgan and Bella out of the car. "You and Bella go play until Raven gets here. She should be here soon," Ethic stated. He rubbed his goatee as he watched Morgan and Bella run down the grassy hill that led to the park. Out of frustration he hit the hood of his car and he began to pace back and forth as he continuously checked his watch. *Come on, ma, just come back home,* he thought as he felt himself become emotional. His cell phone rang and he answered it quickly hoping that it was her.

"Hello?"

"Yo', fam, we got that mouse in that trap. We finally caught up with that nigga Mizan. We're following this nigga Audi right now. When we get him out in the clear we gon' blaze on him and make that little problem of yours disappear. The ticket on that still the same?"

Ethic hadn't put in an order for murder in quite some time, but he refused to let Mizan live. Whether Raven showed up or not, he would not let her go back to Mizan. Under no circumstances could he allow her to end up with him again.

"Yeah, fam . . . handle that for me. Make sure that nigga don't walk away from it. Wet that bitch up and make sure he's not breathing, n'ah mean?" Ethic stressed. "I got fifty for you when the job is done."

As Ethic hung up the phone he knew that half of his battles were over. In a few minutes Mizan would no longer exist; now all he had to do was get Raven and leave town.

The closer Raven got to Ethic the more tears slid down her face. Knowing that she was running late, she drove like a bat out of hell. Her heartbeat was erratic and she could barely see through her teary vision, but she kept going. She refused to let her fear convince her to stay. More than her life was at stake. She hid behind the dark tint of the luxury car as she whipped through the city streets. The sound of her cell phone ringing caused her to jump out of her skin.

"It's Ethic," Nikki informed as she handed Raven the phone.

"I'm almost to you, Ethic . . . please don't leave. I'm coming right now. I'm like five minutes away," Raven said. She was so focused on getting to her destination that she never noticed the blue SUV following her.

"I'm not going nowhere without you, Raven . . . just hurry up, ma," Ethic replied.

"I can't come with you, Ethic, Mizan will come for me. I just need you to take care of our son," she whispered as she whipped through the city streets like a NASCAR driver.

"What?" Ethic stated.

"He's yours, Ethic . . . I never slept with anyone else . . . he's your son. Mizan told me if I didn't end things with you then he would kill you. He had someone watching you at the cemetery that day. I had to go along," she cried into the phone.

Ethic beat himself in the chest when he heard her revelation. He instantly felt confident in the decision to give the green light on Mizan's murder. "You don't have to worry about him, Raven. My niggas are taking care of that as we speak."

Raven pulled onto the block and saw Ethic standing at the end. "I see you!" she cried in joy.

Ethic frowned when he saw the black Audi round the corner as the blue SUV followed behind it.

"You're in his car?!" Ethic screamed into the phone as his heart began to pump in devastation. "Raven, no!" he ran toward the car, waving his hands in the air frantically as he watched his own soldiers hang out of the side of the SUV, automatic weapons in hand. The windows of Mizan's Audi were tinted too dark to see that the wrong person was inside. "No!" Ethic screamed as he saw the sparks fly from the pistols. His world went in slow motion as he ran full speed toward the gunfire. The car rocked on its four wheels as bullet holes filled the body of the car. Ethic took out his pistol and ran up to the truck. Rage filled him as he let his cannon bark on his own workers, killing without hesitation. Smoke filled the black Audi as Ethic ran over to the driver's side. As soon as he opened the door Raven fell out into his arms. He looked over and saw that Nikki was slumped against the passenger door.

Raven gagged and choked on her own blood as he held her close to his chest, while blood filled her lungs stifling her last words. As she looked up at him she desperately wanted to speak, to tell him she was sorry, to tell him that she loved him, but all she could do was gasp as she drowned in a sea of red as the life drained from her body.

"Raven!" he heard Morgan scream in the background as he cried, burying his face in her hair.

Raven's eyes penetrated his as she tried to speak. She held onto his hand tightly. She needed him now more than ever. At her side he supported her even in death. She could feel every agonizing bullet hole and every failed attempt at breathing.

"I . . . Eth . . . ." She couldn't get her words out.

"Shh . . . don't talk, ma . . . I love you, Raven. I love you more than life, ma, just breathe," he cried. "Somebody help me!" he screamed urgently. The sounds of a baby crying filled his ears. In his heart he knew that it was his son, but he couldn't tear himself away from Raven as she slipped away in his arms. The shrieking invaded his brain as he held her close, blood staining his white collared shirt, making it look as if he had a bleeding heart.

Raven's eyes looked into the sky and saw a moth flying. It was so beautiful and free as it floated above her face displaying the symbol of her life. As she watched it float she remembered her mother's words:

Don't be the moth that flies into the flame.

I should have never come back to him. It was the last though that crossed her mind. Her grip of Ethic's hand loosened.

"Don't let go of me, ma. I love you, Raven, just hold on."

She heard his pleas and she wanted nothing more than to hold on to him forever, but she had no more strength left. She was tired of fighting. The more she tried to tighten her grip on him, the more she felt her fingers let go. His voice became a whisper in the distance and she faded away. There was nothing she could do. It was too late. A final tear slipped down her cheek as she gazed at the moth as it flew upward into the heavens . . . leading her back home to rejoin her mother and father in grace.

Epilogue

One Year Later

Mizan sat in front of his connect, Dot, as he nervously anticipated meeting the main supplier. He was at the top of the city's drug trade, but he knew that if he could buy directly from Dot's connect then he could take over the entire state, maybe even the Midwest. When Dot had first called him and informed him that she was getting out of the game he knew that it would kill his business. She had the best coke in the city. He knew he would not be able to replace her, but when she offered to introduce him to her supplier he saw dollar signs. As he sat in Dot's bakery he watched as she yelled at a little boy who was running around her shop.

"You got to excuse me, baby. I don't get to spend much time with my great nephew. He is only here for the day and I'm telling you he is wearing me out," Dot said as she chased after the small toddler.

"Yo', when dude supposed to be coming? I don't got all day to wait," Mizan stated arrogantly as he fidgeted in his chair and leaned back, extending his left leg to make himself more comfortable.

"He will be here any minute. He's going to give you a good price, too. I'm getting too old for this business. It's time for me to settle down and act like an old woman. I can't be dealing with this game anymore. I'm not a young'un anymore. I've got to help my nephew take care of this little boy right here," she stated. "His mother died about a year ago and I've got to do my part to help, you know?"

Mizan nodded as if he was listening but he couldn't care less about what the old woman was saying. When he heard the bell above the bakery door ring he rubbed his hands together greedily. He could already feel the money between his fingers. He stood, but when he looked up into the face of his new connect pure panic and fear took over his face. He had been expecting to be hit with some bricks; instead he was hit with a fate that was a long time coming. Ethic stood deathly still as his goons came out of the back of the bakery and slipped a pillow case over Mizan's head. They dragged him kicking and screaming to the back.

Ethic leaned in to kiss his Aunt Dot on the cheek. "Lock the door," he stated in a low, authoritative tone. He pulled out a copy of Raven's autopsy report. It showed every broken bone, bruise, and injury that she had ever suffered. It had been obvious to the coroners that she had been abused and Ethic planned on showing Mizan exactly how it felt to be in Raven's shoes. He was about to make Mizan experience every injury that he had ever given her first hand. "We might be awhile," he stated. He unbuttoned his Ralph Lauren tailored shirt and placed it neatly over the bar stool. Before going to the back of the shop he picked up his son and kissed his chubby cheeks.

"After today, Mommy can rest in peace."

Other Novels by Ashley and JaQuavis

Dirty Money

Diary of a Street Diva

Supreme Clientele

Trophy Wife

Girls from da Hood 4

The Cartel

The Cartel 2

The Cartel 3

Kiss Kiss, Bang Bang

The Prada Plan

The Prada Plan 2

The Dopeman's Wife

The Dopefiend

Pick up your copy today!

If you enjoyed *Moth to a Flame* . . .

You can contact Ashley at:

streetlitdiva@aol.com

myspace.com/streetlitdiva

WWW.ASHLEYJAQUAVIS.COM